DAY INTO NIGHT

C.L. QUINN

Blak Kat Publishing
May 2017
All rights reserved

One

The road before him looked endless, stretching into the distance and the unknowable future. He loved it, and always had. *Thwump, thwump, thwump*...ah, nothing like the sound of his tires striking the ancient asphalt.

The long road. Poets had written about journeys on lonely highways for centuries as metaphors for the journey of life. *Yes*, Will thought, it could be, but, for him, the road was never quiet or lonely. It was an old friend he knew well, happy to be traveling it once again. To him, this was home.

And this time, it may lead him to where he needed to be…he'd learned recently that destiny was true and it might have a plan for him. At moments, it pissed him off that there seemed to be a guiding force that had already designed his path, and at other moments, he'd found serenity in surrendering to inevitability. In his purest moments of honesty, Will could admit that somewhere in his mind he'd always known that his life wasn't entirely his own.

He breathed easier with the wind in his face and hair. It was as natural as the grass and sky to him. Will caressed the long curved handlebars as he glanced to his right to watch the setting sun.

Time to find food and shelter soon. Riding through the darkness wasn't as safe as it had been when he'd started his riding career twenty years ago. Changing transportation modes left little room for throwbacks like him. Lift-cars filled the skies in busier places, but out here on these isolated roads that stretched between North and South America, only an occasional flying car whipped past him on air currents just slightly above his head. Most people preferred to keep the lift-cars low and that posed a danger to old ground-based vehicles like his Harley-Davidson motorcycle.

Moving his eyes back to the darkening pavement, Will smiled. Even if he slid and went down against the ground, the Mother would protect him. She'd keep a layer of compressed air between his fragile human body and the hard surface between him. They'd come to an understanding, he and the living planet. He took care of her and she reciprocated. There were times it all still felt surreal. Now, moving close to her, was *not* one of those times.

Increasing lights ahead indicated a village where he could stop to rest and get something to eat. Maybe treat himself to a fine whisky if such a thing were available. Food and spirits could be a crapshoot south of the border. Unless he was in one of the larger cities, the fare was specific to the region, which suited him well. It was part of the charm of traveling. Almost anything was welcome after a day of dust and wind.

Breezing into the village, his speed slow, he appreciated the decades old classic architecture, stucco in bright colors lined the two lane road that fed past it. His bike's roar had dropped to a soft purr as he noted a bright yellow building in the center of the village sporting flashing red lettering in the windows; a cantina advertising local food and drink. Perfect.

Sliding the bike into a slot just right for its size, Will leaned against it to appreciate bright green double doors that bore a hand-carved wooden sign that said, in English and Portuguese, *Welcome.* The narrow slot that fit his bike well told him that he wasn't the only visitor here who rode in on a motorcycle, although the others were likely jet-bikes. Still, there was a commonality shared in the experience of the open road.

After securing his travel pack, Will pitched his fone into his pocket and pulled one of the green doors open. Whoever had designed this cantina had created the tropical vibe common for many clubs in South America, every corner filled with lush tropical plants and dwarf trees bred for darkened indoor spaces. Festive multi-colored lights made the small spaces glow with warmth, appreciated after the cool night air. He was the only one in the cantina at the moment.

"Welcome, sir. Did you wish to dine?"

Accented, the soft female voice drew Will to his left to watch a flamboyantly dressed woman approach. She twisted a brightly colored towel in her hands, every finger circled with silver and bejeweled rings. Smile welcoming and genuine, her beautiful eyes twinkled. Will couldn't help but respond to her overt sensuality, his own smile matching hers.

"Dinner, yes, please." He paused. "I'm *very* hungry."

The statement hung there as she nodded her head to show she understood him perfectly. A twist in her hips as she moved closer to curl a hand around his thick forearm told him that she was possibly interested in helping him with his *hunger*.

"Sir, I never let a man leave…" Now *she* paused for effect. "…unsatisfied."

Her fingers caressing his bare skin, she drew him to a table in the back of the room. "You are new here? Passing through or plan to stick around for a while?"

"Passing through."

"Ah. You have somewhere you need to be."

"I do. *Where* that is, I don't know, but we'll see how it turns out."

Her dark eyes regarded him quietly for a few moments before she nodded. "Yes, I can see that. You have a wandering spirit. An earthly spirit, I think."

Her comment startled him. How could she know? *Did* she know? Only supernatuals would and she didn't read as supernatural.

Suddenly she laughed. "Don't try to figure me out. Many have tried and *all* have failed."

"Well you are a lovely enigma."

"What a charmer. Here, let me bring you our traveler's special. It is guaranteed to fill up a big man like you."

"Thank you, uh…"

"Cochita. Most call me Chita."

"I'm not most. I like Cochita. It's barely big enough for the vibrant personality I see here."

"Be careful, stranger. I might fall in love with you and weave my spell so tight you could never leave."

"Fate worse than death?"

"Ah, sir, you would die a little each day. Happily. I will return with your meal."

Will dropped into a carved seat at the table she'd led him to, pleased with his prospects for the evening. What an intriguing woman. A nice meal, perhaps this senorita's company, would make the end of his third day on the road a real pleasure. He had a long way to go and he'd learned that you take your joys where you could find them.

While he'd been assured that his lifespan was longer than normal humans, Will wasn't sure he believed it, and even if he did, life still came and went in a flash. After the past few months, he'd come to understand how beautiful that gift could be. Years of self-torture for an accident he'd thought was his fault had finally given way to accepting a new truth…that what he *was* was vastly more complicated and beyond his experience than anything he could have imagined. Lost in thought, he was surprised when Cochita placed a bottle of tequila on his table. "I believe you need a night devoid of stress. May I join you?"

"Please."

Lifting a curved whisky glass, she carefully poured tequila into one and then a second glass until each was nearly full. With an artistic flair, she whipped her full skirt aside and sat in the chair across from Will.

"You're a dancer," he commented, because he knew instinctively by her movements and grace that she was.

"Yes, I am. So, Mr. Traveler, I wait anxiously for your story. This is the most fascinating part of my job."

Will lowered his eyes to his glass as he picked it up and killed a long swallow.

"Everybody's got a story," he finally responded.

"They do. Tell me yours."

"Nothing much to tell." *Like hell there wasn't!*

"You wouldn't believe half of what I've experienced in the past six months."

"And you would be surprised." Her gaze was measured as she matched his deep sip of tequila.

Silent again, staring at the glass of clear liquid, he shifted his gaze back to Cochita's. "I'm a human supernatural with bizarre abilities that helped avert a global disaster last year. Now, I'm blowing in the wind because, somehow, I know I'm not where I'm supposed to be and I'm not sure how to find out where that is. How's that for a story?"

Cochita didn't lose his gaze as she lifted her glass and one, two, three sips later, slid closer. "Riveting." Pulling both of Will's hands into hers, she closed her eyes.

Without moving, both sat speechless for several long seconds before she lifted her eyelids. "You will find your place."

She stood abruptly and walked a few steps from the table before she looked back. "But not tonight. Tonight, you eat the best of what we offer and then you and I...we fuck like rabbits the rest of the night."

His breath hitched, Will watched the lovely temptress disappear behind a swinging door and dropped back against his seat, the glass in his hand, as he recovered his breathing.

"Damn," he whispered, now taking only small sips of the tequila before he reached for the bottle to refill the glass. The night had just gotten far more promising. It seemed that lately the people who came and went in his life were much more than they appeared. His mind went to the gorgeous vampire he'd rescued just days ago and returned to her friends in Vegas. Even now he almost wanted to turn around and go back to find her and learn more about *her* story. Then tonight, this woman, human as far as he could tell, who seemed to understand things she probably couldn't about him, and made it clear that she wanted, *and would*, be with him in his bed after he ate.

"Bring it on," he said aloud as he started on the second glass of alcohol, on his way to being thoroughly drunk so he could tamp down his tiresome inhibitions and just enjoy this beautiful woman's company tonight.

Dinner over, and the entire bottle of tequila now empty, Will's eyes locked on Cochita, who stood to grab a second bottle and plopped it in the center of his table. She moved around behind him, her hands rubbing his shoulders slipped down his back and curved forward to outline the tight muscles that formed the masculine V shape of a well-muscled back.

"You are strong." Her voice purred into his ear, her lips close enough to brush it as she spoke.

As Will pushed up from his seat, he turned to lift her chin and capture huge dark eyes lined in black. "When do you finish your shift here?"

"When I wish." Moving away, she snatched his hand and pulled. "Which is now."

In rapid Portuguese, she called out to an unseen person behind the door that led to the kitchen, then tugged Will to a stairwell behind a huge potted plant. The stairwell ended into another that took them back outside to cobbled steps which led around behind the cantina. A two-story building painted in teal and brown bordered by elaborate tile work faced the stone trail.

"This is beautiful." Will let his hand slide along an old-fashioned iron fence.

She stopped to survey his face. "I like beautiful things."

Her smile electric, she bounded up stairs lined with the same iron rails and pushed open the second door. "It is time to play. Mr. Traveler, this is *my* sandbox."

Once she disappeared inside, Will followed even faster, closing the door to the hot, dark room illuminated with a single flickering flame as she lit other candles. He lifted the bottle she'd placed on a table near the door and popped the cap.

Finishing with the final candle, Cochita faced him, lifted a fat rolled paper, lit it, and took a long puff before she held it out to him. "This is peyote, but not like you've ever known it. There are magical spirits in the world, Will. All is not as it seems."

Oh, he knew about magic and spirits and the unseen world. He hesitated only a moment before he took a healthy swig from the bottle, reached for the roll and drew hard on it.

Smiling, Cochita led him to a mattress in the corner covered by bedding that looked like an artist's palette had spilled over it again and again. "We'd better get down here and naked before it hits, my friend."

It was already hitting. Will watched brightly colored wall hangings that covered all four walls of the room begin to dance and swirl.

"Kicky," he said, then dropped his eyes to watch Cochita slide her dress off, and on her knees, crawl to him across the mattress layered with heavily-patterned bedding. Naked, she reached for his jacket, popped the release snaps, pitched it away, then his shirt and pants were gone too. Now, naked too, Will stood on his knees and pulled her slick warm body against his. "You think what we just smoked was magic? Watch this."

While he knew he shouldn't show off his earth magic, Will's compromised judgment controlled him and he brought his *own* magic up from the ground, wrapping them both in cool air. Giggling in delight, Cochita groaned and fell backward, pulling him with her. Fueling their sexual frenzy, she opened her legs to cradle his body as Will buried himself in her, and for the next twenty minutes, neither had any interest in anything other than the pounding of skin on skin and eventual release that left them both gasping, collapsed against the bed.

They didn't move again until the sun blazed into the smaller windows at the back of the room.

Awareness arrived slowly for both of them. Her hair tousled, Cochita shook her head. "Aye, yi, yi."

She stopped to stare at Will. "I know we…"

"Yeah," he added as he sat up. "It's all a bit…fuzzy."

"Too much peyote…and spirits, eh?"

Falling back to hug a pillow, Will yawned. "Yes, too much."

Suddenly, she pushed off the mattress. "But I'm sure we had an amazing time." Her eyes moved over Will's naked back and ass. "Yes, I am sure." *Although she wished she could remember.*

"It will come back. Nothing important is ever really lost. Get up, traveler. You told me you need to get back on the road early. You have somewhere you need to be."

Squinting, he looked up at her. "Not yet."

"Aye, you do. Something is waiting for you. Or someone. You do not know until you find."

Nodding, because he didn't know what to say to her, Will rolled upright and stood, his head pounding. Pulling his clothes on quickly, he let Cochita lead him from the room to face a warm morning and the rising sun. A light mist covered bountiful blooms all around the landing, sparkling with moisture in the nascent light.

"Magic *does* live here," he whispered, and followed his lovely companion down the stairs to the front of the club.

She kissed him softly and ran a hand around his jacket to straighten the collar. "Do not doubt, your destiny is waiting for you to come to it. You will find it. *And her.*"

Back on the road, the miles pushing his night behind him, Will thought about Cochita's last two words and the woman from a year ago with a cloud of dark hair surrounding a face he knew he would never forget.

It all felt too improbable, and too big a concept after a night of chemistry-accented sex.

Revving the engine, Will slipped the bike onto the pavement and continued to the main road again, the miles pushing his night behind him. Yet his mind went back to the idea of destiny and fate. *Was* there something waiting for him, designed by the universe? His connection to the living planet had proven there was. Whatever that destiny might be was unknown, or unrevealed as yet. *How do you search for the unknown?*

Although it seemed cryptic, he thought he knew the answer.

"It's in the search that you find the hope," Chione had told him before he left Colorado last year. Even *she* had seen something in him that let her know that something waited.

"Perhaps it's true," he whispered into the wind.

Memory led him back to the first moment he saw her. Olivia, smiling as he walked toward her through the hot desert air, naked, fascinated. He'd felt she was something special, something wild, someone outrageous, someone he wanted, even at first glance. Events had never allowed them to pursue those feelings. Was it too late?

Olivia was unfinished business, *hope* suspended, possibilities unexplored, pleasure untouched. No, it wasn't a surprise that it was *her* face that came to his mind as he confronted the accusation that he was on a quest.

All right, universe, he thought, *let's see how this plays out.*

Five days later in Brazil

Road weary, wearing the dust of the long journey, Will brought his bike to a stop in front of an uninspiring building nestled into about an acre of cleared space. Varieties of small trees had surrounded him for the past ten minutes of his ride. He scanned what looked like a large warehouse clad in metal siding, spacey but utilitarian. This was where Ife had Vtex'd him to come to join her and her Amazon basin restoration team. Not the usual dwelling of vampires, but he'd been surprised before.

Leaning against the seatback, he closed his eyes and drew in fresh air tinged with moisture. Even his breathing had changed…in, out, fuller, deeper. Resting comfortably, he lifted his eyelids to scan the horizon, where the sun hovered. Scarlet and golden light spread across the dying blue and tangled with clouds set aglow by the brilliant colors. The departing sun's rays highlighted a newly planted forest where sturdy trunks stood tall against the sky.

Swinging his leg over the seat, he stood for the first time in six hours. After lifting one knee, then the other, flexing his muscles, Will placed both feet on the earth, the connection here, so close to her heart, Mother Earth's magic reached through the ground to touch him. Here was life and love and hope, the very basis of earth-based magic. Uninhibited joy infused Will as his gaze moved right and left in sweeping glances to take in the wide panorama of a once stunning rain forest now burgeoning with life again. Could there be anything more beautiful than seeing life endure?

He'd always appreciated the beauty of the world, but now, with his tentacled connection to the planet beneath his feet and the sky above her, moments like this left him awestruck.

"Mesmerizing, isn't it?"

Hearing that voice again for the first time in almost a year, Will turned to the woman who spoke.

The last time they'd been together had been under circumstances that he still had trouble believing.

Will and a rag-tag group of supernaturals and humans had faced a devastating battle, the end of life on a massive scale, prevented it, came back victorious, bruised, bloodied, but not beaten, and then parted to return to lives interrupted with little idea how to do it.

He searched the young woman who stood beside him now, confident, smiling. She looked good.

"Scottie. Damn. You look happy, girl."

Never one to initiate physical contact, Will found himself reaching for her and pulled her into a loose hug. Scottie returned the embrace by pulling him closer, tears in her eyes.

"I am. More than I ever thought possible. This land has become a part of me and I think *I've* become a part of it."

"Won't be returning to New York?"

"The concrete jungle? No. Now that we've activated our powers, I doubt any of us can go back to our old lives. Have you?"

A shake of his head answered Scottie's question. Will lifted his eyes to the scarlets now streaking across the wide sky. "No. I've been unsettled since Yellowstone. That's why when Ife called, I didn't hesitate. I felt a strong pull to be with you guys again. I can't describe it, but…"

"You felt incomplete?"

Will looked back into Scottie's eyes. "I guess. Maybe this is where I belong."

Scottie lifted a hand to push back a heavy swath of hair that had fallen over Will's face. "Earth man, you absolutely do. Chione reminded us before we split up that, even when we went back to our lives, we will *always* be connected. Hey, you gotta be tired and hungry. Come on in and we'll get some food in you. Ife has a superb chef."

"God, yes."

They watched in silence as the departing sun left a navy sky fading fast to black. Will was accustomed to pitch dark skies and the Milky Way-patterned skyscape in the southwestern deserts of Arizona, but it was different this far south.

Reaching for him, Scottie wrapped both arms around Will's right arm to draw him into the large building.

"Come, the others can't wait to see you. Especially Caed. He's outnumbered by chicks and sometimes it makes him nervous."

As they passed sliding doors, Will looked around, and smiled. He wasn't shocked to see that the unassuming warehouse hid a huge high-ceiling semi-circular room filled with large plush furniture in natural shades, the walls clad in local grasses weaved into leaf-like patterns. The décor and open spaces had been designed to feel as if the outdoor continued inside. Coming off each side of the semi-circle were heavy doors that he knew would lead to each member's private rooms.

One of the doors opened just as they entered, and the ethereally lovely Ife walked out, scrolling through a small tablet in her hand. She looked hurried until she glanced up to her right and saw Scottie leading Will toward her.

"Willoughby, you're here!" Always quiet and reserved, Ife's exuberance showed him how grateful she was that he had actually come to help her and her team re-populate this irreplaceable rain forest.

She glided forward, her movement silent and elegant as only a first blood vampire could do.

Scottie released Will as Ife, less uninhibited than Scottie, gently took his hands with an easy smile, her pale eyes sparkling. "This means so much to Brazil. Will, your magics are the final piece we need to resurrect what has been lost and to recreate this forest. Please, we are just to begin first meal. You must be famished."

"Yup. Especially since you vampires eat so well. I hope you have enough."

"My darling traveler, I suspect we do." Ife laughed and moved her eyes to Scottie.

"Would you mind taking Will to his chambers, then bring him to the dining room when he is settled in?"

"Sure, Boss."

"Scottie, how many times..."

"Yeah, yeah, don't call you boss, I get it. But you are. Kinda."

"We are all equal. I am merely the one who guides this effort."

Scottie grinned. "'Cause you're the boss."

Ife sighed and looked back up to Will. "She's untrainable. I'll see you soon."

Once settled in a bedroom at least four times larger than his cabin in the desert, more like a suite with a big sitting room and vidscreen, Will followed a chatty Scottie through a corridor that held native plants, past a big gaming room, and into the dining room. Voices floating through the doorway let him know they weren't the first to arrive.

Ife was already seated at a round table in the center of the room, large enough to have pleased King Arthur. Trays filled with towering food faced the diners. She looked up as he entered.

"Will, come, have a seat next to me."

Scottie pushed him toward her. "Teacher's pet."

At a buffet table near the back of the dining area, Crezia and Caedmon turned when Ife called out.

Caedmon, shaking his head, surged forward.

"Oh, thank the gods! Another male!"

"Is that a complaint?" Crezia chided as she reached Will first and hugged him. "Welcome to the sweat box, Will."

"Thank you. I'm happy to help."

A loud yawn drew everyone's attention to the entrance where a swiftly moving young woman breezed past everyone and headed straight for the coffee.

"Caffeine please. *Oh, please.*"

Another pleasant surprise. Smiling, Will moved toward her. "Dani."

Dani, a steaming cup in her hand, turned to the voice behind her, sleepy eyes squinting. "Will?"

Accepting an embrace from the big man, Dani held the cup out to her side. "Will. What are you doing here?"

Pleased to see another earth warrior that he'd trained with in Africa and fought beside in Yellowstone, Will shrugged. "I think the same thing you are."

"To party like there's no tomorrow?"

Laughing, he stepped back so she could take a sip of the coffee she'd sought in desperation. "Okay, maybe not the *same* thing. I'm here to help with the restoration."

"Oh. Cool. I'm here to visit Scottie and get a little R & R before I begin working with Cari's crew. It's, um…" Dani shook her head, glanced at Scottie, then looked back up into Will's amused eyes. "It's pretty frantic around here. Kind of wild. Have you ever met Dez and her gang?"

A quick shake of his head answered Dani while she took a longer sip of the coffee.

"Oh, it's a gas. You'll love it. Hot men and women, endless drinking, music, games, just a freaking amazing good time. But it'll wear you out. I'm more exhausted than I was after the big battle last year."

Scottie pushed in to pull Will back to his table.

"Get something to eat, my friend. Dani's just a lightweight when it comes to all-night partying. I'm training her, though."

"Ugh. I hope I survive." Dani grinned. "Although if I don't, I'll die with a smile on my face. And then, Will, there's the *mystery*."

Seated now, Will looked up as he filled a plate with bacon and eggs. "What mystery?"

Crossing to the table, Dani snatched a slice of bacon from his plate. "Ife hasn't revealed it yet. Ask her. See if she'll tell you."

Dani lifted her voice. "I love a good mystery, but I'm dying to know more about it." She leaned across the table, staring at Ife. "Tell us?"

"Now that Will's arrived, I can. After first meal, everyone, we'll gather in the lounge. Yes, something quite interesting is going on. Now, eat, enjoy, and then we'll meet and I'll tell you what it is."

"At last." Dani dropped into the chair next to Will and began to fill her own plate. "You look good. We need to catch up."

He shrugged. "Not much to tell. My life is pretty much back to ordinary."

"That's about to change," Scottie announced.

Over an hour later, a group of 14 blood-bonds that worked with the vampires, Dani, Scottie, and Will had taken seats in the high-ceilinged lounge he'd first seen when he came into the building.

Dani looked down at Will, sprawled on a teddy-bear brown sofa, a hand on his gut. "Oh, boy. I remember my brother and half a dozen steaks not long after we arrived in Colorado. It wasn't pretty. That's a complication of living with vampires, they can eat ten times what we can, and never suffer or gain weight. Yet we still overdo."

Will groaned. "Worth every pang, though. I've had days when I get ready to hit my bed and realize I haven't eaten."

Watching the huge man with deep roots to the earth, Dani wondered how well he was adjusting to the new life thrust upon them all this past year. She had the support of her brother and the close bonds she'd built with Cairine and her friends in Colorado. Her innate ability to intuit people's truths let her know that he was unsettled. Coming here to this family that Ife had built might be exactly what he needed.

Reaching for Will, Dani slid her fingers along his shoulder and down to rest on his wrist. "This should be interesting. I think you're going to enjoy your time here."

Nodding, Will watched Dani. He'd only had a minimal relationship with her before now. Once they'd finished their mission at Yellowstone, he'd left without delay. His eyes moved over her face, lovely, with perhaps one of the most engaging smiles he'd ever seen. Her wild hair, longer than it had been when he'd seen her last, created a curly halo around smooth milk chocolate skin and eyes he'd learned could see past the surface and into the depths below. He sensed in her a genuine concern for him, a need to connect with him as a friend and compatriot.

Without forethought, he lifted a hand and caressed the back of hers as it lay on his other wrist. "I hope so. I needed...*something*."

"I feel that when I touch you. If you want to talk, anything, while you're here, just come to me."

"I will."

Their eyes locked until Ife and others surged into the room. Voice levels rose while the new arrivals found seats until Ife spoke.

"So, our little mystery." She settled into a high padded chair, one leg drawn beneath her. "Two weeks ago, Crezia, Scottie, and I were in an area we call Section 12, a garden filled with native flowers we've replanted. Most of the varieties were nearly extinct. Luckily, we've been successful in reintroducing them and they are flourishing. Caed was helping me carry a new sprayer that we planned to use to supply natural nutrients."

Caedmon laughed. "I'm the Back."

"And a beautiful one." Crezia rubbed along his spine, fingers spread, to punctuate her point.

"We couldn't do without you," Ife continued. "So this is what happened that day."

(Two weeks ago)

"Ife, is this where you want this?" Caedmon asked, anxious to drop the heavy container. He might be vampire and strong, but not only was it heavy, it was bulky and awkward. Grateful when Ife called out with an affirmative answer, he lowered it, as carefully as he could, and lifted up to rub his shoulders.

"Anything else I can help with?"

Crezia, already on her knees checking the roots of their newest seedlings, looked up. "Not right now, my love."

"'Kay. I'll be nearby if you do."

Scottie drew Crezia's attention back to the ground, and, his eyes on the three busy women, Caedmon turned to search the gardens and wandered away when he noticed large rock formations some distance away. Curious, he glanced back as all three women, on the ground, examined the health of the new plants. They wouldn't miss him, so he headed toward the boulders.

"This row looks stressed." Ife lifted a seedling from its roots and showed it to Scottie and Crezia.

"They do. We'll use the nutrients we just brought here, then Scottie and I will give them a power boost." Taking the seedling from Ife, Crezia examined it, and reached for a tool to poke a hole in the ground to replant it.

Ife began to rise when Crezia looked up abruptly into Ife's eyes.

Calmly, Crezia shifted her gaze to Scottie and then back to Ife. "Caedmon fell into the earth."

The comment was so bizarre, Scottie and Ife didn't respond right away. A second later, Ife dropped back down to face Crezia. "What do you mean? Is he hurt?"

Crezia shook her head. "He's fine, but we'd better go check on him. He can't get out."

"Of course," Scottie agreed. Reaching for hand-held LED torches, she passed one to Ife and had to run to catch up with Crezia, who had already taken off.

Ife worked to keep up with Crezia, and although she was moving fast, she didn't break into air displacement. "Zia, where is he?"

"I'm not sure. Our connection is strong, we can communicate psychically through distances, but sometimes I can't get details. I know he wasn't injured or in danger, there isn't any panic or pain."

The three women followed a crooked path through several of their planting projects toward an increasing amount of huge boulders and a solid rock cliff.

Half an hour later, weaving through several large upright stones, Crezia came to a stop on the far side of where they'd entered. Pausing, after searching through numerous walls of rock, she pushed through a narrow slit between two of the largest formations.

Scottie shrugged and followed, Ife right behind.

"Down there." Crezia pointed to a fresh break in the ground, a dark hole, widened from where it had been disturbed.

"He's down there?" Ife asked, and Crezia nodded.

"How deep is it?"

"I don't know. Too deep to jump out or he would have instead of letting me know he was in trouble."

Scottie moved closer and looked into the hole, so dark she could see nothing beyond. "How do we get him out?"

"We'll figure it out."

"Can you speak with him?"

"Not exactly. Our communication is more *sense* than words. It's tough to explain."

Suddenly, she grinned. "He's exploring. He can't see much, but he thinks it's an enormous cave."

By now, Scottie leaned over the opening, squinting.

"The locals make rope ladders. Long ones. They might do the job."

"Of course!" Ife exclaimed. "Scottie…"

"On it."

Scottie was gone immediately as Crezia leaned over the broken earth at the edge of the hole. "I'm going in."

Ife sighed and nodded. "I'm not surprised, but Zia, are you sure it's safe?"

"It's safe. Caed has traveled some distance past the opening. With my help, we can create light balls and see what he has found. "Just…get those rope ladders, Ife."

"We will. You have your fone?"

"I do. See you soon." Crezia stopped to smile to her friend. "It's exciting, isn't it?"

"We'll see once we know why the earth gave way here, and what's underneath us."

"I think the Mother Earth is in a generous mood. I don't know exactly what Caed is seeing down there, but he's feeling something kind of intense."

"Send me a Vtex when you create light and see the space. Gods, I *am* curious, but be careful, Zia."

With a last nod, the LED torch secured against her, she took a deep breath and dropped blind into the opening, aware that the bottom would come up fast and that she'd hit hard.

Watching from above, worried in spite of Crezia's assurance, Ife heard the distant thump as her friend landed brutally.

"Are you okay?" she called down.

Silence at first was followed by her fone chiming. Ife grabbed it and punched to accept the call. "Zia!"

Zia's voice, even labored, seemed fine. "I'm okay. Um, I'm going to try to find Caed. I'll keep this line open."

Minutes passed as Ife sat above, her eyes wandering over and over to the opening. She toyed with the idea of joining them, the purpose being that *three* first bloods should be able to use their magics to escape the underground cave or whatever the hell this was. The ethereal connection Crezia and Caedmon shared was unique; the other first blood warriors were more effective with physical contact. Without a conduit like Chione or Cairine, it was difficult to share and maximize their power.

Using her skills, she listened for Scottie or any of the locals who helped them during daylight hours, mostly trusted blood-bonds, but she didn't hear or see any movement through the scruffy brush that surrounded the rocky outcropping.

The decision made suddenly, she palmed her fone to Vtex Crezia.

Zia, I'm coming down. Make way.

A final momentary hesitation became solid determination and Ife jumped, for the first time in her life, into a dark chasm, unaware what waited, and felt her body fall almost in slow motion, her arms out to her side as if they could slow the descent...and felt unrestrained exhilaration. That split moment when she jumped pitched her heartrate into maximum overdrive and for those seconds, she felt weightless and free, a wild sense of joy that she breathed and lived. Fear became her companion in this reckless and awesome act.

Always graceful, Ife had a fraction of a second to acknowledge that, with the effects of gravity, she would crumble upon landing, but it didn't happen. The ever-elegant vampire landed hard enough to jar her teeth, but on her feet, stunned for the first few seconds.

"Holy shit. Ife, you all right?"

Caedmon's voice penetrated her state of shock and euphoria as pain surged from her ankles up into her legs, her knees buckling at last. She felt Caedmon's strong arms support her as she nearly went down.

"Ow," Ife whispered as Crezia started to laugh from somewhere in the darkness to her left.

"Understatement of the century, darling. Try to relax. If you didn't break anything, the pain will subside quickly."

"Whoa. That was incredible. Not sure I want to do it again, but wow. It was a longer drop than I expected."

"Yeah. I tried the vertical jump to get out and I couldn't pull it off. With the three of us, maybe we can rise through the air."

"Scottie has it covered if we can't. Caed, let's make some light and see what we've found."

"You feel okay to stand on your own?"

"My legs are shaky, they ache, but I think I can."

Ife's feet were still pinging with nerve pain, but it had lessened significantly already. Vampire healing rocked. Stepping forward to take Crezia's hand, she reached for Caedmon's.

Now touching, the three first bloods created well beyond balls of light; they summoned excited molecules and created a bright glow that illuminated the entire space they stood in, its secrets no longer covered by the lightless cave it had been before Caedmon's mishap.

Speechless, eyes locked above them, the three vampires, still holding hands, unmoving, couldn't believe what they saw. The curved ceiling of a vast cave spanned the wide space overhead, every inch of the surface, above them, down the walls until they struck the floor, covered with large sparkling crystalline formations in colors that ran from pale pink to pale green. The glowing light they'd created twinkled off faceted surfaces in what had to be one of the most beautiful places on the planet.

"Ah..." Ife expelled.

"Holy..." Caedmon, blinking, couldn't believe something like this had been underfoot all this time.

"Wow," Crezia murmured. "We've found Mother Nature's jewelry box. Ife, you have any idea this was here?"

"No. No one did. This is one of the most miraculous things I've ever seen, and you guys know what that means with all the miracles we earth warriors have experienced. Usually with openings this size, the crystal formations are radically different. I can't imagine how this formed."

"They aren't diamonds, right?" Crezia inquired.

"They aren't." Ife tugged free of her companions and moved into the center of the cave, spinning to take it all in.

"It's magnificent."

"Yup. We let the world know it's here, they'll decimate it," Caedmon said, his voice reverent, quiet.

"That we all know. We'll need to return for samples so we can identify the composition of the crystals. To see how old it is. Aw, our geologists in Colorado will love this!"

Ife's fone chimed. "It's Scottie, ready to get us out of here."

(Present day, back in the lounge)

As she finished her tale, Ife watched her audience.

"So, pretty cool, yeah?"

Will thought about a cave far below the ground that no one else had ever touched. He couldn't wait to climb down and touch the earth deeper than he ever had. "Did you find out what the crystals are made of?"

Shaking her head, Ife's eyes sparkling, they moved from face to face. "That's the mystery, kids. We've sent samples to Cari's team, to Fia's labs in Paris, and to a vampire team in the U.S. that handles the history of geology for the planet. They cannot be identified as anything we've ever seen before. These crystals are unknown to the world of science."

Dani sat up and leaned forward. "No shit? Holy hell. They didn't mention it to me before I left."

Ife lifted to fold both legs beneath her, and dropped back into her seat. *This*, she loved, surrounded by family and friends, by fascinated and fascinating minds, by earth-born, and starborn magic. They were doing good things here in the Amazon basin for both the planet and all life that depended on her.

"So, whoever would like to come, we've placed secured sturdy rope ladders at the opening."

Will stood, his gastrointestinal trouble forgotten.

"I'm in. Can we go tonight?"

Ife nodded. "Of course. Will, you sure you don't need some rest first? You look quite exhausted."

"Sure, yeah, but I can hold it together for a few more hours. I need to see her."

Like Dani, Ife felt an overwhelming need to touch Will, but she refrained. "You really are the earth's sentry, aren't you?"

"We all are, but it does seem like I'm locked in. Shit, I can't even fly without magical intervention."

"I remember that. Will, it seems the earth has chosen you. Your magic is linked to her even beyond the other earth warriors."

"Naw. I'm not anyone special. Some days, I barely hold it together."

Now Ife reached for him, her fingers moving along his arm and down to his hand, just as Dani had. "You're special, and the fact that it isn't easy makes you even more remarkable. Will, I think this part of your journey will bring you full circle. My empathic skill is somewhat limited, but

I'm reading your agitation, you're very private, yet I'm also reading your aura and the future attached to you. I believe that, here, in Brazil, is where you find what you seek."

Surprising himself again, Will pulled her hand to his lips to kiss the palm gently, his eyes on hers.

"Ife, I hope you are right. I guess we'll see as the days go by."

"That's how the future reveals itself. But you'll have a lot of fun too, Will. We spend weekends at a complex just thirty minutes south of here run by Dez. Have you met her? You'll love her and her facility. We work hard, but we play hard too. Oh, and Will, Brigitte will be visiting next week. I'm sure you remember my sister."

Brigitte. Will remembered her; hell, she was unforgettable. The exciting, no-holds-barred sex was hard to forget. Extraordinarily beautiful in the way of the first bloods, she'd kept him sane and focused through all the shit and craziness last year. Yeah, he'd love to see her again.

"Sounds good," was all he said, then lowered Ife's hand. "I'll be ready whenever you guys are."

"Be out front in ten minutes."

Two hours later beneath the surface of the earth

Moving in a circle around the perimeter of the high-ceilinged sparkling cave, along with the vampires, Dani and Scottie, and at least twelve of the blood-bonds, Will lay his hands against the rough surface of the wall for the fifth time, then placed his cheek against it too and closed his eyes.

Ife, Crezia, and Caedmon had been watching him and now that he'd moved around the entire edge of the vast space, Ife stepped closer. "Amazing, isn't it?"

Not moving away, Will nodded. "Truly."

He didn't elaborate and didn't see Ife shrug to Crezia and Caedmon. They'd hoped he would be more helpful, but he just lay there, his face scraped, a tiny bit of blood on his forehead. Suddenly he lifted away and faced the three.

"They're not hers."

After a moment of concern, Ife spoke. "I'm sorry, what do you mean?"

"The crystals. They're not hers. Mother Earth's. They didn't come from this world."

Ife looked back to her companions and then to Will.

"You mean, they really are extraterrestrial?"

"Yes. And they've been here for millions of years."

"So not from the beginning."

"No."

"The mystery deepens. Look, we've been down here for a while. Let's get back, let you rest, then we'll debrief further. I think *you* more than anyone may be able to help solve the origin of these jeweled walls."

Muffling a yawn, Will agreed. Right now, he was a walking dead man. Tomorrow night would come soon enough.

Two

FOUR WEEKS LATER IN LAS VEGAS

Leaving her business in good hands, Olivia had packed sparingly, and now sat in her lift-car, her eyes on the spectacular 360 degree view that surrounded her on the roof of her building 75 stories high. Parked on the top of Serenity Tower, her home as well as the finest nightclub and restaurant in the city, she searched the brilliant multi-colored lights that drew massive numbers of travelers to the jewel of the U.S.

Even leaving Vegas for a short time was tough. In her very long life, little brought her greater joy than this city and the life that she'd built here, with family and friends nearby. This city left her breathless.

So had he.

Always the first in line for adventures, she'd prided herself on spontaneity, the wild need to seek excitement in any form, her free-spirited dedication to creating ecstatic moments of joy with new people in new places. So why did she sit here, frozen in place, when she knew exactly what she needed to do and where she needed to be?

"Why are you so afraid of this?" Olivia asked out loud as she toyed with the lever that would raise the car from the roof and move her toward South America. At this moment, she felt cowardice wrapped around her like a mantle.

Yes, she *was* afraid to see him again. That moment in the desert when she'd seen him for the first time, dripping, naked, ripped like a god, walk out of that dismal pool toward her in candlelit glory, haunted her dreams. On the nights when the dream came to her, it played through from the moment he lifted himself from beneath the waterline to the moment he stood in front of her, her breathing labored. Olivia always woke startled, horny, wet, in desperate need that would not get quenched. No matter how many times she dreamed of him and hoped that, at least in the dream, she would get to fuck him, the dream always stopped at the moment they stood, confronting each other, strangers and yet, curiously not, both sexually stimulated, yet eventually walking away from each other.

This time, she planned to walk toward him and finish this, one way or the other. Even after so many lovers over the past centuries, she'd never been in love.

That's why she'd walked away back then. He was Shoazan, and mate for a vampire. At that moment, the idea of taking a mate seemed ludicrous, something she couldn't imagine.

Yet here she was, a year later, unable to forget him.

"Willoughby Jasper Collins, I guess we'll just have to see how this farce plays out."

"So let's go," she whispered to the fool she'd been.

Finally, decision made, she pulled the elevation lever backward to lift off.

She'd passed her 300th birthday, had bedded more hot men than she could ever recall, and yet still felt a tickle in her belly and pulsing between her legs at the idea of seeing Will again. The intense attraction they'd both felt on that hot summer night in the desert needed to be addressed. At the very least, confronting the attraction might be the only way to purge this strange obsession.

With the air calm tonight, it didn't fight the car as she headed to the airport to take her slick new jet to a rendezvous that almost seemed destined to happen. During the six hour flight, she would rest in the light-tight chamber built to protect a vampire during what had always seemed the most vulnerable type of transport for someone who could never allow daylight to touch them.

Once she landed, secured the car, and entered the jet, Olivia nodded her thanks to her pilot.

"I'm ready, Manuel."

Moments after sealing herself in the safe zone, she used the intercom to let him know he could take off. Settling into a custom-built seat, she pressed the number 1 on her fone, smiling when a brusque voice answered.

"Dez, I'm on my way in. I'll see you soon."

"Brilliant! Your bedroom awaits, my love. We're all exhausted here. Young vampires have arrived from all over the globe and we are partying every night. It's been wonderful, but now, with *you* here, it will be perfect."

"Young vampires? Who's there?"

"Ife, of course. Crezia and Caed. Brigitte stopped to visit and hasn't gone home. And now you. We are enjoying the company, my darling girl. It was time for an infusion of young first bloods."

"Wow. I didn't know. This will be a mini-reunion. Okay, I'll see you soon. We're going wheels-up in a few moments."

"Safe trip, my darling. See you soon."

"Goodnight, grandmother."

Closing the call, Olivia lay back against the soft leather that retained its coolness even in the heat. Leather was still particularly desired, but it was no longer made from animal skin. The resource wasn't there anymore, but most of the world had long ago moved to cruelty-free production. Nearly all food items were bio-chemically produced now to provide high nutrition and taste with no animal products. It was the only way to achieve sustainability.

"So many first bloods at Dez's. Interesting."

Closing the lights out, she reclined the seat and tried to sleep, but it didn't come easily. Olivia had trouble shutting down her mind to rest. Usually the only thing that helped was the vampire imperative to sleep during daylight, but sunrise was hours away. When she finally allowed blessed unconsciousness to come, the dreams that arrived were otherworldly and made no sense at all. They were erotic, and somewhere buried in the disjointed scenes, her dream-self searched for something or someone.

Waking hours later, Olivia shot upright, parched and unsatisfied, well aware that she wouldn't fall asleep again.

The intercom pinged.

"Ms. Olivia, we are on final approach to Desiree's."

"Thank you. I'll let her know."

Ringing in, Olivia smiled when her grandmother answered her fone with an enthusiastic, "Hi, baby!" Loud music almost overwhelmed the greeting.

"Party tonight, gran?"

"Yes, we have the group in from the Basin and we're having a dance competition. Hurry up, darling, and you can still get in on it."

"Oh, I don't know about that. I'm pretty whipped. But I can't wait to see you and Zach."

"You're staying a while, yeah?"

Olivia didn't know quite how to answer that. "I'm not sure what my plans are, *Grandmére*, but I may be."

"I will take what I can get, Livie. See you soon."

The plane landed safely on Dez's private runway and taxied back to the entrance of the building.

After thanking her pilot, Olivia hurried through a cooled corridor that led underground to the rear of the main housing section. In the past thirty years, Dez and Zach had completed remodels that expanded the underground chambers to accommodate larger numbers of visitors that came and went year around. Before she even reached the inner door, Olivia heard pounding music, the percussion felt beneath her feet. Her grandmother *did* know how to party.

Computer controlled automatic security stopped her at a heavy entry door, but it recognized Olivia following a brief thorough scan. *Welcome, Miss Olivia*, the pleasantly-accented AI voice said.

Without pause, she moved inside, dropped her travel pack in an alcove to her left, stepped down a short flight of steps, around a second corner and down a wide corridor painted with images of a Tuscan garden. The corridor opened into a beautifully lit room with high chandeliers and multi-colored lights facing several large mirror balls. Other lights in the room were off to create a darkened nightclub ambience, the result electric and welcoming, enjoyed now by a generously-sized crowd. Drinks in hand, most of the partiers were dancing and eating, some doing both at the same time, while they watched a smaller group of dancers finishing what looked like a competition of an old-style dance from the late 1900's. Dancers with great rhythm recreated classic hip-hop moves while others, some highly inebriated, stumbled and laughed as they attempted to match the steps.

Scanning the dancers, she tried to make out the faces, and only recognized Scottie, Rodney's daughter, as she sauntered around the floor.

"Hey, pretty girl."

Olivia turned to a voice she knew well, to the man sitting at a table lost in the shadows behind her. Moving toward him, she smiled. "Zach. Hey stranger."

"Join me. Here, have a glass. Ife's father sent us some of their special MoonShine wine. I could live on this stuff."

Sliding into a chair beside Zach, Olivia reached for the filled stemmed glass he handed to her. "I remember. I'd hoped to get some for my restaurant, but he only sent me a small amount for my private use."

"No, they don't make it in that kind of volume. It's unique. Nice to see you, Livie. Dez know you were coming?"

"Yeah."

"A nice long visit I hope."

"Um…we'll see."

Zach clicked his tongue. "Ah, ha. Something else is afoot. I know you love to visit us here, but I suspect there is another reason you've shown up so suddenly?"

Lingering on slow sips of the exceptional wine, she finally answered. "There *is* a reason that I've come this time. I think. I hope."

Olivia scanned the man she'd had a special friendship with from the first moment they'd met in Austria. The low-light shone off his blonde hair, tied back at the nape of his neck. Sexy, just like he'd been so long ago before she found out what she was.

Zach lifted his glass. "To journeys. Unknown paths and destinies. A vampire's life is rarely dull."

"True. Speaking of...why are you alone here in a corner?"

"I like the solitude." He used his wine glass to point across the room. Olivia's eyes followed to where Dez, her skin-tight suit sparkling, moved sensually among her guests. Dez threw her long black hair over her shoulder, laughing as she ran her hand up the back of a handsome local man.

"She's so comfortable with this life. One of my favorite things in the world is to just sit back like this and watch my woman work the room. I'll never get enough of watching that mesmerizing witch do what she was born to do."

"I can see why. You remember how she challenged me the night I met her?"

"Every moment. That was the night she came back to me."

Olivia would never forget either. It was the night she met Dez, and would find out soon after that the woman she'd developed an odd relationship with was her grandmother. Her life had changed forever that night when she not only found out that she was a first blood vampire, but that she wasn't alone in this world. Zach had found his mate and she had found a family. The past century had been the best years of her life.

"Penny for them?"

Pulled out of warm memories, Olivia reached for the bottle of MoonShine. "Zach, sorry. I zoned."

"You did, and Olivia, you *don't* zone. Are you sure you're okay? You gotta clue me in. What is it? Or should I ask *who* is it?"

As he spoke, she'd been scanning the dancers. One of her favorite romantic songs had replaced the hip-hop tunes, and the couples that dominated the floor now were dancing close. Ready to turn back to answer Zach's question, her eyes slid across a pair dancing together some distance across the floor. Taller than most of the couples, the man and woman were plastered against each other, their hips moving in perfect sync. As they slowly turned, the dim lighting revealed the man's features, enough to identify him. Heat infused her face, her hands stilled, as she processed the image. Will, grinding on another woman, their relationship obviously sexual. Squinting through the darkened space, she tried to see who the woman was, but she was turned away from her.

Gulping down the rest of the glass of wine, she gingerly set it back on the table. Well, this changed the course of her visit. Even so, Olivia couldn't take her eyes from them. Against her will, she found herself focusing in on every detail. Will's right hand lay low on the woman's buttock, the fingers curled around the curve. As Olivia watched, Will lifted his left hand to her face and lowered his to hers. He kissed her with passion and familiarity. *Who was this woman?*

Olivia didn't want to acknowledge the tightness in her throat, the disappointment, the unexpected sense of loss, even though a relationship with him had never existed. Pressure behind her eyes threatened tears, and she wondered why her reaction was so strong. She couldn't deny that it hurt to see him so intimate with another woman.

"Olivia?"

Eventually, Zach's voice penetrated. "Olivia, are you okay?"

Unable to pull her eyes from Will, she finally responded, well aware her answer was clipped.

"Fine. Never better. Do you know that tall man?"

Zach searched the floor to land on Will. "Oh, yeah. He's a regular at Dez's weekend parties. He's human, one of the earth warriors Chione found last year. Hell of a dancer, hell of a fighter." Zach laughed. "Hell of a lover. Since Brigitte arrived, you can barely get a molecule between them. Watch. Within the next half hour, they'll stumble to one of the guest rooms and won't come out until daylight. Will goes back to Ife's compound to work, and Brigitte stays here for her rest. They're good together. Make a smashing couple."

Zach stopped to top off his glass. "Liv? You look upset. What…" His eyes moved from her gaze, locked on Will and

Brigitte, and back to notice the moisture in her eyes. He got it now. "Liv, you're interested in him."

It was a statement, he already saw it in the cold glare and tight set teeth. "How do you know him?"

"I don't. Not really." Olivia turned those big blues that reminded him so much of his mate's on him. "Chione needed help tracking down one of her human warriors, a stranger that lived in the southwestern desert, with only a nickname and vague location. She knew that I could do it. That's pretty much the story. I found him, got him to Africa, and came home."

Zach shook his head. "That wasn't *pretty much the story*, it was just the outline. What happened in between the *I found him* and *came home* part?"

Several more moments passed. Sighing, Olivia looked toward Brigitte, the kiss highly sexual now, and averted her gaze back to Zach.

"Nothing. Honestly, Zach, we were never together. It's me, not him. Unfounded expectations. A spark of a relationship that I never let ignite. A woman suddenly wondering if she'd let go the man who might be *the one*. Don't judge me, Zach, I'm ready to rip someone a new one and you're the closest to me right now. I'm okay. You know I'm always fine. I just came down here chasing a dream, but dreams aren't real. Anyway, it got me away from work and here to visit you guys, so no complaints, right?"

"None. Dez is always over the moon to see you. Why don't I go get her?"

"I like that idea. I'll stay here and protect the MoonShine supply, right?"

"I'm not sure I trust that glint in your eye. I remember you could drink me under the table in Siberia."

"Hmmm." Bypassing her stemware, Olivia lifted the second bottle to her lips.

"I'll hurry," Zach groaned.

Lowering the bottle, Olivia let it hover above the tabletop. Zach needn't worry about his wine supply; she wasn't in the mood anymore. Still, the bottle in her hand, she lifted it again, thinking that, mood or not, being drunk with a magically produced wine might be the only thing that would get her through the night without becoming maudlin.

The bottom of the bottle still lifted, she shot a quick glance to where Will and Brigitte had been practically fucking on the dance floor and saw them moving toward her, now only about ten feet away. Still wrapped around his partner, weaving a little, Will wore a genuine easy grin, something that she'd never seen, when he suddenly glanced up, his eyes scanning around him until they landed on her. His expression revealed shock when he saw her.

Surprised he'd noticed her in his current inebriated and horny state, Olivia waved at him with the bottle.

Pulling Brigitte to a stop beside him, Will stared at Olivia, unaware that Brigitte's eyes followed his to the beautiful vampire at the table, then back to Will.

"Olivia," Will whispered.

"Biker." Olivia did *not* whisper. The nickname she'd known him by before she'd known his real name felt more intimate, but she reminded herself that it was a mistake to bring up that memory. Will was with another woman. Her eyes moved from his to those of his companion.

She summoned a smile for Brigitte, even if it couldn't quite reach her eyes. She'd always liked the beautiful child of the moon.

"Hey, Bridge. How's Zambia?"

Brigitte's smile was warm, real, although Olivia could sense her concern. "Um, great. Everyone is doing perfectly. When did you get here?"

"Just arrived in time to see the end of the dance contest."

"Ugh!" Wrapping her arms around Will's waist, Brigitte laughed. "We were hardly stellar, were we, babe?"

Olivia's eyes went to the hug. And she noticed the endearment. Staking her claim?

Will nodded, his head stiff. "No, not quite." His discomfort was obvious. Pulling away from Brigitte's tight embrace, he glanced at Olivia. "Well, it's nice to see you again."

If she hadn't been so unsettled about finding the man she had come all this way to seduce in a clinch with another woman, Olivia would have found his discomfort amusing.

Brigitte shrugged as Will pulled her away. "See you later, Olivia."

As they cleared the room, Olivia rolled her eyes, and whispered, "Not if I see you first." Childish she knew, but she didn't care.

Brigitte was a sweet girl. And Will had no idea that Olivia had come here for him, so both were innocent in this. Didn't matter, though. Olivia lifted the wine and sucked down a quarter of the bottle. She couldn't purge the image of Brigitte's legs wrapped around Will's waist.

"My girl!"

Dez blew in like a hurricane, enveloping Olivia in her huge presence and warm arms. Like a lifeline, Olivia held tight to her grandmother, one of the brightest points in her life since she'd found her family.

Dez pulled back to absorb her granddaughter, still one of very few fourth generation first blood vampires.

"I think you need to *move* here. I miss you way too much to have you all the way in the U.S."

"I'd love to, but my business is in the city of night-lights, and you know I love it. Although, of course I miss you too."

Zach stood behind the two women, so alike in spite of the generation that separated them. Life had become one big party after another since he and Dez had finally mated, and he wouldn't change a moment. He stepped forward, a hand on each of their backs.

"Why don't we retire to the dining room and let the rest of these guys burn out as dawn arrives? Get a nice *quiet* last meal."

"Perfect idea." Dez winked at Zach. "With all the belly dancing earlier tonight, I need to recharge."

His grin wide, Zach lifted his eyebrows. "From my point of view, it was worth every tiring gyration."

Dez ran a finger down his chest and stopped just below the beltline of his jeans on the obvious mound.

"Perhaps after some calories, I'll give you a private encore before we rest."

Following them, Olivia faked a choking sound. "Ugh. Should granddaughters have to listen to their grandmothers make sexual deals?"

Especially when her own erotic adventure had just blown up in her face.

His eyes on her, Zach stopped and pulled Olivia forward. "I know what *you* need. Come look at this."

He led her into the dining room and toward the buffet table near the kitchen that was just now being set for last meal. "This is it, Liv."

Zach lifted a large stainless-steel cover from a tall tray with a flourish.

Olivia couldn't help shooting him a wan smile. Aware of her heartache tonight, Zach knew precisely what a woman needed to help salve a wounded heart. A three tier chocolate cake glistened under the lights over the table. Dark chocolate icing dripped down the side over thick milk chocolate buttercream icing that covered all three layers.

"It's filled with rich white icing," Zach elaborated.

Olivia, her back to her grandmother, sent him an air kiss and mouthed *thank you*. The man knew what a woman needed and this would do nicely. As the moments passed, she felt more raw at the way the situation had turned out. She'd waited too long, it was that simple. Taking responsibility for her own choices that led her here at this moment of lost possibilities didn't mean that she didn't deserve that cake.

Two hours later, filled with wine and a massive dump of sugar, a little drunk and a lot exhausted, Olivia left her travel pack on a padded bench at the foot of the bed in her room. Decorated with natural colors, the wall hangings on the room shimmered under soft crystal lighting. Like Dez, Olivia loved sequins, crystals, anything that sparkled or shined, creating a space that felt like home.

After her flight, in need of a quick shower, Olivia donned a thin robe and headed from her room to the nearest of three enormous bathrooms that served all the rooms on this floor. Her mood had improved, both from Dez and Zach's amusing company, and the effects of the

MoonShine. Smiling, humming a tune that had been playing in her room, she hurried down the hallway, low-lit since, while it was daylight outside, it was a vampire's *night*.

As she reached the big double door, she dropped against the wall, frustrated that it was occupied. Pushing away, she started to head toward the other end of the corridor to the next closest bathroom when she heard the door open. Good, she could get her shower now. Turning back, she watched Will, wrapped only in a damp towel slung around his waist, walk from the bathroom into the hall, his eyes lifting from where he'd just secured the towel to meet hers.

Neither moved at first, both stunned to meet like this, still surprised to have met here tonight at all. Finally, his tongue moving around his lips, a hand pushing wet hair from his face, Will nodded to her.

"Olivia."

She shook her head. "You already said that. Earlier. Tonight."

Uneasy, Olivia shifted her weight and let herself enjoy the unexpected view. Gods, he looked, *smelled*, impossibly arousing. Instantly, she felt the tug of sexual desire between her legs. Inhibition still compromised by the MoonShine, she couldn't control what she felt and found herself saying what was on her mind.

"You looked almost exactly like this when we first met, except that you didn't have that towel, you know, where it is now, covering…"

Easing closer, her hand moved out to touch the towel exactly where it covered a rising mound. "Um, here."

Although the pressure was light, she could feel the hard length of his cock as it continued to fill, and she pressed harder, her fingers curving around the long thick shape. She smiled, and wondered if he could see the regret, then dropped her hand to take a step back.

"I remember."

Will fought the urge to pull the towel free and bring her hand back where it had been a second earlier. "What are you doing here, Olivia? I'm sorry, that sounded rude. It's just, I've been here for a month and I've never seen you."

"Dez is my grandmother."

"Oh. I didn't know that. Although, now that I think about it, when I first met her, she reminded me of you."

"Aw, how sweet."

His erotic response to her deepened as his eyes moved over an almost sheer robe she wore, highlighting rather than covering dark nipples pressed against the soft fabric. This was not right, not after he'd just fucked Brigitte harder than he ever had. He knew it was because of Olivia's unexplained presence tonight. Just seeing her had brought surprise, confusion, resentment, guilt, an entire concoction of ridiculous emotions that he didn't really know or understand. Yet here he was, a few hours later, on a chance encounter, and his fucking cock was begging for her to touch it.

I'm a pig, he thought. *Beautiful, sexy, giving woman in my bed who I've been having sex with for the past three weeks, and here I am, drooling over a woman who wouldn't give me the time of day before. Get it together, man.*

Was she coming on to him? Just teasing him? It couldn't matter. While he and Brigitte were only having a good time like they had in Colorado, no commitments had ever been proclaimed for either of them, he was still *with* her. No matter how intensely his body reacted to Olivia, it wasn't happening. Backing away, he smiled.

"Well it's all yours. Have a nice visit."

Her eyes shifted to the floor and back to his. He could almost swear he saw indecision, but that didn't make sense. Whatever it was, he needed to go before the erection got any bigger or he lost his ability to control the unwelcome desire for this unbelievably beautiful woman.

"Good-night."

Moving like the devil himself was chasing him, Will walked with purpose and speed back to the suite that Dez had assigned to Brigitte since she'd been in South America. He himself had slept there with her every night since she arrived.

They had a perfect relationship. He liked her, a lot, and she liked him, a lot too. The sex was hot, athletic, satisfying, and since they already knew each other's bodies and preferences from the days in Colorado, they'd fallen right back into comfortable patterns.

This was what he needed. What he wanted. Nothing serious. Will knew, admitted to himself only, that if he'd started something with the intriguing Olivia, it would never be just casual. It would be scorching and something they would likely have trouble walking away from.

I'm not ready for that, he promised himself as he stepped inside Brigitte's room. *Right?*

"Right," he whispered out loud to himself.

Brigitte slept, the deep sleep of a vampire after aggressive sex and the arrival of daylight hours. He needed to get dressed and back to Ife's home, where he still lived most of the time, and get back down to what they all now called the *Cavern of Starlight*.

Pressing the door to the now empty bathroom closed and dropping back against it, Olivia closed her eyes, her right hand sliding down to squeeze the thick nub that had been begging for attention. Just seeing Will again had reignited the fire she'd felt that first night he'd come from the sand-pool in the desert, turning her on immediately.

Water had cascaded from him then as he walked from the pool, and even though he was merely damp tonight, Olivia, aware that she was drunk, enjoying the freedom it provided, had nearly pushed him down and licked him top to bottom.

"You'd have enjoyed that," she whispered to the man who wasn't there. Her eyes landed on the tiled floors and walls that covered the back of the oversized bathroom, still wet from Will's shower.

Moving slowly, Olivia dropped her robe and stepped onto the stone-colored tiles, toeing water droplets that might have slid down his body. Eyes closed now, she imagined him there, naked, no towel, the cock she knew was incredibly generous erect and weeping for her. She glanced up at the rain shower head and a hand-held wand that provided powerful pulsating water at the touch of a button. Leaning against the tile wall, she turned on the water, and as it cascaded over her head, she reached for the wand. It would have to do.

Six hours later at the *Cavern of Starlight*

Will laid his snack pack on a metal table set up the first week that Ife's team had started serious investigation into the cave system of off-world crystals. Certain now that the crystals had been here for millennia, everyone waited with fascination to find out more about their nature and why they were suddenly revealed. Had they been put here with a purpose? Was there a reason the cave had been revealed at this time? It was indeed the mystery Ife had told them it was.

But not to Will. From the first moment Caedmon had led him down here, the second his foot had touched the earth at this depth, he'd known that this cave had opened for *him*. That the buried treasure of universal gifts had been waiting for him. That Mother Earth welcomed him home. His earth-borne power had dug into the living planet at the same moment that it had reached up to him. What these crystals were, how they had come to be buried so deep within this world, what their purpose was, he did not know, but he *did* know that *he* was the one destined to touch them and deliver them to the world.

As he had that first night, and every time he was here alone since then, Will turned off every light that the vampire's had placed around the huge domed cave. Instead of total darkness, as Caedmon had found when he fell into this opening, Will lifted his eyes to watch an unparalleled display of refracted light glow from every crystal that covered the ceiling and walls of this magnificent place. He'd discovered something that he hadn't revealed to anyone else yet. It's why he came here alone during daylight hours. Will wasn't ready to share with anyone yet that when he was alone here, the cave and crystals absorbed his magic. They resonated now with light and sound that made the mystery even grander.

At first, when he'd felt the power exchange, the crystal cave reaching into him, feeding power to him, he'd worried about what they wanted from him. Were they trying to drain him? Had he been given this gift to only hold for them awhile?

Now, he knew, without doubt, they were taking from him, but they were feeding him too. This symbiotic relationship had always been written in the stars.

"I can feel you," Will whispered, moving slowly around the perimeter of the cave, fingertips sliding along the wall, surprised anew at the infusion of warmth that tickled his skin as he went.

After a full circle, Will reached for his pack and removed two bottles of water and some dried fruit. After dancing all night, he was as tired as Brigitte, but here is where he needed to rest. Finishing half the fruit and one bottle of water, he sat on the ground, which became warmer and warmer with each passing moment, then lay back to seek the greatest contact possible with the living world. Here he would stay until the others arrived after sunset when they would start again the pragmatic part of the research. He would help them *study* something that he already understood completely.

Eyes on the waves of color overhead that moved much like the Northern Lights, Will let his mind relax. He was unsurprised where it went. Olivia's image filled it, leaning against the wall, breathing deep, drunk, her touch where he'd imagined it more than once...*and that thin robe!* Minutes after aggressive sex with Brigitte, mostly to try to purge Olivia from his memory, he'd taken a cold shower, finally calmed his frazzled nerves, and walked out, nearly bare, to find her big blues on him.

"You're cruel, Fates, you know that, right?"

His voice bounced off the walls and fed back to him. After hooking up with Brigitte again, they had reconnected and he admitted that it could become serious. When he was ready to share his life with a woman he truly respected and cared about, Brigitte might have been the one...until Olivia showed up, the one woman who had haunted him from the moment he laid eyes on her.

She didn't want him, she'd made that clear. When he'd accepted Ife's invitation, he'd come to get away from his unsettled life, and Olivia had been part of that. He'd had no idea that Olivia had ties here in South America. Had he known, he might not have come.

Closing his mind off now, he allowed himself to sink into the earth, almost literally, as his body seemed to burrow into the soft ground several inches deep. Who was he fooling? He'd always have come, he was meant to be here. And somewhere, deep in his unconscious mind, he'd known that she might have been too.

"Trying to slip away from me?"

Torin's booming voice brought Will's head up.

"No, just getting an early start."

"You know better."

"Yeah, I do. You're here now."

"Go ahead."

Will's watchdog scooted up on a table, music playing in his ears as he sipped a cold coffee.

Will dropped his head back down and closed his eyes.

AT DEZ'S PLACE AT FIRST MEAL

Olivia shook back her hair, tied in a high ponytail with scarlet-tinted loose tendrils cascading around her face. Tonight, her grandmother and Zach were taking her to see the big mystery of the region, Ife's newly discovered cave. Never mind the fact that, after Siberia, she'd have figured the last thing any of them wanted to do was climb deep into the ground again. It hadn't exactly been a pleasant thing back then, and she couldn't see a reason to do it again.

Her eyes moving over the crowd gathered for first meal, she discovered that, reluctantly, she was searching for Will and Brigitte. A sharp stab in her chest let her know that she really should keep her distance and ignore them, but she found herself seeking them out anyway. When neither showed up, she finished piling up her tray and joined Zach and Dez at the main table. After finishing off an excellent omelet, she glared at Zach.

"You're really going to take me down a ladder into the bowels of the earth again. I know it's been a while, but didn't we get enough of that at Lake Baikal?"

"No," Zach parried. "This is nothing like Siberia, although you'll be thrilled to know that Nikolai has been working with us on this discovery. No, *this* cavern is warm, solid, and stunningly amazing. Liv, you *have* to see it."

"Oh, I'll go, of course. When have I ever turned either of you down? Don't answer that. Some questions are obviously rhetorical. It sounds neat, so I'm there. After more cake please."

An extended groan carried across the entire room from the doorway as Brigitte entered, dressed, but wearing a bathrobe over her clothes, a hand to her head. "Why did you guys let me *do* that? Between dancing, boozing, and fucking, I think I saw my life flash before my eyes."

Laughs cascaded through the group. Mostly vampire, they understood and appreciated the feeling.

"Coffee. Stat!" Brigitte filled a cup the size of a small mixing bowl with the hot brew, poured a generous splash of cream in, leaned against the buffet table with her eyes closed, and savored the first sip. An orgasmic moan later, she pushed away with a wide smile.

"Better. Dez, would it be awful if I bow out tonight and spend it in bed. I'm not sure I've ever been this exhausted."

Watching the gorgeous vampire approach the table, Dez sat back to study her. "Still tired? Willoughby must be quite the sex machine."

Dez didn't notice Zach's expression as he reached for her. She continued. "Humans can't easily wear out vampires."

Brigitte, hands wrapped tight around the big cup, grinned, her eyebrows raised. "Well, *he* can. *Did*."

Zach tugged hard on Dez's arm. "Dez, don't…"

Laughing, Dez touched Zach, still unaware he was trying to stop her. "Then he's a keeper."

Brigitte shrugged, the grin softening to an easy smile. "I think he is."

"Dez!" Zach called out, exasperated.

"What?"

Finally getting his mate's attention, Zach lowered his gaze and leaned closer to place his lips to her ear.

"Stop. I'll explain later, but get off this topic."

Lifting her head, Dez nodded, then turned back to Brigitte. "Yeah, perhaps an extended rest will do you good. We're going to the cavern today and you've already seen it."

"Yup. Pretty. Don't need to see it again. Thanks."

She lifted her eyes and looked to the other side of the table where Olivia sat silently dicing a tall stack of pancakes into child-size pieces.

"Wow. You're really focused on your task."

Olivia lifted her eyes from her plate. "What? Oh, yeah, I've always liked tiny food."

"Um, Ooo…kay. We didn't get a chance to catch up last night. How about we get together for second meal? I heard Cari and Eras spent a few weeks with you in Vegas recently. I'd love to hear the details."

It's not her fault, Olivia had to remind herself. *You cannot be upset with Brigitte.*

"Sure, that's fine. They had a smashing time, and of course, hated to leave. You haven't seen them recently?"

"No. I'm heading to Colorado right after I finish here."

"Bridge, what brought you here?"

Olivia wondered if it had been for Will, or had they just met back up accidently.

"To see Ife. I haven't seen my brother or sisters in a long time, so I'm visiting them one by one. I've just, um, lingered here longer than I expected to."

God, don't start talking about sex with Will again. I already look like an idiot for pulverizing my food.

Awkward silence brought the uncomfortable conversation to a close and Brigitte stood, the coffee cup still firmly held. "I'll see you all tonight. Enjoy the sparkly cave."

As she wandered back toward the door, Brigitte scoped out the breakfast buffet, filled a plate high with a variety of items, and took it with her.

Once Brigitte disappeared, Dez's eyes shot to Zach.

"Well everything about this meal since Brigitte showed up was straight up weird. You care to fill me in?"

The bullet-quick gaze went to Olivia. "And you, what the hell was that? *'I like tiny food'*? Tell me."

Zach took his cue from a silent Olivia, who just pushed the pancake bits around in her plate. It was up to him to begin the story. "Your granddaughter is happy to be here with us, but she actually *came* here for Will."

"What? Will? Olivia, you've been seeing Will? Why wouldn't you tell me that?"

Feeling like a teenage girl caught by her parents in bed with a boy, she shrugged. "Dez, there's nothing to tell. I *haven't* been seeing Will."

"All right. Then I'm confused."

"Let me fix that. Do you remember when I told you that I helped Chione find one of the human earth-warriors? Will was the one. I didn't elaborate because the two days I spent with him were strange. You two know I've never had a long relationship. I've never been in love, which suited me just fine. Too many hot sexy men in the world to get tied down to one. I went to find Chione's missing soldier in the desert in Arizona last year, and well, let me say that the first time I saw him, he was soaking wet and completely naked. For some reason I still don't understand, he got to me right away."

Dez placed a hand on Olivia's. "Darling, love doesn't ask permission. It's a bitch that way."

"I guess I discovered that. When I entered Will's spirit realm later that night to show him what I was, to *prove* that he had to believe me and trust me, I saw his nature too. I saw the latent power that shouldn't have been granted to a human being; it was overwhelming for him. He'd suffered so much, Dez. More interestingly, I saw that he was Shoazan and could be a vampire's mate. It spooked me, so much that when I left him in Africa, all I wanted to do was forget him. And I did. At least, I *thought* I had until about a month ago when he rescued Corri and brought her back to Vegas. Since then, I haven't been able to purge him from my mind. Last week, I finally had to admit to myself that I didn't want to. I needed to find him, and here I am. Too late."

"Livie, you don't know that."

"No, I won't walk over whatever he and Brigitte are building. I'm too late, it's that simple. If they're together, if they've fallen in love, it's great. Brigitte's a darling and Will deserves to be happy. I'm not even sure what I'd have to offer him. My feelings are out of whack. All I know is that I wanted to see what we might be together. Now, it's set. We're meant to remain only friends."

"That coffee looks good." Olivia pushed her seat back, stood, bent to kiss Dez on the cheek, then Zach, smiled, genuinely, she hoped, and lifted her mug. "Let's not think about Will today. I'll make it an Irish coffee and go back to my room. Zach, let me know when you're going to leave, okay? I can use the distraction."

Zach started to say something as she walked away, but Dez laid a finger over his lips. "Don't."

"But she needs to know that Will is likely to be there."

"Darling, no she doesn't. Let's allow the course of events to chart its own path."

"But…"

"My love, do I need to find something else for you to do with that mouth?"

Three

"Wakey, wakey!"

From deep in his spirit merge with the earth, Will heard the familiar voice and smiled. He truly believed that man could wake the dead. As he floated from the merge, he sat up carefully, aware by now that it took a few minutes to regain his equilibrium after several of these sessions. He felt Torin's hands on his back, supporting him.

"Easy there, 'bro."

"Thanks, Tor." Will felt fine now, opened his eyes and easily pushed off the warm ground to stand. "What'd you bring tonight?"

"Phoenix bananas."

"I've never heard of that."

"That's my mission. Feed you food you've never heard of. With this, you take bananas that are so far gone, you'd think they must be spoiled, then you mash them, add one each of eight different spices and blend it into a topping poured over jalapeño-infused mixed vegetables. The bananas, like the Phoenix, rise again. Spicy, sweet, amazing. You'll have a happy mouth, I promise."

For the past three weeks, Torin often brought local foods when he came down at dusk to check on Will. Once Ife realized that Will went down into the cave every day by himself while her vampire team still slept, she'd assigned Torin as an assistant slash caretaker.

Will had been pissed at first, but eventually accepted the local man's help. Since then, they'd fallen into almost a brotherly friendship. A close male friend Will had never had. Because he himself was large and imposing, a loner at heart, men had never tried to befriend him and he'd been okay with that. Now, with the easy camaraderie he'd developed with Caedmon and Torin, he knew what he'd missed.

"I'm starving, so let's do this."

Torin used a delicate silver cake-server to scoop out two large portions from an equally delicate-looking tray. He routinely swiped items from Ife's warehouse compound because he told her that the facility was "too fancy and had too much," when many of the local clans had so little. He had seen in her eyes that she agreed and an unspoken agreement that he could take what he wanted had been born. Since then, she'd happily noticed some of the elaborate items that her mother routinely sent her being used with joy in the villages she often visited. Torin was doing a very nice job in redistributing her wealth.

His plate full, Will dropped back down onto the ground and scooped up his first bite, followed by a moan of pleasure. "Shit, Tor, this is fantastic. Might be the best yet."

"You said that two nights ago."

"You keep excelling. God, this is good. What are you trying to fatten me up for?"

"So that hot little vampiress dumps your chubby ass and comes to me."

"Hah! Not happening. I mean, look at you, then look at me. No contest man."

Friendly chiding was all it was. Will was handsome in a rough-guy kind of way, big, his body highly-toned, the muscles deeply chiseled. But Torin was every bit a woman's idea of desirable manhood, at four inches above Will's height. While he carried another thirty pounds, he was built like solid rock, muscles just as carved as Will's from hard work. Most women looking at either of them might wonder what it would be like to have him beneath her or above her.

The comment wasn't a surprise. Will had known from the beginning that Torin had the hots for Brigitte. Hell, yeah, he would, the girl was stunning and vampire, which meant endless stamina, and in *her* case, inventive aggressive sex. The girl loved to fuck. It was what she and Will had most in common; what brought them together back in Colorado and again here in Brazil. But it turned out, it wasn't the only thing. They truly cared for each other.

"Sorry, dude, just saying that if the opportunity presents itself…"

"It won't." Will surveyed the thick braids that Torin wore wrapped around his head, raven's wing black, his beard neatly trimmed. Yeah, Brigitte wouldn't hesitate to jump on a man like that, except that right now, she was fully committed to what she and Will had built since he'd been here.

As he lifted another forkful of the banana mash, Olivia's face sudden filled his mind and he forcibly tamped it down. No, *no!* He was with Brigitte. For how long, he didn't know, but this relationship they had was an unspoken, if temporary, pact to be together instead of with others. He had to, *would*, honor that pact. Besides, Olivia was here to see her family, not him, so there was no conflict anyway.

"Ife up yet?"

Finishing his plate by licking it, Torin looked over at Will. "Yeah. They're going to work in the gardens before they come here. She asked to let her know if you had any new epiphanies for her."

"Not tonight. I felt like I was…how would I describe it? Sort of like I was in a…soup of light? Maybe that's as close as I can get. But it was all sensations, nothing that I can use to inform Ife or her scientists about its origins, purpose, or power."

"Too bad. It'll come, though, I have faith. I've felt your power."

Will nodded. *He had.* Two days after Ife had assigned Torin to keep an eye on Will, he'd come down into the cave to find him lying on the ground, seemingly unconscious, breathing shallow, his color pale, his skin cold. Startled, worried, he'd knelt beside Will and tried to rouse him. The contact had pulled Torin into the bizarre power exchange between Will and the living planet, feeding him into the power wave. Terrified, Torin's first reaction was to fight, but

Will calmed his nerves with magic, and once done, his body dormant beside Will's, Torin experienced something normal humans rarely did…earth magic up close and personal. Instantly, he discovered that there was a world much greater beyond everything he and his ancestors had ever known…that there was so much more unseen than seen in this universe. As he woke later, tears filling his eyes, the bond with his new friend deeper than he could have imagined, he knew he was changed forever.

"I am humbled to have been given this glimpse. What you are, my friend, is greater than mere mortals."

Will had placed both hands on Torin's shoulders. "No, that is not true. What I am is a conduit, a part of you and this world, all of us part of the whole, all of us vital to existence. I am just like you, Torin, other than the gift I have been given that I never feel I deserve. I serve this living world and so do you. In different ways, yes, but we all serve."

From that day, their relationship had become so close, they knew without fail, that they would remain companions for the rest of their days.

"So, your girlfriend coming down tonight?" Torin asked.

"No. Brigitte finds this cave fantastically beautiful, but she doesn't have any desire to revisit it."

"Well, if she did, you can go back up, Willie boy. This would be a fine place to…"

Will punched Torin in the arm, pulling very little of his strength.

Rubbing the spot, Torin, grinned. "You know, the girl deserves a great orgasm."

"Ah, *that's* not a problem…over and over again."

Standing, Torin began to pick up the remnants of their dinner. This area was so sacred, neither would spoil it with even a sliver of trash.

"I guess my chances with the lovely vampiress are low, but if she ever dumps your big ass, I'm next in line."

"Fair enough, buddy."

Noise moved easily through the cave, so when voices and sounds traveled down the access corridor, both men faced the ladder that led from the surface.

"Someone's coming," Torin commented.

Above the cavern, Olivia glanced over the edge where a solar-powered lantern's light disappeared into a dark hole.

"Yep, that looks familiar. Sans snow and ice. And I think the last one was a real ladder. Is that rope? It looks swingy."

Zach nodded. "It's swingy, and kind of fun."

"I'm a wuss, Zach, and I admit I'm all kinds of girly. Can you carry me down?"

"Ha. I've seen you in action, lady. You are a wild woman."

"Was. Now I'm just a lady. I'll go first. Can I just jump?"

"Not wise. It's too deep."

"I'm fourth generation, I got mad skills."

Dez grabbed Olivia's hand. "Sweetheart, don't. Use the freaking ladder."

"Worrywart. Okay. Last one down buys drinks all night."

Olivia used the freaking ladder, but jumped the last dozen feet. The easy drop felt good. Even vampires needed to keep their bodies moving and she'd been particularly sedentary lately. Add to that the emotional confusion from her failed attempt at romance, and it was clear to her that she needed to change a lot of things in the coming months.

Zach dropped beside her, smiling, because he'd done the same and pushed off the ladder far before the final steps, then waited for Dez to come down each one, careful not to damage the high heels on her boots. Zach played the gentleman and reached out to lift her into his arms before she hit the final step.

"I wish you had worn one of the six pairs of hiking boots I bought you this year."

Dez slipped onto the soft ground. "Traipsing through the jungle and climbing down into a hole in the earth is no reason to abandon sexy footwear."

Kissing her grandmother on the cheek, Olivia turned to head down the dark corridor. "It kind of is, Dez. So, what do we find down here anyway?"

"You'll see," Zach answered. "Just keep going."

The corridor proceeded for another thirty feet or so to where she saw low flickering light ahead. Aware that Dez and Zach were just behind her, Olivia continued until the corridor ended into a vast cave, high-ceilinged and brilliantly dazzling where an unknown light source flickered across what looked like millions of large diamonds. Not true diamonds, she imagined, but incredible nonetheless.

"Oh, my…" Olivia's voice a whisper, her head back, eyes cast upward, she turned to take in the view. Coming around, she noticed two figures behind a shadowed wall. Male, both big, they walked out into the light, and she held her breath. Will was one of them, his eyes locked on hers, a wave of emotion curling off him as she realized in that moment that the connection they'd had last year in Arizona was still there. Whatever he had with Brigitte, he still had feelings for her. The realization took her by surprise.

"Willoughby Collins. I was told you might be here, and as expected, here you are."

God, how lame. Olivia decided it was time to shut up and let the others in the room handle the conversation, since they really *hadn't* told her. Zach and Dez knew how she felt, so they could crawl her the fuck out of the embarrassing situation.

But they didn't need to. The other man, who she hadn't paid any attention to other than acknowledge that he existed, moved forward to take her hand.

"Hello, lovely lady. May I introduce myself? The name is Torin Almada."

Surprised, Olivia switched her gaze to the man who was even taller than Will, his look exotic and fascinating, his scent that of a wild animal. This intriguing man, Will, and the most spectacular natural formation she'd ever seen, here in this hole in the earth in South America. She had to admit, things had gotten interesting.

"Olivia, at your service sir," she said, mirroring his proper demeanor. Without warning, her eyes shot back to

Will. He hadn't moved, standing just beyond the darkened shadows with a bag in one hand and a bottle in the other.

"A friend of yours, Will?"

"Um, yeah. A friend."

"Brother, more like, these days." Torin hadn't released Olivia's hand, and now slid a finger into the palm. "Here to see the sights? Quite unrivaled anywhere else on earth, isn't it?"

"It's...astounding." Her eyes moved to Will, silent, still, waiting to see how she reacted. Shifting back to Torin, she smiled. "Why don't you show me around? Tell me what I'm seeing."

"It would be a pleasure."

Keeping her hand in his, Torin led Olivia to the other side of the cave while Dez and Zach remained beside Will.

"Handsome man. A friend, eh?" Dez watched Will as he watched Torin with Olivia. He wasn't happy.

"He is. We've bonded through both common interests and magic."

"Magic? I sense no magic in him."

"No, he's perfectly normal, but he's traveled with me into my connection with the earth. It was accidental. I didn't know it was possible, but he touched me while I was fully immersed and it drew him in. Since then, he gets me and I get him."

"He likes my granddaughter."

"Of course he does. The guy has great instincts and taste, and Olivia is extraordinary."

Moving closer to Will, Dez touched his wrist and read his emotions. It was as she suspected. Will's heart was racing, breathing too quick, and he couldn't take his eyes off Olivia. Whatever relationship he had with Brigitte, this man had deep feelings for Olivia too. Watching her with another man, even his friend, upset him. There could be no doubt; he cared for her.

Dez would keep his secret. She'd learned a long time ago that in matters of the heart, it was best to let things unfold naturally. If he was meant to be with Olivia, he would be. The year she'd discovered that she was first blood had shown her that when magic was involved, the universe had a way of seeing to it that what should be would be.

"It'll be all right," was all she said, and stepped back.

"So, Will, how's the progress here?"

An hour later, their guests gone, Torin turned to Will.

"I think I'm in love. What a glorious woman. Vampire, right?"

"Vampire. First blood, like Brigitte."

"Damn. Well, you're making it work with Brigitte. You think I have a chance with Olivia?"

Will didn't know what to say. Olivia wasn't his, he was with Brigitte, so he had no right to interfere with Torin's interest. It wasn't right to discourage him. Anyway, Olivia might not even be attracted to him. Immediately, he admitted that wasn't likely. Torin was *exactly* her type. Big, alpha male that oozed sexuality. Will had seen his effect on women, even Brigitte.

He nodded. "She *might* like them big and dumb."

"Ha, ha. I think I'll go get a nice long shower before we head to Dez's tonight to party."

"Have a good time. I think I'll stay in and get some rest."

"No way, brother. We can make it a foursome."

"I'm coming off very little sleep from *last* night."

"So what, you mostly sleep while you're down here. Come on."

"Not tonight, Tor, but good luck with Olivia."

"Won't need luck, got skills. Okay, I'm heading up. I'll take the bags. I guess I'll see you tomorrow evening."

"Deal."

After Torin left, Will did his final lap around the cave, his hand against the crystal wall as he walked. No matter how hard he tried, he couldn't keep his mind off Olivia. She'd looked so perfect tonight, but it was the image from this morning that filled his mind. Barefoot, drunk, playful, her hand on his cock. Even now, alone here, sacred though it was, the cave also held a sensuality, and since it often fed off his emotions, an intense wave of need washed over him. Somehow, it carried Olivia's scent, which still lingered here, to him and he breathed it in as his hand lowered to pull his zipper down and release the tightness as his cock responded to just the essence of Olivia.

Will let the hand touching the wall drop too, and walked back to the center of the cave.

"What are you doing?" he barked, his eyes on the ceiling as he shoved the nearly erect cock back into his pants and forced the zipper back up. "You're feeding me her scent. It isn't going to be easy for me to be around her while she's here. Don't make it harder."

Pissed, and not sure why he was, Will finished his lap and climbed to the surface, stopping to appreciate the light breeze. The temperature was always high in the cave, the air sometimes stale, making the return to topside refreshing every time. Ife and her group would arrive soon and although he usually hung around to greet them and let them know if there was any new information, tonight he'd had enough of everyone and everything. All he really wanted was to crawl into his own bed, alone, and sleep until the sun left again.

Will had grabbed a cup of non-caffeinated coffee, a tray of fruit, and retired to his room. Door locked, fone keyed to low, he finished his snack and crawled onto the top of his bed to let his body and mind crash. As tired as he was, he fell immediately into a dreamless sleep.

An incessant beeping interrupted that deep sleep, and Will came awake slowly as awareness told him that someone was trying to wake him. He finally identified the beep as his door chime.

"Ah, what the hell..."

Right now, he didn't want to open his eyes, let alone move. He wondered if whoever it was could hear him if he just called out. Doubtful, since the bed was in the back of the room and behind a heavy screen.

Fully awake now, he sat up and swung his legs off the bed, reluctance tugging at him as he reached for his shorts and pushed himself up, scratching his belly like he remembered his father doing decades ago.

Instead of calling through the door, he pressed a button on a panel several feet away.

"Yes?"

"Willyboy, we have a date."

Brigitte. Shit. He knew what this meant and he knew he couldn't say no. Oddly, with her, he never could, and it had nothing to do with compulsion. She was just so fucking cute and persuasive.

A second button released the locks and the door slid open. Will took one look at her and rolled his eyes.

"Yes."

Grinning, Brigitte walked in, closed the door panel, and loosely locked her arms around Will's neck. "I haven't even asked you a question."

"It doesn't matter. The answer is yes."

Moving closer, she snuggled into his wild bed hair.

"Ummm, I love them when they are well trained. Saves time, but I guess I'd better ask anyway. Come with me tonight to Dez's. I'm in the mood for more dancing, more camaraderie, and more *you*. So I guess we're going then."

"I guess we are." He didn't want to. As much as *she* was in the mood to party, *he* was in a mood to stay here and brood. Thing was, he'd never disappointed Brigitte and he couldn't now.

"Let me get cleaned up."

Purring into his ear, Brigitte lowered a hand to slide it beneath the shorts. "I can help you with that."

One hour later at Dez's compound

Torin scoped the room, his eyes sharp, his desire strong. That stunning vampire had to be here, he had to find her. The more he thought of her, the more he convinced himself that they might be good for each other. Touching her arm tonight had left an impression.

Dez's place was hopping tonight. The tables were already filled and the dance floor busy with people who had obviously been partying for some time. That was possible; Dez didn't really completely close down the nightclub rooms in her compound. If someone wanted to stay and drink, stay and dance…hell, stay and fuck, they could.

Accustomed to the lifestyles of vampires, Torin found everything about their behavior completely normal now. They lived life fully and without hold, all the pleasures, all the joys, full on. Fucking, most of all. As only a human, he wondered if he could ever measure up, but the idea was ludicrous. No, he couldn't, but he knew that vampires fell in love with humans all the time.

So why couldn't this lovely Olivia fall in love with him? He intended to see where they could go from here.

In her room, Olivia debated between what she wanted to do, which was stay here and sleep, or do what she *should* do, and go enjoy the company of her family. Making the right choice, committed to the action, she put on her sexiest dress, smiled at the image in the mirror, forced a cheerful look on her face, and went out into the corridor, up one flight, to find Zach and Dez. The situation with Will stung, there was no doubt, but she needed to get back to living the life she'd built.

"Find a good man and fuck him hard." Good advice that had served her well more than once. Long lives bred bad days with great frequency. Olivia had years ago discovered that simple physical pleasure could heal a lot of wounds if one gave it time and effort.

Tonight, she planned to give it a lot of effort. Entering the nightclub area of the compound, she looked at the large group of partiers, most of whom were already feeling no pain. "Right back at ya, friends," she murmured.

"What was that, Liv?"

Zach came up behind her and dropped a kiss on her nose. Acting like her grandfather, Zach failed to accomplish the task. He was a few hundred years younger than her and appeared to be the same age, even though, technically, as Dez's mate, he tried to assume the role.

"Booze, Zach, and a lot of it. Quickly."

"As you wish, young lady. Come with me."

"You make a handsome grandfather, Zach."

"I know. Something I could never have imagined when I was an attorney in L.A. so many years ago."

Her gaze softened, a hand slid up to his cheek.

"I bet you were quite striking as a human."

"You'd win that bet."

Nostalgia for the life lost as a human being was rare, but there were moments when a memory struck and regrets surfaced. Briefly in most cases, certainly true for Zach, who loved being vampire and mated to Dez.

"Had a lot of fun, I admit it. Some friends I miss."

"How did it happen for you?"

"I decided to go out on a date with a pretty girl. She was abducted by a vampire, I tried to help her, got nearly murdered, and she saved me by making them convert me. Reluctantly, Dez offered to do the deed, and vampire I became. It was a fucking crazy ride."

"It had to be. I'm glad you're here with us now. Dez is so *gone* for you."

"She saved me, in more ways than one. I can't imagine a happier life."

A happy life. Yeah, that's what mattered in the end, what everyone sought. Olivia watched the writhing bodies enjoying Dez's hospitality. Perhaps her reaction to Will was only a recognition that it was time to find someone special to share this journey with. Perhaps it didn't have to be *him*.

"I think it's time I look for some of that myself. Hey, isn't that Will's friend from the cave?"

She and Zach watched Torin at the bar, smiling at the friendly barmaid. Zach nodded.

"Yeah, it is. He seemed to like you quite a lot."

"I think I'll go see if he'll buy me a drink."

Zach stopped her with a hand on hers. "You deserve your happily ever after, Olivia. Open yourself up to it."

Her eyes on his electric blue ones, she tipped her head in acknowledgment. "I think I'm ready to. Have a good night, *grandfather*."

Her fingers sliding off Zach's, Olivia walked slowly across the room, her eyes on Torin. He was a truly attractive masculine specimen, every bit as sexy as Will. She had no doubt that they could have a good time together. As she watched, he lifted his drink, his head back, he brought it to his lips, a laugh finishing, when his eyes moved toward her. The smile widened and he lowered the drink.

Olivia didn't stop until she was within reach of his breath. "Hello, Will's friend."

His eyes moved over her, dropped to her body briefly, then back to her face, to her lips, then to her eyes.

"Hello. *Will's friend* will do. I'll earn the right for you to remember my name."

"Fair enough. Please order me a generous glass of Glenfiddich."

"Without delay."

Torin turned to place her order, presenting a nice view of a strong back, and thick arms. Olivia smiled as her eyes moved over his head and long sleek dark hair that would be nice to hang onto during an orgasm. Yes, this was a good plan.

Brigitte kissed Will as they moved through the nightclub where the floor pulsated to blasting percussion, vibrating off the walls as well. Her arms around his neck, she pulled back to search his eyes.

"I'm happy you came with me. You seemed a little distant this morning."

"No, Brigitte. I just partied too much last night and the work is taking a lot of my energy right now."

"Perhaps I can help. If you need a magical conduit to share the load while you merge, I could join you."

"It isn't like that, Bridge. It really is a one on one fusion with my innate earth powers. I'm fine, I just need some rest." *That wasn't exactly true, but he couldn't let her know that Olivia's presence had affected his connection to her.*

"I'm sorry, I guess I shouldn't have pushed you to leave your bed. Say, let's just go back and I'll crawl in with you."

Will almost nodded and lifted her in his arms to carry her back out of the noisy room when he saw Torin at the bar, an arm around Olivia's waist, lift a stemmed glass to her lips. *Torin and Olivia, together.* It shouldn't surprise him, but it did. There couldn't have been a worse development. If Olivia *did* fall for Torin and they were to become close, would he be able to deal with it? How would he handle hearing Torin boast about how great they were together?

As much as he wanted to, Will couldn't walk away.

"No, we're here, and you really wanted to be out tonight. Torin's at the bar. Why don't we join him?"

"Are you sure?"

"Yeah, sure. Come on gorgeous."

Satisfied that all was well, Brigitte took Will's arm and followed him to the bar, happy to see Olivia there.

"Livie!"

Olivia, caught in the circle of Torin's arms, peeked over his biceps to see Brigitte beside Will. She smiled at her friend, but her eyes slid to Will before bringing them back to Brigitte.

"Hi, Bridge. You two are out again tonight, eh?"

"You know me, Liv, I like to play. My parents tell me that I'll settle down some day and get something done, but so far, life's just one long party to me."

Carefully, Olivia pushed Torin's arms down to his sides and turned away from him. "Looks like you might have found something to settle down *for*." Her point-blank stare at Will wasn't cloaked, she wanted to see if Brigitte was serious about Will. *Needed* to see.

Brigitte's gaze followed Olivia's to an uncomfortable Will.

"Stop it," he barked. "No one is talking about mates right now." But when his eyes landed on Brigitte, she wasn't smiling, her eyes shining with moisture, locked on Will, as she reached for him.

"I don't know, Will. I mean, no, I'm not ready to consider anything like that either." After a pause, she continued with one word. "Yet."

That word rocked Will. *Yet.* They had been having fun since she arrived, just as they had in Colorado last year. There had been no talk, *no thought*, of anything serious. He adored her, the sex was amazing, he would do practically anything for her, but the idea of signing on with her forever, possibly converting to vampire...it hadn't occurred to him. This moment, though, he realized, it had occurred to *her.*

He didn't know what to say. Olivia was looking at him, eyebrows raised. Torin's grin was sly, and Brigitte's face was flat-out serious. "Bridge..."

A second stretched into eternity before Brigitte smiled easily and lifted her hand to ruffle his hair, leaving the strands sticking out in all directions. "Relax, frat boy. I'm not ready either, but I'm not ruling out anything for the future. Now, I just want to dance. You look thunderstruck. Sit and recover. Torin, take a girl for a spin."

She touched Olivia on the arm. "You don't mind do you? Torin *is* a better dancer than Will."

"Um, no, of course not. You two go for it."

Torin threw a glance back at Olivia as Brigitte yanked him out amongst the frenzied dancers.

Left alone, Olivia and Will avoided each other's gaze for a few moments, then their eyes collided as they both looked up at the same time.

To break the silence, Olivia stayed on topic. "So, it looks like you have a keeper. She's an incredible young woman."

Eyes still focused on hers, Will shook his head. "I didn't know. I mean, we've become close friends, I am crazy about her, but..." Will trailed off as he reached for Olivia's whisky and swallowed the several shots still left in it.

"You know more than anyone that with my history, the idea of committing to someone seems impossible."

Olivia sighed. Her eyes hadn't left his either. She didn't want to, she *loved* looking at him, and more than that, in spite of everything, she needed to touch him.

Reaching up, she twisted her fingertips into the messy strands of his hair, then smoothed them down. "Oh, Will. Yes, I know about your past, how unkind the fates have treated you and those you loved. I know how impossible it's been for you to understand and accept your power. Above all, I know what a generous and beautiful man you are, and that you need to love and need to *be* loved. It's what you deserve, my sweet warrior. You were never meant to travel this journey alone, of this I am certain."

Her fingers, sliding against his scalp, lingering, titillated him, even though he doubted she intended it to do so. If there was ever a moment he considered the idea of forever with someone, this was it. The innocent, simple touch of a woman who ignited his body and mind, who was out of his reach, had been all it took to take him from shocked at the idea of committing to a life with someone to wanting it more than anything.

She wasn't his, had no interest in him, not like that. He had no need to be jealous of his friend, Olivia likely just wanted to enjoy him, to find pleasure in him, and bring pleasure to him as well. Surely it was unlikely she would fall in love with him. *Gods, let it be unlikely.* At this moment, he had to admit that he wasn't, *couldn't*, be in love with Olivia, *but it was possible that would come.*

He wanted to lean into her, then lift her and carry her to his room. As much as he knew she would be shocked, so would Brigitte.

Will let himself enjoy her touch, but when she pulled her hand back and smiled up at him, he smiled back casually. "Thank you, Olivia. You give me far too much credit, but if I ever needed someone to write my press releases, it would be you."

"I believe in you. I always have. Don't forget, I've been inside you."

Oh, that was a mistake. He could see that she realized it as soon as she said it.

Will's cock reacted instantly, growing hard while trapped in his jeans. *I've been inside you...* No, she hadn't, not the way he wanted, but oh, fuck, he wished he had, *could*, and *now*.

"I, I mean..." Olivia stuttered. "You know what I mean."

"Uh, yeah, of course."

Yeah, he did, but it didn't stop the desire that surged, the physical reaction. What was he going to do with this hard-on?

"Would you tell Brigitte I'll be right back?"

"Sure."

Will turned to find a private place to deal with his situation, stopped by Olivia's touch, which did not help.

"Biker, I...I'm sorry."

"Sorry?" What was she apologizing for? For causing this erection? He hoped she hadn't noticed, then remembered that she could read him. Yeah, she knew.

"You've nothing to apologize for. Uh, yeah, I gotta go, Olivia."

"I know. I wish..." She stopped. "I mean, go. Take off." *I wish I could help you with that* was what she wanted to tell him.

Will strode purposefully through the crowds at the edge of the room, and Olivia watched him until he disappeared from view. A deep sigh released a long-held breath. "Oh, Willoughby, I could *really* take care of that for you."

When a desperate desire to throw all caution to the wind and follow him nearly won her mental battle, Olivia forced herself to watch the vivacious, gregarious Brigitte heating up the dance floor with Torin, trying hard to keep up. It was a reminder that she must do what was right and honorable. Brigitte was an earth warrior like Will, and a great-hearted first blood. Olivia felt it was her duty to protect these soldiers, and that she would do. Will was off limits.

Breathless, Brigitte led Torin through increasing dancers. "This guy can really move," she told Olivia as she passed him back. "You're lucky I have my Will. Thanks for the loan, Liv. Where'd Will go?"

"Gentlemen's room."

Torin, shiny from sweat, his eyes sparkling as he looked at Olivia, did indeed look sexy as hell. Olivia let her eyes roam over his, top to bottom, her intention clear.

"Bridge, please excuse us."

After hooking a finger around the top of Torin's vest, she pulled him past the dancers, past the edge of the room and into the hallway. The thudding base could be heard through the doorway that separated the two spaces.

Moving close, Olivia pulled Torin's head down to whisper into his ear. "You've worked up a sweat. Care to continue?"

A brisk nod answered her query.

"Come then, and be quick about it. I've a terrible need to see if your moves on that floor are repeated in a bed."

Torin had no words to respond to this unexpected moment, but he followed Olivia down into the lower levels where he knew the vampires spent their days. He'd never been below before, but it was apparent now that Olivia had seen in him the same he'd seen in her; a partner for ancient games played on a leveled field for pleasures found no other way. He'd never had sex with a vampire, but as they moved toward her chambers, he found himself interested more in intimacy with Olivia, vampire or not. Something about her was more intriguing by the moment.

"Here," she announced softly, as she opened a double-wide door and led him inside a place right out of a fairy tale.

"Wow," he commented.

Olivia walked to the bed and slipped her dress over her head. "Save the exclamations. You'll need them later. Get naked, and come show me what you can do."

Four

Stretching, Olivia put a hand out to slide it along Torin's back. He was incredibly attentive, but when he was ready to sleep, he'd told her that he always preferred to roll away, which suited her. Olivia, too, was not accustomed to someone in her bed while she slept. For the past two weeks, they'd been together most nights.

"Lights," she said, cueing the system to bring up low illumination.

He groaned. She'd discovered that Torin was *not* a morning person. "Tor, you have to go."

Another groan ended in a growl as he sat up, struggling to waken. After a long yawn, he rolled over on top of Olivia. "I need some *help* getting my motor running."

Olivia pushed him off her, laughing. "I *helped* you all night. Get moving."

She didn't say what was really on her mind; that he needed to get to the crystal cave to keep an eye on Will. As she'd learned more about what Will was doing there, the deep earth-magics merge, she couldn't control her concern. She knew what he experienced when he was in one of those merges. It could be overpowering, but more than that, it could be dangerous. That's why Ife had assigned Torin to be there with him. Luckily, Torin took his role as protector seriously.

"Okay," he said, "I'm up."

"I'm up," he repeated, as if to convince himself he was, but it was another few minutes before he lifted off Olivia's bed and stumbled to his clothes.

After he had dressed, Torin hovered over Olivia, pulled her sheet back, and kissed each nipple, ran his tongue from one to the other and back again, licking the entire path. "Will I see you tonight?"

Her eyes still closed, Olivia moaned. "I'm not sure. Dez may have plans for us. I'll let you know."

"All right. I guess I'll get gone. Sleep well."

After he'd left, Olivia stretched out to take up most of the bed. Torin had been a delight since they'd been together. For the past few weeks, he'd shown he was creative, attentive, and amazingly athletic. She'd threatened to put in a trapeze just to see what he would do with it. Not surprisingly, he was a good lover, something she needed right now, in spite of the fact that he was close with Will.

A vampire's imperative to sleep during daylight took over and Olivia submitted.

AT IFE'S COMPOUND

Dani polished off her third bowl of clam chowder, reminding herself once again that she wasn't vampire and that eating like this would add unwanted pounds. So far, she'd been lucky and still kept the cute figure that brought her a lot of masculine attention these days, although still no *dates*.

"Dani, I need your latest update." Ife breezed through the doorway, snatching a cinnamon bun as she moved past a buffet table to join Dani at her small table.

"Of course. Little has changed since we spoke last though. The elements of the crystals have yet to be identified. Fia's taken the samples to four reliable facilities to see if anyone has any ideas or recognizes the composition. Will remains convinced that with these magical exchanges, he'll eventually know their source and what they are capable of. He still feels they are here for a reason. We're waiting for Fia's lab in Paris. Did I tell you that they are using the same equipment that the U.S.U. uses on Mars? The units are designed to analyze off-world items. Crystals vibrate at different frequencies and these are nothing like any other observed on earth."

"Thanks. It's still so crazy to me that all these centuries we had no idea that the cave or the extraterrestrial crystals existed."

"No, Ife, all these centuries those crystals have *waited* for us. For Will. What is happening is remarkable in ways I don't think any of us can imagine. Honestly, I don't know what Will will be after he's finished with them and they're finished with him."

"I know. He's not worried at all, and I'm increasingly worried."

"We must trust him. Only Will knows what the crystal's power feels like. He's unstoppable in his need to continue this bonding, but I worry too. Torin says that he seems to be completely comfortable during the sessions."

"He seems to be. I tried last week to tap into his spirit realm while he was connected, but it wouldn't allow me in."

"Really? That isn't typical, is it? Cairine's gone into mine and Dylan's a few times with no trouble. Huh."

"You're right, though, Dani, we have to trust him. Will is like no one else I've ever met. I agree, I think he has a special purpose."

"Each earth warrior has a place in the universe, but Will seems to be on the edge of something even grander."

"Another grand destiny," Ife whispered.

Unable to stop herself, Dani walked slowly to the buffet to snag one of the cinnamon buns. *Oh, my ass*, she thought. When she took her seat again, her fingers covered with the generous icing on the bun, she licked her thumb, her eyes on Ife. "Yes, another grand destiny."

At the *Cavern of Starlight*

Torin had climbed down that ladder so many times, he knew exactly how many rungs it had and usually slid down the last five. Lately, he'd found himself whistling after he landed on the deep earth and traveled down the corridor that spilled out into the massive cavern.

His eyes moved at once to Will in his usual spot centrally located, his back, arms, legs, and head pressed into the ground, eyes closed, and checked completely out of his physical space. The glimpse he'd had into where Will's mind, *his soul?*, went, had transformed his concept of reality. Although he'd been with Ife for three years and felt fully indoctrinated to the vampire's world, the magic Will wielded with this living planet blew his mind.

He just hoped it wouldn't blow *Will's*. Working with so much power was inherently dangerous.

Squatting next to Will's prone body, he checked his breathing and color. Surely this had to be finished soon. Today would mark the thirteenth session. Torin laid a hand on Will's forehead, which was thankfully cooler than the surrounding air.

"Doin' okay, buddy?"

Will was deep under, Torin didn't expect an answer, so, lifting back to his feet, he turned to walk away when Will's right hand curled around his leg.

"Tor."

Will's voice was weak, the volume weaker yet. Torin went to his knees, and cupped his head. "Willy boy, are you all right?"

"Tor," Will repeated. "Help me up."

Usually Will came completely out of his merge, and although sometimes he needed a little help to stand so that he could regain his balance, this time, he seemed to be really out of it. Torin supported his friend to the best of his ability, but although he himself was bigger and heavier than Will, it was a struggle to keep Will upright.

"Don't try to stand. Here, let me bring you over and have you sit against the wall."

Not listening to Torin's command, Will tried to remain on his feet, but he wobbled so badly when Torin let him go, he grabbed his arms again. "Will, you need to sit down."

"But I...I have to get some..."

Using force, Torin finally got Will back onto the ground, but supported against the crystal wall. He'd chosen a section where the stones were smoothest and pressed Will back.

"Good. Stay, Will. What happened? You're not right, my friend. You're kind of acting drunk, but I know you're not."

"No..." Will drew out the word, his eyes closed again, and following a deep expulsion of breath, he didn't say anything else. Torin confirmed that he was still breathing, but other than that, he didn't know what was wrong with Will.

After five minutes passed and Will remained quiet, not distressed, not asleep but not awake, Torin decided he had to have help. His fone in his hand, he was a button away from contacting Ife when Will's eyes opened, dropped to the fone in Torin's hand, and he shook his head slowly.

"I'm okay. Don't call her."

"What can I do for you?"

"Just...stay here...with me. And, um...water?"

That was easy; Torin had a sleek water bottle up to Will's lips at once, amazed that he drew down all twenty ounces in one swallow.

Again, Will sat motionless, but this time, his eyes were open and began to move across the ceiling. Torin, frozen beside him, concerned, but willing to trust that Will was all right and that he shouldn't call for help, found his eyes moving upward as well.

"Are you looking for something?" he finally asked.

Will shook his head again. "No. Some*one*."

"Someone? Who?"

"It hasn't been revealed to me yet, but there is another earth warrior who can link with this cave. He or she is near and it is my job, my privilege, to bring us together here for the final meeting."

"Wow. But you don't know who it is?"

"It's how this always works. We'll find each other, of that I'm sure. What I'm not sure about is how I'm going to get back up the ladder. I feel as weak as a kitten."

"No worries. I've always got you, brother."

"Don't say anything to Ife. She worries too much. The last thing I want is for her to think that I have to stop. This is nearly done."

Torin was quiet for a moment before he cleared his throat. "Will, what is this doing to you? I mean, what does the planet, those crystals, this cave, *want* with you?"

Another long pause later, Will answered. "I think that it's changing my power. In my body, I feel surges, a desire to run, full out, across the land, crawl against the grass, lie under the sky."

He lifted his downcast eyes to meet Torin's. "Honestly, I don't know what's happening to me."

"Then you have to stop. Stay away from this hole. Get well again. I've noticed you've dropped some weight these past few weeks. When you feel up to it, I'll help you climb the ladder and then we don't come back."

"No, Tor, I can't do that. Look, I know things are strange, I feel weird in ways I can't describe, but I trust what is happening. It's for the greater good, of that I'm certain. In the end, we'll know what it is and I'll be fine."

Torin didn't buy it. When he started to protest, he felt Will's hand on his chest.

"Tor, you've been there with me, you know there is no malevolence."

"I don't know what I believe right now, except that my friend looks like he's been dropped from a lift-car. You know I'll be with you no matter what, but I think you need to get far away from here for a while. Get well again, anyway. Get some good nutrition. Let that vampiress reenergize you."

"I like the last part. Tor, for now, just help me get up the ladder."

That he could do. Torin used all his strength to lift Will from the ground and help him through the access corridor to the ladder. Standing at the first rung, Will groaned.

"Fuck, this is gonna hurt."

"I'll be right behind you every step in case you need support."

"Let's do this."

It had taken twenty minutes, but the two men made it up to surface level where, thankfully, Will's strength increased enough to make it over the landscape easily to Torin's jet-bike.

Now, entering the compound, Torin tried to supply support without being obvious, but everyone who worked with them was sharp-eyed and intuitive.

"Will, you look like doggy-doo. What happened?"

Dani and her southern U.S. vernacular. She may have phrased her inquiry with humor, but she looked at them with a deadly serious gaze. "You are involved with something we have no clue as to what it is or what it can do. When you look like this, we're going to ask. And you're going to answer."

Ife walked in on the last part of Dani's comment, her eyes moving immediately to Will. Wordlessly, she walked over to place a hand on his forehead and lean in. The room froze as Ife tried to move deeper into Will's spirit realm but she was pushed out again as she had the last few times she'd tried to do so. Pulling away, she stepped back.

"Will, I can't get in, but I can feel your weakness. Are the crystals draining you?"

"No, Ife. Until tonight, I never felt anything less than a euphoric merge. Even today, it was fine, I felt cradled and safe, but later, I don't notice time when I'm merged, I began to feel worse, I can't describe it, but I don't believe it is intended to harm me. Perhaps I'll get more clarity in my next session."

"Which I believe he shouldn't do."

Ife turned to face Torin after that statement. "I'm not sure I disagree. Will…"

"Stop. You brought me down here to help protect this region and what I am doing with the crystal cave may be exactly what you need. The crystals are here for a reason, and there's a sentience attached to them somehow. Not the crystals, I don't mean that, but someone has put them here for us and it is my job to find out why. So, thank you all for you concern, but I'm going into my room to sleep, undisturbed, for the entire night. You go ahead with first meal, I'm not hungry. I'll eat when I wake later. Goodnight, everyone."

Striding with as much purpose as he could, Will crossed the room, aware that everyone's eyes were on him, and gratefully closed the door to his room behind him. It was uncommon to lock doors in the compound, trust in their companions high, but this time, he did so.

Moving into the bathroom carefully, his balance still suspect, Will stopped in front of a wide well-lit mirror and stared at his image.

They were right. He looked bad. His eyes were bloodshot and appeared to be sunken in, his skin tone sallow, and he noticed that his shirt *did* fit looser.

He'd felt the draw as soon as it had begun, a subtle invasion that slowly increased until something inside of him rebelled. It was at that point he'd called out to Torin to help him. All of his actions were clear, he wasn't confused about anything, but why it all happened like that tonight, he did not know.

"Shower and bed," he whispered to the somewhat scary-looking image in the mirror. Peeling his clothes off to step into the shower, Will put his head under the pulsing hot water as it pounded against his skin. Heat and the water massage made him feel better right away, relaxing tight muscles. He knew he would sleep now and heavily. After drying off quickly, he wandered into his room and dropped naked onto his bed. Moments later, sleep took him away from his corporeal needs into a dreamscape built from his own hidden desires.

There, amongst wild flowers on a summer morning, the sun rising in the sky, stood Olivia in a yellow sundress and nothing else. The fabric nearly sheer, he could see her perfect body well outlined and he couldn't look away.

Yes, my own hidden desires, he thought, and walked toward his dream woman.

AT DEZ'S COMPOUND

"I'm not in much of a mood tonight, Dez. Will you forgive me? I need to catch up on lost sleep. Torin has been with me almost every night for several weeks. He called to say he wasn't going to make it tonight, so I think I'll head back to my room."

Olivia really was exhausted, Dez could see it in her movements and eyes. It wasn't just marathon sex, though, that made her granddaughter so tired. Emotional distress could do more than anything to mess someone up, which is what she saw and felt when she looked at Olivia.

"Go, sweetheart, get some rest. I've got plans for Zach anyway."

Olivia rolled her eyes along with a dismissive hand gesture. "All right, no details! I'll see you at first meal."

Hurried, she was in her room in minutes, undressed, and collapsed on her bed. She'd been serious that she was in need of sleep, but there had been a second reason she wanted to retire to this room tonight, perhaps more important than time in bed.

Whispering to herself on the way down the steps, she'd shaken her head at her folly.

"Social animal Olivia isn't feeling social."

Right now, she didn't want to spend an evening laughing, drinking, dancing, with Dez and her guests. While her time recently with Torin had been stimulating and enjoyable, an unexpected sadness had been creeping in and no matter how hard she tried to get her old mojo back, she hadn't been successful.

Many of the evenings with Torin had started in the company of Will and Brigitte, and although she'd accepted the fact that the two were a couple, it still stung to spend time with them. Brigitte, highly affectionate, spent a lot of moments wrapped around Will.

Lying alone on her bed with only dim candlelight-style bulbs illuminating the edge of the room, Olivia felt awful to admit to herself, "*I don't want to see them together.*"

Finally, she gave in to her need to sleep.

It was rare that she dreamt, but this night, she found herself in a meadow filled with bright yellow wildflowers. A sun partway up a bright blue cloudless sky warmed her skin through a light sundress. Even in the dream, she was aware that the sun was a forbidden gift, and lifted her face to the brightness. She stayed that way for endless moments as distant memories of joy returned.

"A beautiful vampire in sunlight, that's quite a sight."

Will? The voice travelled from her left, and she whirled toward it. And just as he should be in a dream, Will stood mere feet away, shirtless in the morning warmth, lightweight shorts his only attire. His smile showed he was as delighted as she to be here.

"Biker." Softly spoken, the nickname slipped from her tongue before she stepped toward him.

Expectant moments filled the time before he dropped into the flowers and wrapped his arms around her belly, his face pressed into her just below her breasts. Beneath the thin fabric of her dress, Olivia's dream-self felt his hot breath glide across her moist skin.

"I've wanted to do this since that first night you showed up."

"You couldn't."

"No, but it didn't stop me wanting to."

Her hands buried in dream-Will's thick dark hair, dream-Olivia threw her head back to glance toward the sun. *No, it didn't.*

"Dreams mean something," she commented to the dream-lover holding her. She remembered her great-grandmother's love affair on the dream-realm with her mate. It had been sensuous and beautiful, long before they were together.

But this wasn't a connection in the dream realm like Tamesine and Marc's. This was her own mind wishing that Will still wanted her, and that they could be together. It wasn't true. Still, there were no limits to what they could do while she was dreaming. This couldn't hurt anyone.

The dream-Will seemed to agree. His hands had moved from her waist, and when he tugged at the neckline of her dress, the spaghetti straps slipped off her shoulders and the top of the dress slid down to her waist.

Dream-Olivia lowered her eyes to watch as his lips moved to one exposed nipple, the hot tongue sliding over it, then around in a circle, back and forth until she nearly dropped onto the ground with him. He held her steady on her feet, though, as he shifted to the other nipple and repeated the sensuous pattern and pulled back to survey the results of his work. He lifted his gaze back to hers.

"Huh. It appears I've started something."

Both nipples erect, dream-Will tugged at each with his fingertips, fully aware than when his hands moved from her waist, the dress would fall, and once it did, his eyes went to the area between Olivia's legs, no underwear hiding it.

"And more work to be done."

Yes! Before dream-Olivia could push him down and straddle him, dream-Will surged upright and lifted her into his arms.

"You refused me last year in the Arizona desert. Would you refuse me again?"

"No. I refused you for a reason that makes no difference now. It no longer applies and this isn't real anyway. What you do to me is exactly what I, as the architect of this dream, wish you to do. Fuck me, Will, and don't hold back. Use your strength and make me scream."

"Architect? I don't feel like I'm being directed, but I like the prescribed action."

"Shut up and fuck me."

Lowering her into the grass, dream-Will lifted her legs to let them rest on his back. The sun brilliant now, he ran his fingertips over the inside of her thighs, touching, absorbing her, before he lowered his head to touch his tongue to the same places, nipping as he went. A finger moved to the rigid clitoris waiting for attention, curving around it over and over before he slid it along the entire moist slit.

"Bite."

Dream-Will glanced up at Olivia's face. "Harder?"

"Harder."

It made sense to him that biting would be sexy to a vampire, but he didn't want to hurt her. Still, he moved back down her inner thigh again, traveling back up and just before he reached her core, he bit, hard enough to break the skin, blood seeping from a small tear.

"Too hard?"

Looking back up into her face, he smiled. Olivia's arms were over her head, her eyes closed, lips curled up in erotic pleasure. *No, not too hard.*

No more playing around, Will went right to the center, his tongue moving deep into her sex, pulling back to capture the clit in his teeth before he pummeled it with his tongue.

Dream-Olivia sighed deeply as waves of pleasure overtook her. Her Will making love to her…glorious…*as she'd hoped…*

Her eyes opened for a split second, and, in her orgasmic state, barely understood the strange movement overhead at first. Whirling white clouds sped in to replace the sky, the flowers, the sun. Within the dreamscape, Olivia sat up, joy ripped from her. The dream was ending, and Will was gone.

Wakefulness came easy, her eyes opened, and, unmoving, slid across the rainbow lit walls. Moments later, a groan came as she remembered the illicit dream, intimate touches from Will, gone now as dreams would do.

But memory remained, and for the moment, having just awakened, it was sharp and caused a reciprocal twitch between her legs. She was wet there from her body's reaction to her mind's construct.

Dreams could be beautiful…*or nightmares.* This one was both. It wasn't real and never would be. She could still feel the connection she'd created between them in the dream world, the feelings of love she'd never get to share with him, his touch she would never really feel.

Nightmare. *Not real.* Sleep came again, but a full hour later with no remaining memory of dreams again.

Good. Great. Fine.

It was time to go home. Dear friends and family waited for her in Vegas, missed her, always holding the door open for her. This journey to seek some part of a universal destiny meant for her had failed. Staying here watching Will make love to another woman hurt. Olivia had always been a take-charge, take-no-prisoners type of woman, so it was time to go home, find a big vampire and fuck him until neither he or she could move.

She'd enjoy one more night with Dez and Zach, say goodbye and thank you to Torin, and head home after first meal tomorrow night.

In his own bed, at precisely the same time that Olivia slowly woke in hers, Will shot awake, startled, alert, his hand moving down to a hard-on.

What a dream!

Olivia, under his fingers, beneath his mouth...

Sitting up, he reached for a glass half full of bourbon that had been there for two days and downed it. If dreams were a manifestation of desires, this one didn't surprise him, and although he knew, *knew*, that it wasn't real, every second felt seared into his mind, like a memory instead of a dream. The moment he'd fallen onto his knees to hold her, then reached up to drop her dress, his mouth on her nipples, and later, lower, to lick, to nip, to *bite*, felt as real as the whisky now burning his throat. Her face lying back, arms over her head, her expression of erotic immersion, then the moment it all faded and he woke violently as he lost the chance to see her orgasm.

Feet on the floor, he palmed the rigid cock that had nowhere to go. A man's mind could be cruel.

Time for a cold shower.

Five

Ife walked around the dining room table, her eyes on him, assessing, using her limited empathic sense to read his mood, his mind, his physical health.

"Would you stop that?" Will barked, a spoon halfway to his mouth. "I'm fucking fine, Ife. Go bug someone who needs a vampire babysitter."

Taking a seat across from him, Ife reached out and snagged his left hand. "You're not. You look sick, Will. I should have stopped this weeks ago. Whatever this bond is, it's hurting you."

As he placed the spoon back into his bowl, Will took Ife's other hand in his right. "What you see is simply a very exhausted man who is catching up on his rest. Is the merge draining me? Yeah, a little. Is it dangerous? No. Ife, don't you think I would know if it were hurting me?"

"I think you wouldn't tell me if it were. I think you feel like you *need* to do this. Will, I'm shutting it all down until we have a better understanding of what it is. You forget that I can tell what's going on in your mind, and you've lost focus. You're not yourself anymore."

"I'm completely myself. You know as well as I do that we earth warriors have to go on faith. I'm doing that, Ife. I'm following my path. I can't let you stop me."

"It's my project, my territory, and you will comply with my directives. Will, I'll let you back in, but not until we gain more insight as to what this thing means, if it means anything at all, and what it wants, if it's seeking something from us. Until then, you are to relax, rest, eat, and recover. Tonight, Zia is coming to your room to use her power with you. It will make you feel better, Will."

Ife watched Will's expression go from smiling to fuming. That expression told her that she had been right. For whatever reason, he was addicted to this strange power merge with the cave, the crystals, Mother Earth, whatever the hell he was doing down there all this time. It had seemed manageable, *harmless* at least, at first, but now she had reason to believe the exact opposite was true. Her instincts told her that Will wouldn't pull away regardless of the potential for damage, so it was her duty to protect him.

Brigitte had agreed when they spoke about him two nights ago. If anyone understood the changes in Will's personality of recent, it was the woman he slept with. Her intimate contact showed her more than anyone else might see.

"He's detached, distracted, less interested in being with me. It's like someone blew out his light," she'd told Ife.

"So I'll end this for now." Her response had been predicated on her own observations about Will's state of being. Then there was her question to Torin last week.

"So what does Will tell you about what he's doing while under?"

Torin's eyes had been guarded, and he'd looked away while he answered her. "Not very much. He's going to reveal more once he is finished, which he says will be soon."

Torin's demeanor and body language had worried Ife. Tonight, though, he'd come to her and explained that he thought Will was sick. That he'd barely emerged from the bond this time. That Ife had *better* be worried…

She pushed away from the table. "Will, take care of yourself. That's your only job now. In fact, after Crezia checks you over, why don't you join her and Scottie in the fields? It's what I wanted you to come down to Brazil for in the first place. I think your skills are exactly what they need."

He didn't answer, but she hadn't expected him to. This would take time to understand and accept.

"Okay, then, I'll send Zia to you later on. Please, Will, be in your room and let her work with you. She's incredibly powerful, you know that, and she should be able to help you. Please." Following a pause, she leaned over to capture his gaze. "Will you?"

"Sure. Why not? I'll be there. Getting drunk."

Nodding, she lifted herself up and walked out of the dining room. Well, small victories. Willoughby was a strong-willed and extraordinarily powerful man. Honestly, she thought that if she refused him access to the cave, and right now, she did, he'd find a way to get it back. In the end, she was certain that she couldn't *keep* him out. For now, she'd accept the win.

AT DEZ'S COMPOUND LATER THAT NIGHT

"Hey, gorgeous! It looks like I'm free to spend some extra quality time with you. It looks like Will doesn't need my help anymore."

Olivia downed a sip of wine and glanced up at Torin leaning across the table. *Too bad*, she thought. I have to tell my lover boy that I won't need him anymore either. The question in her mind, though, was why Will didn't need his monitor.

"Really? Is he finished?"

"For now. Ife pulled him out of the cave. It's weird, but during the past two sessions, I think the earth or whatever he's on with down there, is sucking him dry. I love the guy, and I couldn't let him keep at it when I think that it's hurting him. So for now, he's banned."

Hurting Will?

"What do you mean, hurting him? How?"

Torin shrugged. "I don't know. This is all still pretty crazy to me. Will's a big guy, strong, and when I met him, built like a bulldog. You know, meaty and ripped. But he's losing mass and his color is pale. Also, his energy has changed, he's almost a different person lately. Last night, Will couldn't pull out of the merge, and, Olivia, he *literally* called out for me to help him like he was in trouble. And he was. He couldn't stand, he couldn't get up the ladder without my help. The crystal cave is fucking robbing that guy. Don't worry, though, he's going to be fine. Ife and Zia's going to work on him tonight."

Torin scooted his chair back and skirted the table to drop next to Olivia, his knees on the floor and hands in her lap. "So, I'm all yours, vampiress."

I'm not all yours. Olivia smiled into his eyes, spanned his face with her hands and kissed him gently on the lips.

"Ah, Tor, you are a darling, but this is bad timing. I'm heading home tomorrow night. My business needs me."

"Not yet, Olivia. Please, we're just getting to know each other. I haven't even shown you all of my moves yet. You gotta give a guy a chance to impress you."

"Tor, you do impress me. It's not easy to do that when the woman you're fucking is hundreds of years older than you, so rest assured, you satisfy me completely. But I do need to get home." She slid a hand down lower to press against his crotch. "But we still have all night."

He wasn't happy, but he knew that nothing he said would change her plans, so he rose and lifted Olivia off her seat. "Then there isn't a moment to waste. Can we order your first meal in your bedroom?"

"Ummm, that's the best way to eat it."

"I'm only aiming for the best tonight, my lady, so let's go do this."

Arms tight around Torin's neck, Olivia laughed and realized that she *would* miss this energetic sexy man. Perhaps in the future when she got over this fascination for Will, she'd come back down and see if Torin was still available. Or he might like to visit her in Vegas.

Enough with musing about the future. It was something that vampires rarely did. Living in the moment was a default setting for immortals. Trying to deal with the current moment and those yet to come was exhausting and ultimately unsatisfying.

Carrying her down the stairs to her chambers, Torin entered Olivia's rooms with energy to spare, and, placing her on the bed, he rolled over to pin her to the soft duvet.

"How do we get the food delivered?"

She lifted a hand to point. "Press that button, tell them what you want, and presto, here in twenty."

Just as he reached for the button to order the obscene amount of food they would want, Torin's fone chimed. Glancing at the screen, his brows came together.

"Huh. It's Brigitte."

"Answer call," he said, and held it to his ear.

"Tor, I need your help." Brigitte's voice was calm, so he assumed there was no problem, but then she continued in the same calm voice. "Will and I had dinner and I lay down with him so that he could rest. He looks like shit. Anyway, I woke up a few minutes ago and I can't find him. I think he's gone to the cave alone. Ife has forbidden him to continue with the bonding and he agreed with her terms. I should have known he would do this. Hard-headed human."

"I'll come right away. Did you notify Ife?"

"That's the thing. If she finds out he took off without any protection to do what she'd told him not to do, I think she'll send him away. Tor, I'm not empathic on my own, not without channeling my sister, but I think it will destroy him to be separated from the crystals and this deep access to earth magic. I need you to help me get him back here before Ife gets involved."

"I'm on my way."

Torin laid his fone down and started dressing. "I need to find Will. He took off."

"I heard Brigitte through the fone. I'm coming too."

Using hyper-speed, Olivia was dressed, hair brushed and clipped back, perched on the edge of the bed as Torin pulled his shirt over his head.

"What is he thinking? You vampires are too powerful for him to think he can overrule you."

"Will is used to doing what he wants. I suspect that the best way to ensure he does it is to tell him he can't."

Torin stilled to catch Olivia's eyes. "He's not well. You haven't seen him this week, but he's changed. I'm worried that this might be dangerous for him, and so is Ife. She barred him from visiting the cave for a very good reason, Liv, and yet he's sneaking back."

"Don't worry. I'll get him. We won't let anything happen to Will."

Torin didn't know it, but Olivia would move hell and earth to protect that man.

"Let's go. We'll take a lift-car of course."

Twenty minutes later, Torin led Olivia through the standing stones where Brigitte waited at the ladder above the crystal cave.

"Thank the gods you're here. I just came back up. I know he's down there, I *know* he is, but I can't find him."

"That doesn't make any sense. He would be in the main chamber."

"Yet he isn't."

"Are you sure he came here?"

"Tor, I know that man well, and I know why he disappeared without telling me. He's here, I fucking tell you he is."

"Let's go down."

Olivia wasn't messing around. Like Brigitte, she believed that Will either came here or intended to, so they needed to search for him, and if he really wasn't here, then they needed to look at alternative possibilities. This wasn't the time for pointless discussion.

After climbing halfway down the ladder, impatient and worried, she pushed off and dropped the last half to land easily on her feet. She stepped away and headed down the corridor to the cavern using air displacement, and stood in the center of the cave turning a full 360 before she accepted Brigitte's word that Will wasn't present. The last time she'd been in this cave, the area had been lit by solar powered LED lamps as it was now, she assumed that Brigitte had turned them on. The only other thing she noticed out of place from that first visit were quite a few smaller crystals lying randomly on the ground, mostly toward the bottom of the walls, but spread over the entire space. It gave the sparkly cavern an untidy look after the stark perfection of that first trip weeks earlier.

She scanned one last time as Torin and Brigitte arrived at the outside perimeter of the chamber. Brigitte searched the space as Olivia just had.

"See? Where the hell might he be? Tor?"

"Maybe he just went somewhere to cool off. It's been a bitch of a week for him. Maybe he just needed some breathing room."

"That tracks." Olivia approached them. "Bi…Will is a solitary man. He isn't comfortable around groups and this place is nothing *but* groups. If he's ill, if he's upset, he'd seek solace by going away from everyone. Either way, we still need to find him."

"Wait." Torin walked around the cave now, moving his feet carefully around the fallen stones. "What the hell is this? There are fragments and crystals all over the ground. This is not normal." He turned to Brigitte. "Were these like this when you came in the first time?"

"I think so. Honestly, when I saw that Will wasn't here, I didn't pay much attention. I just went back up to wait for you."

"We've been here for weeks and not one crystal has ever fallen off the walls or ceiling. I don't…"

The slight tremor beneath their feet didn't alarm any of the three at first, the movement so minute, they weren't completely sure they'd felt it. A split second later a low rumble preceded a stronger wave and doubt disappeared. When a third even more powerful quake shook loose more crystals, falling like tiny torpedoes around their heads, Torin grabbed Brigitte's hand and held the other out for Olivia. "We have to get out of here now!"

Brigitte started down the corridor as Torin waited for Olivia, but he watched helplessly as she moved her foot on shaky ground to speed to him, but tipped backward as the earth beneath her feet split and dumped her against the wall.

Before she could regain her feet, the ground beneath her tore open and she felt only air beneath her body as she fell into where the floor of the cave used to be. She thought she heard Torin scream through the cracking earth, but she was gone, falling, falling, and all she could hear then was the rush of air, sight lost as darkness replaced the lighted cave she'd fallen from. Her skills were useless because there was nothing to push against, no idea where she was or when she'd stop. Fear barely registered since she knew that, as vampire, very little would kill her, but pain was real, and as she passed jagged stone too close, something ripped her side. What felt like minutes was likely much less, but when she finally landed on a solid surface, her breath knocked from her, her head striking hard, consciousness faltered and she thought she was going out. Tiny explosions and sudden strikes on her skin and head resulted as soil, rock, and crystals fell down the crevasse with her.

But once the cracking stopped, silence and complete blackness surrounding her, Olivia lay still, her head exactly where it dropped, eyes closed again, and struggled to recover her breath. Motionless, eventually her respiration calmed and she opened her eyes to look up. Nothing to see, there was no light down here this deep beneath the surface of the world. Once she regained her senses, she would be able to assess how hurt she was and try to determine how fucked she was.

For now, she didn't move, but focused on controlling panic. Panic was useless, it messed up thought processes and she needed her wits about her. For now, she was safe, nothing was falling and she'd survived. *For now.*

Several long minutes passed, her eyes wide to blackness, she squinted to see if there was any fraction of light anywhere, but her landing point was devoid of it. Could she create light such as the earth warriors did? They fed off each other to do so, but maybe a fourth gen first blood could pull it off. Carefully lifting her arms, the damage to her right midsection stinging, she mirrored the motion she'd seen them do. Nothing. What she *could* do was create a flame, she'd done that before, so when she rose, she'd light up at least a small space to get a glimpse of what she had fallen into.

Finally ready to try to sit up, Olivia pressed her hands into soft dry ground, and pushed when a glow began to her left. Sitting now, she watched as the glow brightened, then a dark form moved through it to resolve into the shape of a man.

"Olivia?"

Will. *It was Will!*

"Biker!" she called, her voice still weak.

He was beside her in seconds, shirtless, the glow following him, enough light to easily see his worried face. Knees on the ground, he hovered over her, his fingers moving against her waist.

"Olivia, are you hurt?"

Pale, butter-colored light glowed unnaturally all around them as Will's fingers moved over her.

"Not really. Well, not my arms or legs. I think something scraped me as I fell down this rabbit hole, but it isn't serious. Not for me, anyway. Will, how did you get down here? Did you fall in as well?"

"She drew me down. The mother planet opened up and swallowed me. My landing was softer than yours, I imagine. I'm sorry, Olivia, you weren't meant to be here."

Olivia processed his comment before she asked her next question. "But *you* were?"

He nodded as he slipped his fingers along her side to check out her wound. "I was. I was always meant to be here in this chamber of power. Olivia, you're bleeding."

The warmth of Will's fingers moving across her skin distracted Olivia, and she pressed her own fingers over his.

"It's okay. I'm vampire, remember?"

"I remember, but this is deep."

"It will heal." Her eyes had adjusted to the limited light that came into the darkness with Will. "Are you bringing the light?"

Nodding again, Will looked up at the soft illumination.

"Earth magic. I don't think anything is more powerful. I don't actually have the power to do this, but I have the ability to channel the power of the planet beneath us."

"You are remarkable, Biker. I knew that from the first moment I saw you."

Instantly, erotic images surged in her mind and her body reacted with moisture. *Not good*, she thought, *the two of us trapped here together*. They really had to get out of there. "Let me get up from here and we'll see about escape from our little earthy cell."

"Let me lift you up."

"Will, I can do it myse...*ow!*"

Pushing away from the ground, the tear in her side hurt so much worse than she expected. Finally on her feet, Olivia lifted her shirt to see about a six inch gash on her right side from just below her breast to her waist. The blood had begun to clot, it was only seeping, but it was clear that she'd sustained more damage than she thought.

"Olivia..." Will whispered, his eyes on the torn flesh. "*You need blood to help you heal."*

Not from him, oh, hell no, never from Will!

"No, it'll just take a little longer, that's all. See, I can walk."

She could, but her pace would be slow. Her injury hurt even more than it looked like it did, but enduring it was a much better idea than a blood-draw from this man. Just his touch was almost too much since she'd desired him for such a long time, *un-satiated*.

Will watched Olivia struggle with moving along the narrow corridor provided by the crystals that would lead her to another cave. Since the walls of the corridor were close, at least they provided support.

He smiled to himself. Olivia was as stubborn and determined as he was not to reveal her feelings. Although he had committed to the relationship with Brigitte, for the time being, she wasn't unaware of his intense reactions to Olivia.

Or hers to him.

It seemed that right from that first night, the night when his world had changed forever, for the *worst* and for the *best,* their timing had been off. She'd refused him during those first few days when their sexual chemistry threatened to create an explosion, and now, a year later, he was bound by honor to remain faithful to another woman. At least until this unfortunate event had, literally, dropped her into his lap.

"It's only about twenty feet ahead. Just take it slow. Believe me, it's worth the journey."

"I just hope there's a nice place to rest for a moment. And by the gods, is there any chance we can get some water? I'm parched. It's almost like I fell through half a mile of earth."

"Ha, ha. Olivia, I think you'll be properly pleased."

Rounding a final turn, Olivia felt like the narrow corridor spilled her out into paradise. The cavern wasn't as large as the sparkling one she'd just fallen from, but it was majestic, filled with clear crystals in different shapes. Long chandeliers made of shining spikes of crystal hung from the geode coated ceiling, pointing toward stacks of stones covered with glittering patterns formed in delicate lace-like crystals splattered everywhere on the ground that looked like it was made of glass. Along the back wall multiple paths of water trickled down another wall of crystals and emptied into a bubbling pool of water lit from below with the same infusive pale yellow light.

"Oh, Biker. I don't think the word beautiful begins to describe this. *How* is this here? Why are *we* here? What does this mean? And oh, God, I want some of that water. Is it clean?"

"Whoa, lady. I will answer your questions, but let's get you into that pool so you can get a drink. It's also filled with healing minerals, which you need, plus I'll warm it using my abilities. You can just relax and soak."

"Are you sure, Will? You are that certain of what you've been brought to down here."

He shouldn't, he knew it, but he did it anyway. Will moved close and took her face in his hands, which felt right in ways he didn't want to explore. "I am that certain. My journey, my destiny, it's here. This is what I've been brought to South America to do…to reveal this wealth to your community and ultimately bring it to the entire world. All here is pure, is right, is good. Get in the pool and let the waters restore you. I feel guilty, it's my fault you're here in the first place. You came to look for me, didn't you?"

"Yes, but I wasn't alone, Will. Brigitte and Torin came too, but they were on the other side of the cave when the earthquakes broke out the ground beneath my feet. I hope they are safe."

"No one has been hurt in these caves. Other than your injury in the fall, I mean. Olivia, please, get into the pool."

The nagging pain in her side brought her eyes back to the inviting bubbling water, and while it was compelling, she couldn't take her clothes off around Will. That would be only slightly less dangerous than giving him a blood draw.

"I'm fine."

"Stubborn, is what you are. Okay, whatever you want. I, however, am going in. I imagine that my friends have told you I've suffered from my recent bondings."

Olivia's eyes moved from Will's face to his body and back up. Muscles bunched in his arms as he flexed his hands, his torso presenting the defined abdominals, but he was slimmer than the last time she'd seen his body without clothes. "Yes, and I can see that they are right. You're too slender now. Your face is almost gaunt."

"I realize that. This pool is energized by an infusion of healing minerals as well as the power of the crystals. Its purpose is to heal and that is exactly what I need, so forgive me, but *I* am going in."

"Huh." Olivia's eyes moved over his body again, lingering below the beltline. "Naked?"

Will's eyebrows lifted. "Naked. You have a problem with that?"

Oh, fuck yes, I have a problem with it!

"No. I've seen your equipment already."

His eyes on hers, he snapped the top of his jeans, hooked his thumbs around the edge of the waistband and tugged them over his hips, lower, over a cock that popped free, growing erect, as her eyes stayed on it. The pants on the ground now, he stepped out of them and recaptured her gaze.

"Olivia, join me. It's safe."

She watched him step into the water and wade deeper until the delicious cock bobbed at the surface before it was submerged as he went deep enough to begin to swim across to the opposite side just below the trickling water.

Lifting her eyes back to his face, she wasn't surprised to see a wide grin.

"Still thirsty? Come on in, the water coming down the wall is cool and pristine. I can't bring it to you."

Cool water on her parched throat was the least inviting thing in that pool. Could she undress and get in with Will without fucking him? Unlikely.

"Not now. Maybe later, after you're finished."

The humorous expression on his face changed. He lingered against the wall for a few moments longer before he suddenly surged across the pool and out, the water splattering as he shook his hair. Unexpectedly, he lifted Olivia off her feet and carried her with him into the water, still dressed, still wearing her boots and dropped her into the middle of the pool at its deepest point.

Sputtering, treading water, the boots tugging at her feet, Olivia surfaced, shoving soaked strands back over her head, fire in her eyes. "What the fuck, Biker?"

"You want me. Even I can tell that's why you didn't want to get into the pool with me. Get over it, take your fucking clothes off, and come over here to let the water heal you."

"You motherfucking...you think you're irresistible? Hardly asshole! *Dick!* Jerk!"

"Wow, all the classics. Call me whatever you want, just get over here, relax, and heal."

Still treading water in the center of the pool, Olivia admitted she needed this, admitted he was right, but she was still pissed at him for forcing her into the water. Since she was already in and her clothes were now soaked, she might as well see if the water really *was* so magical.

She wouldn't make it easier for him either, though.

Swimming back to edge, she lifted herself from the pool, dripping from every square inch, and pulled her boots off. *Watch me now*, she thought, *see how it affects you*.

Locking her eyes on Will, Olivia pulled her sodden shirt over her head. The thin lace bra she wore held her breasts high, and when she released the snap and let it fall to land on her discarded shirt, full breasts, nipples taut, stayed in place. She smiled when she saw Will's eyes on them, and his hand drop beneath the waterline. *Good, motherfucker, suffer.*

Her jeans came off next, exactly as Will had removed his, slowly, revealing herself to him, her legs spread apart slightly as they fell to the ground. She turned away from him to pull them over her feet, her rounded bum on display as he stared.

Will couldn't look away; he wanted her more now than ever. Together in this setting, an intimate hot springs that smelled like gardenias, he had no doubt, he wouldn't be able to stay away from a woman he hadn't stopped thinking about since the first moment he saw her.

"Is this what you want?" she chided as she reentered the pool and swam over to where he leaned against the edge, his hands still below the water.

Buoyancy let her breasts stay in sight as she treaded water in front of him. *Yes, it's what he wanted, and so much more...*

But he said, "It's what we need. Come, get comfortable over here. The stone wall is warm and will aid in your healing. Olivia, relax and let your body rest."

Shooting daggers at Will with her eyes, Olivia did as he requested and, only two feet from him, settled in, her back up against the wall which did feel amazingly warm and healing. After closing her eyes, she let her mind drift to the ever-repeating image of that first time when he walked toward her dripping sparkling drops off his hair, his arms, his cock, *just like tonight*. Keeping her eyes closed was good, *wise*, she had to do it. Otherwise...no, there would be no otherwise. *Brigitte. Keep seeing her sweet happy face when she looks at this man. He is not yours, he will never be yours.*

I could devour him.

Olivia opened her eyes but kept them raised to the crystals that lined the ceiling. Unbelievably beautiful, more so than those in the cave above. Gently floating, relaxed more than she'd been in a long time, the water caressing her, she let a sensuous sigh slip out.

Beside Olivia, feeling much better, the water having already rejuvenated his flagging strength, Will felt a primal tug in his loins when Olivia sighed in pleasure.

He opened his eyes and turned to her. Her head back, still damp, the globes of her wet breasts bobbing on the surface of the water, her lips curled up, happy, Olivia was healing too. Will didn't know a lot in this world with so much that was unknowable, but this, what he *had* to do, he *knew*.

The water held his big body afloat as he moved around in front of Olivia. His hands moved down to curve around her waist, the fingers of his left hand sliding along the injury. Damn, the slash was nearly closed and well on its way to healed.

Vampire healing and earth magic in tandem, anything was possible, including a rare fourth generation vampire accepting a night of depraved sexual fantasy with a mere human male. *Right?*

Fuck, he didn't need permission. Unless she made it clear she had no interest in him, he was going to fuck her until she saw the stars.

Olivia opened her eyes when she felt hot fingers curl around her waist, and had to quash a moan.

"Will?" His name came out in a whisper, she had no doubt why he had touched her. When she looked into his eyes, filled with need, no other words followed.

Lifting her hands to his hair, fingers tight in the strands, she pulled him to her, perhaps too brutally, and his mouth sought hers as hungrily as she sought his.

Tongues warred, twisting, her hands pressing him into her, harder, seeking him. She wanted to feel him, to taste him, to crawl inside him. Their mouths sealed against each other, she plastered her body to his. Her breasts pressed to his chest, her legs lifted to wrap around his waist, and there, cradled between them, his hard cock grazed her between her legs. Heat built and she pulled away from the kiss enough to speak.

"Fuck...me...now." Breathless, she made it clear what she wanted, and Will, given the permission he had thought he'd never have, moved to make room to lift her legs to his shoulders to kiss her there, the beautiful slit, shining with her moisture, the tongue that had been in her mouth now inside her, the same deep seeking, the same licking at the place begging, begging, needing...

While it was incredible to feel Will's lips on her, nipping that most sensitive organ, twisting it around his tongue, his hands curved around her bum, sliding along the contours as his tongue laved her, it wasn't what her body craved. He felt it before she could ask and moved backward yet again to lower her legs so she could bring them to his waist again. Will lifted his cock, his fingers scoring his own weeping slit and fed it into hers, the thickness growing wider as he pushed inside, hard, *too hard? No!*

He began the ancient strokes that brought pleasure to man and woman, *in, out, in, out, in, hold, feel her, let her feel you, out*...forced an orgasmic reaction that often meant a claim for eternity.

What neither noticed, neither realized, was that the universe marked the moment too, sprinkling scattered lightning flashes all around the already sparkling cave. All Olivia saw was Will, his handsome face, so near her, his eyes soft, focused only on hers, and when he began to ascend to orgasm, pleasure enough for both, as their orgasms arrived seconds apart, hers driven by his, and he emptied himself into her, pumped, pumped, until he collapsed into her, his breathing hard, arms tangled around her.

"I don't want to let you go," he whispered seconds later. "I'm afraid you'll disappear like my dreams."

What? "Your dreams? You dream of me?"

He groaned. "When do I *not*?"

He dreamt of her. Whatever he had with Brigitte couldn't be as deep as she'd thought, not if it was Olivia in his mind and dreams. Then again, she could just be hoping that was what he meant. *Gods, this destiny thing was a bitch!*

Still, whatever the truth was, for this moment in time, this irreplaceable moment, he was here, in her arms, his spent cock nestled inside her.

If he'd had feelings for her since that first night, anything even approaching what she felt for him, then this moment had to come.

"We were inevitable," she whispered.

Moving back from where he'd buried his head beneath her hair, Will slipped his hands around her face. "Were we? I can't read this destiny thing you vampires believe in. I have no idea what it wants of me or plans for me or expects of me. Unless it is…"

The abrupt stop brought Olivia back against the ledge, her eyes searching Will's. "Unless?"

"Unless it's just this earth thing. *That*, I understand. Maybe that's the destiny I'm made for. Nothing more."

"Will, it is apparent that this tie to the living world *is* your path. Other trails you might travel may not be destined, but that doesn't mean there aren't other beautiful things waiting in your life. I know of a young vampire who would agree."

Nodding, Will let himself float another twelve inches away from Olivia, the vision of her elegant arms stretched along the rock ledge, lifting full breasts above the waterline enough for the nipples to perch on the surface, her face glowing, he thought he might be falling in love with her all over again.

In love? Was he? Was it real or just the culmination of finally being with the woman who had haunted his dreams for so long? What about Brigitte? The relationship he shared with her was real. He couldn't deny that they'd been building something over the past year. The great companionship and amazing sex had been satisfying.

Gods in the heavens, where did this go from here? He had just been inside Olivia, and all he wanted was to crawl inside again. He watched her and when she smiled suddenly, it lit up this already magical cavern.

"Will, don't let what we just did torture you. Life takes turns, takes its time, leads us astray, leads us where we need to be, and leads us home. In other words, relax, it will all work out in the end. Whatever the universe has planned, however destiny sets us on our path, it is all okay. I know you have a lot going on now, and I won't be something that makes it harder."

Olivia moved closer to wrap her hands around his waist. "Making love wasn't wrong. We have an attraction to each other, we're here in this magic-filled place in a warm pool and naked. Honestly, what else was going to happen? We have nothing to feel guilty about. I mean, you and Brigitte aren't exclusive, right?" There was one more word she had to say but it stuck in her throat. Finally, she let it come. "Yet?"

"I can't define our relationship, Olivia. I respect Brigitte, we've had a lot of fun together. We're connected, of course, but is there a future for us? I don't even know how she really feels. You guys are immortal, I'm not, so I don't have a clue what you need."

"The same thing everyone does. Look, let's just work on getting out of here. You were right. I'm already healed. And Will, you have undergone a transformation. Can you feel it?"

He lifted his arms, filled out again now, his chest fuller.

"I feel strong again. For the past few weeks, I've felt drained, like I could barely hold onto my bike. I haven't missed the fact that my clothes have fit looser and my appetite's been weak. Yeah, right now, I feel incredible."

"You look it. So, let's get out of this heavenly pool and get our clothes on, because, Biker, if you're looking for truth, here's some. Little has changed since I first saw this body naked coming out of the muddy pool in Arizona, and what we just did, as perfect as it was, barely touched the surface of my desire. But once will have to do, so get dressed while I linger in here and let me know when you're covered."

Will stared at this supernaturally radiant woman floating in front of him who had just admitted how badly she'd wanted him and still did. With a comment like that, if he'd been fully free, he would have pulled her from the water and pounded into her on the more stable surface of sand on the floor of this cave. Could he admit the same to her? That his need to be inside her wasn't even marginally satisfied? Brigitte's smiling face filled his mind and he lowered his gaze to the sparkling water.

No. He wasn't fully free. Best to agree with Olivia's statement and leave her to continue healing while he pulled his clothes on. There would be time later to find out exactly where they would end up from here. Will pushed himself out of the pool.

Soaked, he shook his hair, squeezed the excess water out with his fingers and reached for his jeans. He'd told himself to keep his eyes averted, but they slid to Olivia anyway, and collided with hers. She leaned against the ledge again, watching him.

"Sorry, couldn't stop myself. Gods…" she moaned. "If I ask you to come back in, will you?"

"No." The word came out strangled, the struggle to decide what to do ended. "*You*, come here."

He didn't move, barely breathed, when Olivia smiled and swam forward, her arms graceful in the water until she reached the center and stood to walk out. She lifted her hands to capture her hair as the water sluiced over her shoulders from the sodden strands and curled down full raised breasts to drip from her nipples. Will didn't miss a drop. He reached out to snag his fone from where it lay on top of his discarded pants and held it up to capture Olivia at this perfect moment.

"I hope you don't mind, I couldn't let this image fade away."

The water sliding lower and lower as she moved from the pool, it revealed her curved waistline and belly button before she rose from it enough to show dark hair around the V between her legs. *No, once could never be enough*.

"Biker," Olivia whispered, standing inches from him, her breasts touching his chest.

"Vampire," he answered, his refilled cock pressing against her, ready once more.

Will had been standing, then he wasn't, with no recall when he had gotten there, but he knew *how* he had. Now lying on the sandy floor, Olivia straddled him, and he was buried deep inside her. She did not move.

Leaning over him, she pushed his hair away from his neck. "May I drink?"

He remembered how sensual it was to feed Brigitte. To feed Olivia, to be inside her while she fed, he couldn't have refused it to save the world again.

A simple nod had to do, he couldn't speak since Olivia was already licking him along his neck, grazing sharp lines on his skin, but she hadn't broken the skin yet. Her hands moved into his hair as they dug into his scalp, and simultaneously, she bit into him and raised to stab herself with his cock, feeding him into her core, and feeding his blood into her mouth. Heat soared into Will's mind and body and his hands went to her buttocks, holding her close, pulling her closer, grinding into her as she sucked.

Feeding Brigitte had been sexy, but this, this with Olivia, he felt like he was on the edge of an orgasm the entire time, his skin and cock on fire. Somewhere deep inside of him he knew, he had no doubt, he belonged to her. If he had ever been searching for his destiny, she was it, she was where he had always been meant to be. He could *live* inside her!

The transfer of blood from his body to hers fed every nerve ending in both their bodies, every sensation heightened beyond belief. When Olivia finally finished drawing the life-giving blood from Will, it felt almost as orgasmic as what his cock was doing inside her.

Lifting away after sealing the wounds, Olivia rode Will, hard, fast, her thighs moving on his, her breasts touching his chest when she lowered herself to lick his lips just before ecstasy drove them both to a unified orgasm, Will holding her tight to his loins as he pumped into her once more, *her* fingers locked into his chest. Her moan mingled with his groan as the lights scattered through the cave again, this time bouncing off the diamond-coated walls and ceiling to flash radiantly throughout the space.

Spent, exhausted, Olivia collapsed to the ground beside Will and neither moved or spoke. Minutes passed, and although at one point, she started to move, it was all she could do, and she let herself lie still again.

Never, in all the centuries of sex, had she been this drained, this satiated, this turned on. Will was *it*, the mate she'd been waiting for. The connection they'd shared just now was beyond any normal sexual connection. It was as if the universe had built him for her.

But was it the time to tell him? Finally able to move, she rolled her head to look at him. Had *he* felt it?

A smile curled her lips. Yes, he had. Would he know what it meant? Maybe.

Olivia rolled onto her side to look at Will, and slid her finger over his lips.

"Well, *that* might have done it."

Still lying on the ground, he turned his head to face her. "I think so. If we did that again, it might kill me."

Unable to read his expression, Olivia let her eyes roam over the big body pressed against her smaller one. She could make love to him for centuries uncounted, but she still couldn't figure out how he felt. For now, let the life-changing sex just stand as it was, a moment in time between two people who fit perfectly together. But she still couldn't stop herself from asking.

"Will, are you okay?"

He didn't answer at first, just searched her face with those eyes that she felt held eternity inside, and then he sighed, reached out and pulled her to him. "I'm better than I've ever been. We're made for this, aren't we? The second we laid eyes on each other last year, I guess I knew. When I told you I didn't want you, and you told me I did. When I knew that the reason I didn't want to be with you was because you were the kind of woman a man falls in love with."

"I followed you here. Corri told me about you, and I could barely breathe. When she said you were leaving, that you had a journey ahead of you, I felt abandoned. I knew then that I had to come find you, to see if what we were was real, to see if we belonged."

Sitting up, Will pulled Olivia into his lap and looked into her eyes. "We have something, my lovely vampire. I'm not wrong, am I? You've seemed happy with Torin these last few weeks. Brigitte told me that you don't commit to lovers, that you enjoy them and move on. Am I *that* to you? A fine fuck? If I am, if that's what this was about, just tell me. Don't mislead me, Olivia. If that is how you roll, I need to know."

"What about Brigitte?"

"You know I care about her, but if we're talking destiny, that strange idea that people were meant to be together, I don't think that Brigitte and I have that future."

Olivia slipped off Will's lap, reached for his hands and pulled him to the water's edge. Glancing around the cave, to the waterfall, and back to him, she leaned against the stones. "Look at where the planet has brought you. Will, it brought me, too. If we're talking destiny, then, I agree with you. Biker, I think you and I *do* have that future. Of course, Destiny is a bitch and she likes to leave us, vampires and mortals, all alone to figure this shit out."

"Then let's figure it out. I think we're already there."

"I think we already are. Will, thank you for the most beautiful moments of my life. We will work out the details as they come, but I'm starving. Can we see about getting out of here?"

Will pulled Olivia to him, warm bare skin to warm bare skin, and kissed her. If felt like he needed to feel her breath on him. As she pulled away, he looked around the tight cavern, walls solid, no light other than the one magic created, and had no idea how they would get out.

"Are your magics up to the task?" he asked.

Reaching for her torn shirt, Olivia looked up at him.

"Are yours? This is unknowingly deep, Will. I don't know how far I fell, but it was long enough that I know it was beyond what I am capable of jumping."

"Torin and Brigitte will have alerted the others and they'll already be trying to get us out."

"Oh. In that case…"

Dropping onto her knees, Olivia lifted Will's cock, tongued the tip, and nipped. "We have time."

Will nearly fell onto his knees when she touched him with her teeth. "I was right. You're going to kill me."

Hungry now to taste him, Olivia laughed and moved closer to pull him into her mouth when she felt the ground beneath her knees shudder.

Will pulled her up and into his arms, shielding her with his body. "It's earth magics. I think she's opening up the chamber for us."

"How? How can the planet take us up?"

"It brought us down."

"You're right. Should we move to the walls for shelter?"

"No, it won't hurt us. I can feel the magic reaching out and all it's doing is opening a port to the surface. Steps, Olivia, stone steps built into the cave millennia ago."

"This is too bizarre. Will, I'm a fourth generation first blood vampire, but I swear, in many ways, you are more powerful than I am. Just by virtue of your connection to this world. You are something that has never been seen before, Willoughby Collins."

"I can't imagine. Still, we're going home."

Six

Brigitte raced to Will as he emerged from the crack in the earth, covered in dirt, but looking little worse for wear. Her eyes went to Olivia, just as filthy, but unhurt, too, and felt the oddness in her gaze.

She'd suspected something after Olivia arrived. Will's attitude had changed, his attention more distant, his lovemaking less...*loving*. Last year, in spite of the serious nature of their mission, they had truly enjoyed each other, the sex wild and fun with no ties. They'd fallen into the same caring, enjoyable relationship right away after she'd arrived to help her sister with this project, with one difference. Their connection seemed closer this time, and after a few weeks, she realized there was a chance it might be serious. The thought of having lost him beneath the ground had almost destroyed her. It was time to admit to herself that she was falling in love with her fellow earth warrior.

Holding him now, tight to her, careful with her strength, she glanced toward Olivia, now embraced by Torin. Yes, Olivia was a kind woman, lovely, but Brigitte decided at that moment that if *she* wanted Will, well, let the games begin. Last year, he'd been fine with her no-strings-attached offer of sex. The situation had suited both of them well. Now, they were building something, so that beautiful vampire was going to have to go back to Vegas to play.

Moving back, she scanned his shirtless body, across suddenly redefined muscles, his skin healthy again, darker than it had been the past week.

"You scared the hell out of me! Will, I can't believe you came here alone. I was afraid I'd lost you."

Although he smiled into Brigitte's concerned face, when he lifted his gaze to meet Olivia's over Brigitte's head, Brigitte grabbed him in another tight embrace and he buried her into him.

Standing distant from the clinging Brigitte and Will, a warm blanket around her hips, Olivia watched Brigitte pour her heart out to a man she was obviously either in love with or well on the way.

The connection she and Will had shared in the cave had been beautiful, perfect, felt like it was destined, but the reality was that they had succumbed to sexual heat that had been there from the first time their eyes had met. Sex with him had been glorious, and while she remembered the aurora-type lights that had filled the cave when they orgasmed, it only meant that she had been with a man who had within him the nature to be a vampire's mate. It didn't mean that he was *hers*.

Torin's fingers slid along her cold cheek. "You seem okay, thank God. Vampires are durable, but that fall you two took, I'm surprised it didn't *kill* Will."

"It was a great drop, but the magics protected him. I believe they brought him there to heal, to learn."

She glanced back to Will, Brigitte now holding his hands. Turning to Torin, she smiled. "He's better now, Tor."

"Liv!"

Dez, arriving with Zach, winked at Olivia and stopped in front of her to stare with an amused expression before pulling her into her arms.

"I would have taken it amiss if you'd been buried beneath this rock."

"Like you wouldn't, literally, move heaven and earth for me."

"I would. Let's get you home into a hot shower and warm bed."

Her gaze shifting to Torin, Dez caught his eyes. "Go home. She needs her rest."

Compelled, Torin turned without response and walked away.

"My lift-car is over here," Zach said as he hugged Olivia and led her past the rock face, his arm around her, Dez close behind. "You okay?"

"It's not my first underground cave, Zach. I'm fine. Got a nasty wound on the way down, but it's all healed."

Zach's eyes moved to Dez's. Wounds always healed for vampires, but, this quickly, only with blood.

Olivia smacked him and shot a menacing glance to Dez. "Stop it. Stop speculating." A few seconds later, she shrugged. "Maybe I just heal really quick. I'm fourth-generation, you don't know."

Zach didn't need to know. With what she'd told him about Will, her mostly morose visit, and now that luminous look in her eyes, he knew that Olivia and Will had been together.

"It seems like an interesting bedtime story."

"Not one I plan to tell either of you. Take me home, guys."

Daylight imminent, vampire energy waned as the sun rose. Zach figured they would clear the sky with only minutes to spare before the ball of ultraviolent crested the horizon.

Olivia couldn't stop herself, she looked down as they flew past the rescuers leading Will and Brigitte from the collapsed ground. It didn't hurt that Will lifted his eyes to watch her fly away. Some hard truths had come tonight, but no matter how the future arrived, her time in the deeper cave with Will, learning, finally, how love felt, how making *love* felt, had been transformative. She'd always wondered if she just lacked the capacity to commit her life to one man. Now she knew...*yes*, she could, if it was the right man.

There would be a reckoning, discussions, and decisions made as they moved forward. How this all played out in the end, she didn't know, but for now, she just wanted to sleep.

After arriving back at Ife's compound, after a long shower to wash off soil and sand, and calm sore muscles, Will crawled into his bed with a satisfied sigh of relief. *Yes, sleep, please, for a day or two.*

He was nearly out when Brigitte crawled in beside him and slipped onto his chest. She sighed too, her warm breath moving across his skin.

"Will, I don't know what I would do if something happened to you." Before he could respond, she spoke again. "I'm falling for you, you big human lightning rod. Don't do that again. It would destroy me to lose you."

Holding her close, the darkness of the room offered protection for his conflicted emotions. *Thank the Gods*, he thought, that she wasn't empathic like Shani.

This gentle loving woman had declared her heart to him, and he couldn't break it. All that they had experienced together, the battle for earth last year, sexual connection on the eve of what might have been their last day alive, this reconnection that had blossomed into a true relationship. Did he love her? Yes, he did. Was he *in* love with her, though?

No. Admitting it hurt, because if Olivia hadn't come to South America, if conditions had been right, he and Brigitte might have built a comfortable life together. He'd never thought he would have that again after his fiancée and unborn child had been killed. If Olivia hadn't reentered his life, he and Brigitte could have been happy; he knew it.

He smiled into the blackness as he remembered his mother telling him as a young man that real love was steadfast and true. That burning passion and sex flamed out; that it wasn't real love and it couldn't endure.

Olivia was on her way to Dez's place, likely with Torin, and then on her way back to her life in Vegas tomorrow. The stab of jealousy, envy, *fury*, that struck him when he thought of his good friend lying with Olivia tonight struck with no warning. He felt his muscles tighten, forcing himself to relax his grip on Brigitte, who had already succumbed to her deep daytime sleep.

Will couldn't breathe. Although he was still egregiously exhausted, he couldn't stay here. Carefully untangling himself from Brigitte, he surged from the bed and reached for his jeans beside a crumpled tee shirt lying at the foot of the bed.

"I need air," he whispered as he wrestled with unexpected emotions. Leaving his chambers, he was grateful that no one was around as he walked out of the compound into an adjacent field of fast-growing trees. Most were already ten feet high, and between them, he could see the glowing brightness of sunrise. Long fingers of golden light threaded between row after row of long slim trunks with young leaves.

The clear blue sky and rising sun made him remember his comment at the cantina during his journey south almost two months ago, even more true here.

"Magic lives here."

With crisp morning air and a dawning day, Will was able to slow his breathing and calm his spirit. Dropping onto the damp grass, he watched light change around him with the moving sun.

He was okay; he would *be* okay. This world was staggeringly beautiful, and he was connected to it like no one else above or below it. He *knew* he was its greatest protector, sentry to all life that called it home.

What did he have to be upset about? He'd found his destiny, the place he had to be; a world no one knew existed beneath the ground had literally waited for him. A powerful loving woman wanted him as her mate. Life gave him sorrow that tore him to pieces, but now, it gave him love and hope and purpose. And *peace*, if he chose to reach for it.

To appreciate his gifts, to find joy in this life he'd been granted, to find contentment. *Yes, he chose to reach for it.* Pressure on his chest eased.

The deep blue sky brightened. Standing, Will touched his open hand to his chest, a gesture of gratitude for this perfect morning and moment of clarity. Not ready to go back inside, he turned into the planting field and wandered through the rows. Lost now amongst the young trees, he continued moving and at one point, wandered back to the path that led to the caves. No easy access now, the hole that they had used to climb down into the first cave had filled in, the deeper chamber still open but with no good way to safely climb in or out. They would build one, but it would take time.

He stepped to the edge of the unstable opening and peered down into it.

"Will."

Behind him, Dani had called his name and scared the shit out of him. He hadn't heard her approach.

Turning to her, he shook his head. "Damn, girl, stop moving around on those little cat feet. I'm going to put a couple of bells on you."

"Sorry, buddy. I followed you because I'm worried. Will, yesterday you had a metamorphosis, you know that, right?"

"What do you mean?"

Long seconds ticked past as Dani studied Will, moved slowly around him, his front, his side, lingered on his back, and then moved in front to capture his eyes. She placed a hand on his chest where he had done so earlier, but this touch sent a shiver through him.

Deep brown eyes searched his before she spoke again. "You are not the same. Not the outside, that's obvious. *Inside*. Can you feel it?"

"I..." Physically, yes, that was apparent to anyone who looked at his thicker body and healthier skin tone, but how he felt on the *inside*? *How could she know?* He barely did.

"Dani, tell me what you sense. It seems I remain constantly confused lately. Unsure. Okay, yeah, I *do* feel different, odd, almost like I'm vibrating."

"It's apparent. Not to others, but you know my skill of intuitional empathy. I don't think the change in you is definable other than the fact that you, Will, are a great deal more than just human."

"Aren't all of us earth warriors? None of us is normal."

"While that's true, it barely applies to what you're becoming. Will, we should convene a spirit circle for you."

"What would that accomplish?"

"Understanding what you're changing to. I think something is coming and Will, I don't know what, but I feel as if you are critical to protecting us from this event."

"What? What do you see, Dani?"

"Thoughts. Possibilities. Flashes of the future. When I touch you, I see images. Crazy, unexplainable, beautiful, dangerous."

"Flashes of the future that include me?"

"All of the warriors. It isn't soon. Will, come back to the compound with me. Let's have a nice breakfast and talk about something completely human. I love our lives and our celestial-designed missions, but every once in a while, I like to just be a girl."

After watching Dani thoroughly scan him, Will let his eyes roam over *her*. She'd pulled her hair into a loose bun, and wore a sundress almost the color of the sky. This lovely young woman was one of the most unique and powerful humans on earth, and all she wanted was to be normal. He fully understood.

"It's a date."

Back at Dez's compound

Lying in her oversized bed at her grandmother's home, Olivia, trying to give in to her vampire nature for rest, couldn't sleep. An hour ago, she'd been grateful that Dez had compelled Torin to go home, aware that all he wanted was to come with her, and after making sure she was okay, have sex and feed her.

Images filled her mind, but not of Torin. Will, his lips on her nipples, his tongue inside her, that thick cock finally buried deep in her. Heat and lights and blood, as he slid in and out, over and over, hands on her ass, fingers biting in as he held her so he could move. Brilliant lights filling the diamond-encrusted cavern as they made love in the sparkling pool filled with magic.

And it was love, not just sex. Something between them beyond the physical act had scattered rainbows across the walls, floors, and ceilings of the chamber. She'd hoped it would be a beginning.

It had been a good-bye.

Once *rescued*, Olivia and Will had been pulled apart, and when Brigitte had launched herself into Will's arms, Olivia's heart had nearly stopped. A moment later, Will's eyes met hers, and she'd seen confusion in his.

Olivia knew she needed to step back and walk away.

"If we were meant to be, we will be."

Decision made, she figured she'd go with her original plan to return to Vegas right away; back to the life she'd built over the past fifty years.

It wasn't right to entice him away from Brigitte. Will was hardly a meek man; if he wanted her, he would come for her, he would demand it. Above all, the most important thing was that Will's life would be a happy one.

Outside Ife's compound

After almost a vampire sized breakfast, and two hours of conversation, Will led Dani out the main entrance toward his motorcycle that had been parked too long. "How do you feel about wind in your hair and the sun at your back?"

"God, yes, that sounds like heaven."

"Get on behind me and hold tight."

Winding through inadequate roads, breathtaking landscapes made them stop frequently to view the sights, to enjoy these moments free of complications. No expectations, no decisions waiting to be made, nothing to do except breathe deep, laugh with each other, and climb on the bike to ease on down the road.

Finally, nearing dark, they headed back the way they came, revisiting the same vistas with different late-day light. They stopped just before sunset on a jutting rock ledge overlooking a river below to drink sparkling wine and eat sweetbreads they'd packed this morning.

When Dani, sighing in pleasure, looked over at Will, who did the same, she giggled. "Thank you for this day. I haven't felt this calm in a…since…well, maybe since they found me and my brother that day in New Orleans last year." Her eyes moved back to the view, releasing a long breath again. "I needed this."

"I did too, so thank you for taking this ride with me. I think we can face the night now."

"Amen to that. I guess we'd better head back."

"I guess."

The return trip was just as refreshing. Once the two humans entered the vampire household, Dani hugged Will and tugged on his ponytail. "Let's do that again sometime, right?"

"I'm so in. Rest well, little warrior."

"You too, my friend."

Sliding the door to his room open, Will entered quietly, but saw that his bed was empty. Running water from the shower told him that Brigitte was up and getting ready for her night.

Tired after the day of adventure with Dani, he dropped onto the bed and closed his eyes. Minutes after the water shut off, he felt a hand slide along his denim-covered thigh.

"Hey, wanderer. Where have you been?"

Will opened heavy eyelids to stare into Brigitte's smiling face. She really was a feast for the eyes.

She brushed his hair back. "You look sleepy. I woke and missed you."

"I couldn't rest. I had to get out of here and clear my head, so I walked through the trees right after sunrise, and then spent the day letting Dani entertain me."

"That is one amusing human, I'll give you that. Do you feel better?"

"Much. I'm ready to sleep now, though. Sorry, but I'm not going to be any company for you tonight."

"That's no problem. As long as you're all right, that's all that matters to me. Veg out and I'll come for you in time for second meal, then you can join me. Okay?"

"Yeah, that sounds good."

He was already fading. The last of Brigitte's words didn't register and although he had some awareness that she had placed her fingers on his head, he lost consciousness right after.

Brigitte watched the man she was in love with crashed on top of his bed, still dressed, dirt-covered, starting to snore, but sleeping well. *Good*, she thought, he needed to rest and heal. Even with her limited empathic read, she could tell that something incredible had happened in that new hole. His body had filled back out, even bigger than before, and his fading health was reversed.

And he'd been with Olivia.

It wasn't only that Brigitte could smell Olivia's scent on him, but his reaction to her had changed. It was understandable, he had some kind of history with the Vegas vampire. What it was Brigitte did not know, but there was something.

Fascination, she hoped. Fascination alone was no threat to the real relationship he and she had been building the past month. Besides, Olivia had already announced that she was going home, so that should end the conflict and Will's confusion. At the end of it all, Brigitte hoped to take Will home to spend time with her family.

When Will woke, she would tell him what he meant to her and make it clear that their life together would be spectacular. He would become vampire and join the children of the moon in centuries of joy that celebrated every moment of life and their connection to this world. It would be the perfect place for a man who carried the earth magics that Will did.

First, though, she needed food and a conversation with Ife, who would understand exactly how she felt. Family meant everything to Brigitte. Brushing his hair from his damp forehead, she bent down to kiss him there. "I hope to make you family soon, my love."

Entering the dining room, she sought Ife's gaze, and saw that Ife was already watching for her. Right now, she needed nothing more.

As the night progressed, she and Ife had spent several hours alone wandering through the flower gardens, the discussion about mates a new one for both of them.

Brigitte had never considered one before, and Ife admitted that none had ever appeared to her.

"But one thing I know, my dear sister, is that when you find the right person, you have to do all you can to protect that love. How could anyone refuse you?"

"Right? Thanks, Ife. I needed that."

The two vampires bonded over healthy blooms the rest of the night until it was time for second meal.

When daylight loomed, Brigitte slipped back into Will's darkened room and stretched out next to him. A hand to his chest assured her that he still breathed evenly, a tiny niggling sense that whatever had happened to him in that cave could still be dangerous. She moved her fingers over him, down his side to his penis, now at rest between powerful thighs. Smiling, she began to caress him, then with more energy, she aroused her sleeping warrior, happy when he finally opened his eyes.

"Hell of a way to wake a guy up from a sound sleep."

"Complaining?"

"Hardly." He rolled over to pin her against the mattress. "But I should clean up first."

"Hardly." Brigitte forced him back over and, their clothes gone instantly, impaled herself on him and rode him hard until he grunted as he came, the orgasm quick and intense. After calling out when *she* came, Brigitte lifted off him and pulled him from the bed. "Now it's time to shower, and not alone."

Under the generous spray in a shower built for two, she soaped Will's new body.

"This is magics, Will. You've been losing weight over the past few weeks. Now you look like you've been on extreme training for a year, yet it was only yesterday that you actually looked a little emaciated."

"Dani said that I'd been transformed. Bridge, there was a pool in that cavern that I knew, instinctively, would heal me, physically, from all that I lost during the past month. The crystals took from me, but they remade me too. I don't know why or how, but I do know that it's the truth. I am part of the caves, their magic, and they are a part of me."

"Do you find that worrisome?"

"No, it's what I am. Dani thinks something is coming."

"Does she? Then we need to speak with Chione and Donovan."

Will nodded. "That's exactly how she feels. I guess we need to go to Zambia soon."

Brigitte smiled. "I was thinking that same thing before we even began this discussion. Will, I would like my parents to get to know you."

Water pulsed against his back as Will managed his reaction to a discussion he wasn't ready to have with Brigitte. He was crazy about her, but he was more certain than ever that Destiny might have led him here after all, and that he was meant to be with Olivia. The feelings he'd had when they met last year had only grown stronger. *Love?* Possibly. Lust, *absolutely*. He just had to find a kind way to tell Brigitte.

Brigitte could see his mind working, almost as if she *was* empathic. He couldn't see past his desire for Olivia, and oh, God, she got it, but he needed to hear her out first.

"Will, let's discuss this later. I just need to finish scrubbing you down. Now, let's see, where did I leave off?"

Her fingers clutched the scrubby, filled with soap, and lowered it to grab his penis.

When she'd brought the subject up, she'd seen panic in his eyes, this was *definitely* not the time for discourse.

After thoroughly pleasuring him, Brigitte had a meal brought to the room, last meal in bed, which she grinned at him and told him that she heartily approved.

"Gods, it was good to see you emerge after you fell. If something had happened to you, Will…"

"It didn't."

"I am grateful to the universe that you are protected by magics." Brigitte took a bite of sugared bacon. "And Olivia, of course. Vampires can still be injured, but we heal quite rapidly." She looked up into Will's eyes, carefully wording her next question. "So what did you two do while you were down there?"

Moments passed before Will looked up. "Talked. About the cave, which is even more remarkable than the first one. Olivia went into the healing pool since she'd torn her side open."

"You went in too."

"It called to me. It was *there* for me. That's where my restoration, or transformation, whatever this was, began."

"Huh." Another bite of bacon later, Brigitte looked at him again. "I assume you guys took your clothes off."

This time, Will just nodded as he sipped iced coffee.

Casually, Brigitte laughed. "Well, of course you did. You would have needed warm dry clothes to put back on. I assume Olivia behaved herself. She's got quite a reputation you know."

Will raised his head from his attention to his food. "What do you mean?"

"She's a wonderful woman. Zach told me that she's had a powerful history with lovers. Just not the loyal type when it comes to men. She admits she's all about wild sex and then moving on to the next guy. When I asked her once if she'd ever been in *love,* she laughed with a wink, and said 'Of course! Often several times a night.' I adore her. She's much older than we are, so it makes sense that she's had a lot of lovers."

Brigitte watched Will's reaction to her comments and felt sick. Purposefully trying to discredit her competition didn't feel honorable, but she didn't recant. Sometimes, to make what you want happen, you have to get down in the dirt.

And she did feel dirty.

"Look, I'm sorry I said that. Olivia's a doll, really. Everyone loves her. I'm, uh, going to crawl into bed. It *is* okay if I stay?"

He couldn't help it. The sweet desperation in her voice tore his heart. One way or another, meant to be or not, he did love this girl.

Will lifted her off the bed and swung her around, set her on a high chest, and moved in to kiss her. Tongues together, it ignited them, and within moments he found himself naked again after lifting Brigitte off the chest and carrying her to the bed.

"This, my fellow soldier, is what we have. I don't want to lose it. Or you." Whispering, she moved up as he lifted her to fit himself inside her. The ride was gentle, loving, and filled with promises. Will pumped into Brigitte, aware, without doubt, that she was *not* the one he should be with.

He enjoyed Brigitte, but he *needed* Olivia.

One way or the other, he was going to break her heart.

After clearing away what was left of their meal, he kissed her on the forehead.

"Sleep well, beautiful warrior."

She was already fading, a combination of the nearness of day and a nice orgasm.

Will wondered if it would be their last time together.

The vampires in the compound asleep, Will repeated his previous day, adopting the human habit of spending daylight hours awake. Right now, like Dani, he cherished the moments of normality. Needing distance from Brigitte while he worked out how to protect her feelings while trying to understand if he and Olivia had something destined, the morning sun seemed to provide clarity.

Sitting once again under the trees, he thought about Brigitte's comments on Olivia's sexual history with men. He recognized it as her attempt to tell him that Olivia wasn't the woman he needed, and while he realized the reason she'd said it, he still couldn't get his mind off the subject. Was it possible that he was just the flavor of the month for Olivia? Did they have something real?

He needed to speak to Olivia right now and decided to ride to Dez's compound to find her. Would Torin still be with her?

It didn't fucking matter.

Rising from the warming earth, desire pushed him through the orchard. Silently, he entered his room, snatched his keys, and slid onto his Harley, starting the engine before his leg cleared the seat. On a bike, the drive was about two hours, just enough time to clear his mind and try to work out a way to handle this mess.

Will realized, the way he and Brigitte had been together, that while they had possibly been progressing toward a serious commitment, in the end, neither one of them would have been happy.

Fresh rushing air had been exactly what he needed, his muscles un-clenched, his breathing normalized, and his chest felt calm. The mid-morning sun forced him to stop to don sunglasses, and he lingered to look over the view below. Most roads here winded around high ridges, the valleys beneath now lush again due to Ife and her team's dedicated work. That several earth warriors he'd worked with last year preventing a devastating volcanic event now worked here to help repair two centuries of abuse was no surprise.

No wonder this had felt like home, like *family*, as soon as he arrived. Would he be happy back in Vegas if he and Olivia worked out? Grinning, he knew there wasn't any question; he'd be happy wherever he was if she were by his side. It didn't mean he'd have to leave Brazil forever, it just meant that he'd have to share his time between two beloved places on this planet.

Will arrived at Dez's compound in late afternoon, parked the bike, and started toward the back entrance he always used. One of Dez's largest human sentries met him there.

"Edward, hey buddy, I just need to speak with Olivia."

Edward, despite his intimidating size and appearance, was a soft-spoken man, patient, gentle, unless he needed to be something else.

"She's resting, mate, you know that."

"Yeah, but it's important. Any chance you can let me in?"

"Why don't you wait until tonight? I can take you to the club to wait for…"

"Ed, look, I know you don't like to disturb your host or their guests, and I understand, but, please, can you let Olivia know I'm here? I promise, she'll want to see me."

Will could see Edward assessing him. To his knowledge, *to anyone's knowledge*, Olivia and Will were not close, so he knew Edward might refuse. Then again Edward knew Will enough to trust him. If the man didn't let him in, he'd just have to wait until tonight.

A gruff chuff later, Edward nodded. "All right. Wait here."

Using his coms, Edward stepped away from Will as he contacted Olivia's chambers. Long moments passed where it was clear there was no answer. Edward headed back toward Will, his fone held up, shaking his head. "She's not..."

Edward broke off and spoke suddenly. "Miss Olivia, I am truly sorry to disturb you, but Will has come to the compound and insists he needs to see you."

Silence as Edward listened to the response, then lifted his eyes to Will. "Yes, I'll send him down."

Signing off the coms, he nodded again. "You're cleared to go to her. She's on sub-level two, rooms near the back marked *Liv*."

"Thank you, buddy."

Following directions, Will thought he could be forgiven for his increased heartrate and the fullness in his jeans.

Suddenly awake, Olivia pressed a hand between her legs, trying to still the intense pulsing. An ache moved up from there to the core of her sex.

Will is coming.

He shouldn't, not now, and she had no idea why, but her body prepared her to see that face she could never get used to, that body made to be on top of her, or under her, and inside her.

Will is coming.

Never mind that the very thought that Will was *coming* increased her sexual need. Her imagination had always been excellent, so now, eyes closed, she *felt* him pump into her as he had in the cave, an orgasm beginning to build at the memory.

The interrupting doorchime broke the spell. After a moment's hesitation, she released the lock and the door slid open.

He moved through it slowly, his eyes roving around the room, softly lit for daytime sleep, then came to her on the bed, on her knees, her eyes on him. A thin sheer nightdress covered her, or more accurately, *didn't*, her exquisite body, every feature he loved barely hidden behind a haze of pale peach. Full breasts pushed the fabric out, held by two button nipples he felt sure would be in his mouth in moments. Will forced his eyes back up to her face to see a quizzical look and an amused smile.

"Tough to keep your eyes where you should sometimes, yeah?" Olivia's dropped to where his jeans showcased his expanded girth beneath the strained zipper.

"Did you bring me a gift?"

"Not at first. I mean, it wasn't why I needed to see you right away, but..."

Will was on the bed, his hands moving down Olivia's sides to her waist while his mouth went exactly where it had to and latched onto her breasts, one hard nipple, then the other. He felt her fingers on him after his zipper was down, his cock freed from the snug denim. Instantly, they began to move in circles around his girth, and he hardened further.

"Olivia..." Her name came out on a groan. No, he hadn't intended to do this, only talk about their situation and just *be* with her.

Olivia nipped at the sides and his cock jumped in her hand. She laughed. "I have never purged that scent or image from my mind, so now, a year later, it's embedded in me, and all I want is to eat you up, but after yesterday, I'd better not."

Her eyes lingered on his exposed neck, the desire to bite strong, almost impossible to resist, but it wasn't wise to feed from him. He wasn't ready for that kind of eternal commitment with her, not yet, if ever.

Olivia slipped off the bed as Will pushed to the edge, his feet on the floor. She reached for a bottle of water and leaned against a cabinet.

"You came here for a reason. Sorry I messed that up. What did you need to see me about so urgently?" Her lips turned up again as she glanced between Will's legs. "Or was *that* it?"

"Yes. *No.* I know you were returning to Vegas when you rose tonight. Do you still plan to?"

Cautious, girl, Olivia reminded herself. Don't force him to decide something he isn't ready to do yet. *No pressure.*

"Yes, I do. I've business I need to attend to, and Corri just texted me that my security guy has some concerns. You saved Corri when someone kidnapped her and left her to die in the desert. Which, by the way, thank you. Corri is family and means the world to me, so thank you for protecting her."

"I was in the right place at the right time. I'm glad I was, Corri's a sweetheart."

"She is. Well, Sam, my head of security, has found some anomalies and is concerned that the situation isn't over. I need to head home to see what's going on. We had already realized we were probably facing another threat to our community."

"I should go with you."

"No. I have a great team of both humans and vampires helping me, and you, Will, have a life here. That's why you came to see me today, isn't it? To discuss you and me. And Brigitte."

"What if you need help?"

"Stop. We are not in any danger in Vegas, okay? Once we find the asshole who is doing this, he or she will be neutralized instantly. You need to take care of Brigitte."

That haunted look returned to his eyes. "I hate to break her heart."

Olivia moved closer and dropped at his feet, hands on his knees, her eyes lingering at his crotch now at eye level, then lifted her gaze to his eyes.

"Will, do what you need to do. If we are meant to be together, if it is our destiny, then we will be. Whatever you feel is best, you're a good man, then it is what you must do. Will, I'm not going anywhere. If or when you are ready, come to me."

Placing a hand on his cheek, she smiled.

"I have it on good authority that you know where I live."

Will pulled Olivia up and onto his lap. "How can I let you go?"

"You're a powerful man, you can do anything."

One last time, she wanted to feel his lips on hers, her lips on him, on his skin, on his *neck*. Curling her fingers into Will's thick unruly hair, she kissed him so lightly, he barely felt her touch, then slid her tongue along his lips and gently into his mouth. Moving her fingers lower, she followed with her lips and licked along his collarbone before she moved back under his hair and nipped at his neck. She broke the skin, had intended to, and swirled the drop of blood onto her tongue.

This would have to do. For now, it was goodbye.

Lifting off him, she backed up until she felt the support of the wall behind her. "You'd better go, or I'll break the promise I made to myself not to fuck you."

The frozen smile he offered held such sorrow, she almost backslid on her promise.

He didn't move. "I can't bear the idea of another man inside you."

"Then perhaps it won't take too long for you to come to me."

"Brigitte told me that you're a playgirl. That you *like* sex, a lot of it, both men and women."

It surprised Olivia that they had discussed her. That Brigitte had told him some of her history.

"It's true, Will. I'm vampire with hundreds of years of lovers behind me. Vampires and sex are nearly synonymous, you know that. But Biker…" Olivia closed her eyes and made herself stay away from him. "I have never been *in love* before."

The admission nearly broke him. Will was on her in a split second, his hands buried in her hair, his tongue inside her mouth, the kiss almost brutal in desperation.

"Liv…" His voice cracked and he couldn't finish.

She couldn't take a second painful goodbye.

"Will. Go. Just come to me when you're ready."

Olivia disappeared using air displacement, leaving Will alone in her room to process the last few moments. He realized the choice had been taken out of his hands; Olivia had made it clear that he should take his time resolving his relationship with Brigitte.

And that he and she were not finished.

A smile came as he thought of the promise she'd offered that if they were meant to be, they would be. The days between now and then would seem endless. That she'd left him behind in her wake felt harsh, but it was the right thing to do. Another few moments of breathing her scent, watching her smile brighten, her eyes sparkle, and he'd have abandoned all his fine intentions and fucked her right there against the wall.

Turning, he hurried back through the compound, grateful that Edward wasn't still waiting at the gate, straddled the seat of his bike, but didn't move.

Life, all of its wild turns, the insanity of these powers he was born with, the unexpected future…he didn't know how he deserved it, but thanks to the universe, he was grateful for every bizarre moment.

Firing the engine, he gunned the bike as he flew over the narrow road back to Ife's place to confront the life he'd built down here.

After sunset, a few miles from Ife's compound

Olivia hugged Zach and then Dez, holding on a little longer to her grandmother. "You guys need to come see me in Vegas. Soon. You need to meet Corri."

"We will. Next week, I'm finished with the new project for Luka's community and we'll fly up." Dez watched Olivia too closely. "Sure you're okay?"

"Really, I am."

Zach touched her arm. "What's happening with Will?"

She tilted her head down and smiled.

Zach rolled his eyes. "Never mind. It looks like it's all good."

"It is. We'll be together, but perhaps not for a while. I've learned patience, my family. Fly safe when you come to see me. Namasté."

"You too, my love. Fly safe." Dez stepped back, tugging Zach with her as Olivia moved toward her waiting jet. Moments later, it lifted off and banked to the left.

As it continued north, Zach wrapped his arms around Dez. "She's in love."

"Miracles happen. We're proof."

Zach nodded. "Yup." Yes, thank the gods, his hot-tempered girl had finally come for him.

But it hadn't been easy.

Mid-day outside Ife's compound

Continuing their new habit of getting out of the compound during daylight, Dani and Will sat, full, spent, after a day of exploring the area and a picnic with too many good food choices. Lying beside the picnic basket, an old-fashioned acoustic guitar that Dani had owned since her life in New Orleans waited for her to play some tunes as they watched the sun go down. Now they sat on a rock ledge overlooking a valley already thriving with new foliage, resting against the front of the stone face.

Dani rubbed her belly.

"Ugh. I really gotta stop eating like this. I'm going to be too fat to fit into my superhero outfit the next time we're called up."

"You'll be fine, although I think that both of us may need a siesta before dinner."

"*Dinner*? You're crazy."

Silent now, they watched the sun dropping lower, shadows lengthening around them.

"I'm going to tell Brigitte when she wakes tonight. God, I'm sick about it."

Dani turned to look at Will, who still searched the sky.

"Brigitte's a big girl. Yes, it'll hurt, but I promise you, we *all* need the truth. Anyway, she has to have sensed that you don't feel the same way. She doesn't have to be empathic, she just has to be a woman in love. It won't be as big of a surprise as you think it will."

Dani moved close to tap Will's forearm.

"Vampires live for centuries. She would have learned a long time ago how to deal with disappointments and love affairs that don't go her way. Tell her, straight up, honestly, how you feel. Let her know that you adore her, but that you are in love with Olivia. If anyone needs to live honestly, it's the earth warriors. We understand the truth of the world better than anyone."

"Thank you, Dani. Your wisdom helps. You're right, of course, Brigitte's going to be fine. Hell, as gorgeous as you ladies are, none of you would ever be alone long. I include you in that group."

"Ha! I haven't had a good date since all this began last year. In fact, the last date I had with a promising guy was with Jackson, and he just asked me to dinner so he could reveal that I was this magical earth warrior. And sex? Good God, how long has it been? I can't even remember."

"Poor Dani. That's on my list. As soon as I get to Vegas, I'm going to find you a hot vampire, so you can…"

Dani cut him off, laughing. "Get some?"

"Yeah, get some."

Pitching the water bottle she held at Will, she suddenly shot up. "Ow!"

Lifting a hand to reach toward the back of her right shoulder, Dani searched around with her fingertips.

"Something bit me!"

"What?" Will pushed from the ground so he could help her and felt a sharp sting in the center of his back.

"Fuck! What is it?"

As he reached for Dani, he noticed her eyes close and, gasping for breath, she began to fall.

"Dani!" He called before dizziness began to overtake him, *felt* like he might lose consciousness. He knew then what was happening…someone had shot them with tranquilizer darts. His fingers closed around the dart, confirming his fears, as he crashed to the ground, crushing Dani's guitar.

Shortly after sunset at Ife's compound

She came awake easily, her eyelids lifted, and sadness intruded right away. Sitting up, Brigitte looked around the room. He wasn't there, but when he came, she knew. When they made love before she'd fallen asleep, it had felt like the last time. He would try *so* hard to let her down kindly, an impossible task, to let her know he wasn't in love with her. While she knew it would hurt him to tell her that they were through, she couldn't find the sympathy right now. Tears welled in her eyes and spilled to track down her cheeks.

Well. Staying here wasn't going to change anything. Hungry, Brigitte pulled on a tee shirt lying on the bench at the foot of the bed and reached for her shorts. First meal was serving now and the dining room would be busy. She could have it delivered here, but at this moment she needed to be surrounded by friends and family.

"Moving forward," she whispered and stepped from Will's room for the last time.

Entering the noisy dining room minutes later, Brigitte lifted a plate, her eyes searching the myriad choices on the breakfast buffet. She was hungry, but nothing appealed tonight.

Arms slipped around her from behind. Ife's scent struck, and Brigitte laid the plate down to curl her fingers around Ife's wrists. Leaning back, she sighed.

"Hi, sistah." Ife's quiet greeting told Brigitte that she knew about her sorrow.

"Hey, sistah. Thank you, I need this."

"You always have it. And a whole bunch more. Shani's coming next week."

Brigitte closed her eyes. "You called her?"

"Of course I did. This is hard, Bridge. You need your sisters."

"Bless you."

"Now, I know nothing is going to seem appetizing, but you need to eat, so sit down and let me select the tastiest of everything."

"Yeah, okay." After a pause, she touched Ife's arm again. "Have you seen him?"

"Not tonight. Dani and he are together. She left a text with Scottie that they were going on a picnic."

"Ah. All right."

Brigitte joined a table of exuberant blood-bonds, wiping back moisture that threatened to come again. Ife brought a plate heaping with all the breakfast classics and handed her a fork with dramatic flair. "Eat."

"I appreciate this. I'll eat every bite." Poking the fork into a western omelet, she stabbed a bite and put it into her mouth. The flavors struck her immediately; it was delicious, but pleasure didn't come. She lifted her eyes.

"Ife, do you know if Olivia is still at Dez's?"

"Dez told me she was leaving at sunset. She's probably gone by now."

"Huh. You think maybe Will just hopped on board?"

"Will wouldn't do that to you, so, no, I don't."

Nodding, Brigitte put all her attention on the plate of food and did as she promised. She ate every bite.

Ife, who had been working the room to make sure everyone knew their assignments for the night, plopped into the chair beside Brigitte. "Why don't you join me and the team? We're re-introducing another batch of indigenous flower varieties that went extinct fifty years ago."

"Sure. Yeah. Um, I'm not in any hurry to have my tête-à-tête with Will. A few more hours of delusion sounds good."

As the night wore on, blessedly, Ife stayed by Brigitte's side the entire time, telling ridiculous stories, making fun of silly events that they'd created over their years together, trying to keep the day fun and Brigitte's attention off her looming conversation with Will.

Exhausted, dirty, elated, the team of eight blood-bonds, Scottie, and Brigitte followed Ife home as sunrise neared. Last meal would be served and they would all fall into bed and sleep well.

"Back to my own room today," Brigitte commented when she took a seat next to Ife and Scottie.

"I guess I'll stop before I go and let Will off the hook."

A few minutes later, everyone at the table looked up when Brigitte sighed and said, "Fuck."

She pushed back her chair and stood. "I'll see you guys later."

Step by step, counting each one, she stopped in front of Will's door, hesitating, her finger hovering over the *notice* screen. Finally, she touched the screen and waited for Will to answer. When he didn't, she repeated the summons, but he still didn't respond. Will *always* responded if he was there and he should be.

"Screw this." Brigitte engaged the door and it slid back into the wall. The low lighting she hadn't changed when she'd left hadn't been touched. A quick search showed that not only was Will *not* in the room, there was no evidence that he'd been there since she had.

Had he gone with Olivia after all?

Heading back out, she started back toward the diner, but stopped abruptly. Retracing her steps, she went to another room and pushed the *notice* screen outside the door. No answer. A second try yielded the same results as Will's. Once again, she released the door and entered. Dani had left mood lighting up, the ceiling glowing with pale blue lights. Her bed had been made and everything was in its place.

"Tidy. And you're not here either." She reached for her fone.

"Where are Will and Dani?"

Brigitte's voice boomed into the dining room and everyone looked up. "Neither are in their rooms and usually they're both here for last meal. Anyone know where they are?"

Ife stood. "I haven't seen them since I rose. Anyone else?"

No one spoke, but shaking heads around the room answered the question.

Fishing her fone out, Ife pressed a button and listened for an answer.

"I already tried Will and he didn't pick up for me either."

Punching another button, she tried Dani, and heard only the voicemail kick in. Her pale blue eyes lifted to Brigitte.

"Something is wrong. Scottie, have José track their fones."

Scottie disappeared as she reached for her own fone, bound for their business office in the back of the building. Suddenly it was imperative that she know where her friends were. Both were too reliable to take off without letting them know where they'd gone.

They'd learned that when something seemed to be wrong, it generally *was*.

Seven

IN LAS VEGAS...SERENITY TOWER

When she saw who waited on the other side of the door, Olivia touched the screen and said, "Get in here."

She hurried to meet Corri, who entered on a run and spread her arms and legs in a superman pose, her grin wide.

"What the hell?" Olivia started laughing.

"I thought I'd welcome you home properly." Corri held the position. "Don't you recognize the giant footed onesie pajamas you had designed for me?"

"Yeah, I do, but I never expected you to wear it outside this apartment."

Corri moved closer, pushed a loose strand of dark hair behind Olivia's ear, the grin downgrading to a smile. "I thought you could use a laugh."

Pulling her into a close hug, Olivia lingered with Corri, then took her hand to lead her to the main balcony.

"Laughs, yes, and booze. Lots of strong booze."

"No shortage of either here, love. So, Dori from the new buffet downstairs will be here in a few minutes with a full first meal for all of us. We can do a *girl's only* night tomorrow and you can fill me in on details."

"That works for me. I need to talk with you." Olivia shrugged. "About Will."

"I figured, sweetie. I can read you like an open book. I'm sorry."

"It's the game. So, let me go get some cozies on," Olivia said, her eyes on Corri's onesie. "I feel overdressed."

"Shut up. I'm running back to my apartment to change. Everyone is meeting us here in about twenty. Is that okay?"

"Absolutely. I'll release the locks, and they can just come on in."

"All right. I missed you, my friend."

"Me too."

After Corri left, Olivia dropped onto her bed, her eyes on the champagne ceiling, draped in satin from a central point to create a cascade of softness. Lighting was always kept low, doors to her private balcony nearly always open after dark to bring in fresh air and extend the space to the outside.

Here was where she rested, where she sought serenity and escape when it was needed. This room was also her special place for sensual blood meals and satisfying sex.

The room was heaven to her. One day, she hoped to share it with Will. While her confident promises to Will in Brazil had assured him they would be together someday, she didn't know when that might be. Or *if* it would be.

Destiny kept her hand in the lives of those she guided, Olivia had no doubt, but Destiny was also capricious and often couldn't be trusted.

A deep sigh filled the quiet space.

"Que sera, sera," she whispered aloud, an homage to an old song she loved. *What will be, will be.*

Standing, she dropped her traveling clothes on the floor and lifted a lightweight dress from her closet. Thin, a pale rose that looked incredible with her dark hair, the fabric clung to her body and highlighted her full curves.

"Will would love this." After she slid the dress over her head, she wandered back into her living space, surprised to see two of her guests already seated on the sofa.

"Rochelle! Hi, Gio. How are you two settling in?"

The displaced vampires from Corri's bizarre kidnapping and forced conversion had come to Las Vegas with Vaz, and after a nice reunion with Corri, Olivia had found them both jobs in the building. So far, she'd been impressed with their strong work ethic, and how well they performed those jobs. By now, they were on track to become permanent, valued members of her extended family.

Rochelle popped up and gave her a hearty hug.

"Lovin' this scene, Liv. I'm really good at handling your patrons at the cafe. And I'm surprised how much I enjoy it. Hey, is it okay if I open your bar?"

"Sure." Olivia turned to the dark-haired man who suddenly stood and lowered his head in a bow.

"Ms. Olivia."

Gio. The epitome of a gentleman. Beneath that polite quiet exterior, she imagined the heart of a truly sexy beast beat time waiting for the day it could come out and play. He was handsome enough, that was obvious, but he kept everything bottled up. *One day*, she thought.

"Evening, Gio. And how about you, are you happy here?"

"I'm grateful for the opportunity you gave me. And yes, I am relieved to live a normal life again. You gave me the right job, Ms. Olivia. I am. Happy here, I mean."

"Wonderful. And, Gio, it's just Olivia. We don't stand on formality here. We're all family."

"Forgive me. I'm just grateful for my benefactress and for the freedom you've given me and my friends. Of course, I'll try to loosen up."

Olivia tugged at his shirt collar. "Try to, please. And go get something sinfully alcoholic to drink. Relax, Gio, life is good now. You will always be my hero because you are the one that got Corri away from that motherfucker. Let me take care of you."

"I could have done nothing different."

"That tells me all I need to know about you. Gio, I think you have a big future here with me. Go, get that drink."

When the door opened again, Corri led Vaz through, already having a good night. He'd changed so much since the tortured man he'd been when he showed up desperate to find Corri months ago.

While she kept her welcoming smile in place, it struck her that *love, when it goes right,* will do that for you.

"Welcome, everyone, come on in. This girl has been gone too long, so let's celebrate my return. Now, where's that feast?"

SIX BLOCKS AWAY

"Sir, I have two for you. They are definitely what you wanted."

"Just two?" Frederick inquired, expecting a greater number from his man in Brazil.

"They're all you need, sir. These two are the closest to the vampires you want to know about. If I attempt to take more, they will discover my presence, and then the mission's blown."

"Oh. Sensible, I guess. That's why I hired you. Locktite, bring them to me. The jet has been dispatched."

"As discussed. You're still in the same building?"

"Off Sunset and Wisteria, yes."

"I will see you tonight."

Closing the call without the standard greeting, Frederick Villioth dropped onto a hard chair, relieved. Soon, he would have two humans he could control by compulsion to find out what they knew about the supervamps, or whatever the hell they were.

Finally, he would get his answers. Kidnapping people was distasteful, not something he would ordinarily condone, but he had been presented with no other option. He couldn't just go up to the vampire Olivia and ask what hell she was, not with the violent reaction from that one in Corsica who had the same mysterious skills.

"Did you get anything yet?"

Thalasia entered, and as usual, her voice heralded her arrival. The woman did amazing things with that mouth, but the incessant gabbing was not one of them. It was a pleasant voice, but she did prattle on.

"Perhaps," Frederick answered. "My man is bringing two humans for me to interrogate. Ah, I *do* hate that word."

Thalasia hopped up on the top of the bar counter, swinging her long legs, red spiked heels striking the wood.

"Interrogate? But you do it so well."

"Doesn't mean I enjoy it. However, in this case, it must be done."

"Oh, for that hot vampire babe. Why don't you just go ask her?"

"Because, dear lady, I am quite certain she would use her unbelievable skill to compel me, which she should *not* be able to do, and purge my memory of her altogether."

"Like that big guy in Corsica. Yeah, he was pretty spectacular. Well, you'll get her."

"I don't need to *get* her, I would just like to be in the loop and understand what she and that *Koen* are."

"Yeah, I know. Fred, I've never seen you fail. Once you get what you want, are you going to do what you promised? Are you going to convert me?"

It had been an impromptu promise back in Corsica, and he didn't answer. Dialing his fone again, he spoke as soon as it engaged. "Elmo, prepare restraints for two humans."

"Locktite bringing them in?"

"He is. Tonight."

"Yeah, they'll be ready. He gonna tranq 'em?"

Lord. "Yes, *he gonna tranq 'em*."

"Okay. I'll get to it."

Finally. He'd had three teams working on this mystery since he'd first observed the owner of Serenity Tower use compulsion on a vampire. When it had happened again in Corsica, he'd made a deal with a vampire named Vaz. He would help Vaz find a rogue vampire in exchange for the information on how it was possible for a vampire to *compel* a vampire, but the asshole had reneged and disappeared. He'd distrusted Frederick, and bolted.

Frederick admitted that there was reason to distrust him. His motives were rarely pure, hadn't even been when he'd still been human, but that didn't make him evil.

His only option had been to return to the female vampire he knew was unique, to watch and wait for the opportunity for something, *anything,* to reveal what she was.

After kidnapping her closest vampire ally with failed results, he'd known his best avenue was to find a human being on her inner circle. Humans could be compelled and he would easily have his story. Tonight was one for celebration.

Thalasia's voice interrupted again. "Are you going to take me out of this building finally? Or can I go on my own? I'm bored."

"You remember why we came here?"

"Yeah. You met a vampire who can control…"

"Compel."

"Right. Same difference, really. You met a vampire who can do what they shouldn't be able to do, and *you* being *you*, you can't let it go until you know how they can."

A long sigh of exasperation preceded his nod. "Yes, me being *me*, I need answers. When I became vampire three hundred years ago, the things I could do that mere humans could not blew me away. It still did until I realized that apparently there is yet another level higher to achieve."

"And you have to be at the highest level, right Fred?"

"My dear Thalasia, a man's reach should exceed his grasp, or what's a heaven for?"

Fred watched his favorite blood-bond, her huge eyes wide open as she listened to him. She'd never understand the Robert Browning reference, but it was fine, she was good at fucking and that's all he needed her for. The moment when he'd considered bringing her over had passed. He liked the brazen woman, but a commitment of several lifetimes with her around, he couldn't see it. He wouldn't tell her, of course; why disappoint the poor thing?

"So they get here tonight?" she asked abruptly.

"Yes, and it won't be the failure it was when my first team took Olivia's vampire friend. I'm practically vibrating with excitement. You see, after being alive for centuries, very little surprises a vampire. This, however, exhilarates me like Christmas day used to when I was a child. Oh, to find something new after all these years."

"I can imagine."

Frederick noticed Thalasia's eyes as she spoke, a depth undefined and never before seen. He could almost believe she could.

Serenity Tower's New Night Club

"Whoo-hoo!"

Rochelle was in her element, dancing on stage, the frighteningly brief dress in danger of sliding off with the next cha-cha move, her arms flailing above her head as she wiggled and turned.

Corri and Olivia held onto each other, they were laughing so hard at Rochelle's antics. Dancing around Rochelle and at least half a dozen other women, eight perfectly buff human men wearing only the briefest of briefs tried to do their job entertaining the clients in the club.

"Where did you *find* these men?" Olivia asked.

"Hot, hot, hot, aren't they? I was talking to Cairine about produce the other day and told her that I was looking for male dancers for your new club and she mentioned that a lot of the workers in Australia were really ripped. So I called Eras and he sent me some pics. Whoa, hell yeah, so I contacted them to see if anyone was interested. Forty men were thrilled to send me audition vids. I picked these eight for a limited engagement just to see how it went."

"Excellent choice. They're a hit."

Their eyes back on the hired dancers, they noticed Rochelle with a dark-skinned man she was practically humping as they danced.

"I think Ro would agree."

Sighing, Corri pushed from her seat. Rochelle had limited inhibitions, and humans were less comfortable with blatant public sex displays, even in this type of setting, so she knew she'd better rein her in.

"Unless we want to see more of Rochelle than that tube top she's using for a dress covers, I'd better go get her."

"If there weren't so many humans attending, I'd say let her be, but yes, I think we need to cool her down."

Sipping one of Corri's unique concoctions, Olivia relaxed back into a plush chair identical to every other chair in the club. This newest club, *Persistence*, had been designed for the optimum experience of pleasure and stimulation. Overt sexual acts were kept from the main part of the club, but a series of nicely dressed rooms lined the back where people could go to get a *happy ending*. Her staff was replete with skilled, lovely people of all shapes and sizes, a world palette of skin tones, and any combination of genders. It was an upscale, safe place to explore sexual pleasures.

Now up on the stage, Corri had her arms around Rochelle, trying to detangle her from the Australian dancer. Rochelle, drunk, horny, pulled Corri close, her hands around her friend's waist as Corri led her off the stage.

"Uh, sweetie, let's set you up with a partner."

"I want the gorgeous Aussie."

"Sorry, honey, he's a dancer, not a server. You know you won't be disappointed here."

"Yeah, I know. I miss our days together in the orgies sometimes, Cor."

"Yes, but it's much better now. We're free and happy."

"True. Okay, but I want dark chocolate tonight. I want someone beautifully roasted like me."

"How about Clyde?"

Rochelle slid a hand down her chest, stopping at her nipples. "Oh, yeah, Clyde is exactly what I want."

"Come with me, Ro, but, uh, keep your clothes on until I close the door behind you two."

Rochelle laughed too loud, stomping after Corri, eager now to get to the suites in the *Pleasure Center* of the club.

Leading Rochelle through the crowd, flashbacks of her days with Rocky's troupe, endless sex, naked people everywhere, it struck her as strange that they weren't all bad memories. Much of the time near the end, Rocky had left them alone, so she and Rochelle had just enjoyed young vampire life in Italy. Of course, it couldn't compare to the joy she had now with Vaz at her side and Olivia as family. Happier now than she ever thought possible after she'd been kidnapped and forcibly converted, she was grateful she didn't suffer post-traumatic issues from that horrible experience.

Clyde, a large man with dark skin and hazel eyes, looked up as they approached the *Center*. When he saw Rochelle, he smiled.

"Ro. Shell," he purred. "I hoped you'd come see me again soon."

"Not soon enough, hot buns." Rochelle hooked him with an arm and yanked him into Suite 3, waving behind her back at Corri as the door closed.

Corri sighed and smiled. "Someday, you're going to fall in love, my friend, and your world will change again."

AT IFE'S COMPOUND IN BRAZIL

"José has located their fones. Come on, we'll take the lift-car." Scottie already had the keyfob in her hand and one foot out the door, with Brigitte, Ife, and Torin following on her heels.

Gliding through the dark skies, this lift-car had been fitted with extra lighting beneath the vehicle that, when flipped on, provided efficient ground-directed search lights. Most cars in cities had little use for this type of retro-fit, but ninety percent of the reclaimed Amazon basin was naturally pitch dark again now that the mega-corporations had been forced out. Ife considered that one of her finest achievements.

Using the ground lights, Scottie found the rocky ridge where José had tracked their fones to, and, landing carefully in the limited space, she killed the engine. The sudden silence seemed ominous as the four passengers, using hand-held lights, searched the ground for their friends, the fones, or any evidence to let them know where they could be.

"Here," Scottie called out moments into the search. "Dani's fone. Oh, fuck! She'd never leave this behind. Something has definitely happened to them."

Brigitte's imagination started firing off ideas, scenarios, history, and her head snapped up. "Is there a chance they were swallowed by the earth like before?"

No one answered because no one *had* the answer, so they continued the search wordlessly, radiating out from the center of the area where Dani's fone had lain abandoned. Scottie stood to the side of the ledge, searching through it in case there were any photos, notes, or clues as to their fate. Finally, she turned it off. "Nothing here, guys. Keep looking for Will's."

Five minutes later, Torin barked out, "Got it!," and everyone gathered around him as he opened up the main screen and began to scroll through any recent entries or photos. He was about to announce the same thing Scottie had when a photo came up next as he searched. It stopped him there, stunned. The image was of Olivia, naked, wet, rising from a pool in a cave he did not recognize. He knew it had to have been taken when they both disappeared in that second collapse a few days ago.

God, she was luminous! He also knew in that moment why his friend had been so quiet these past two weeks. Will was in love with Olivia.

Brigitte watched Torin staring at the fone after a long pause, silent. "What is it?"

Closing off the device, he glanced up casually.

"Nothing. Just the usual lame pics. Nothing helpful."

Torin glanced at Ife as he finished and put the fone into his pocket. Once Brigitte wandered away, he touched her arm. "Did you know?"

Ife nodded. "But neither of them had admitted it by then. I don't know if they really have yet. Of course, now Will's missing, and, no Torin, I don't think he's run off to join Olivia in Vegas. I truly think that he and Dani are in trouble."

"Okay. I think so too, but…"

He fished the fone out and turned it toward Ife to reveal the photo Will had taken of Olivia. "I wish someone had told me. I would never have gone after her if I'd known."

"You're a good man, Torin. Will knows that. He trusts you and wanted you to be happy. Let's just focus on finding them and you two will work this out."

A simple nod let Ife know that Torin agreed, and she watched him turn the fone back off and pocket it. As he walked away, she turned from him to face the barely lit valley below. The photo had been taken by a man in love, but it was of a woman in love with that man, too. She hoped like hell this would have a happy ending.

Dizziness moved through her head out of nowhere, and she knew that a spiritual guide was trying to send her an image. Once it arrived in her head, she moaned. No, no happy ending from what the spirit world revealed. Ife didn't care, they needed to do all they could to find Will and Dani.

Scottie walked toward her out of the darkness, the others close behind. "There's nothing here to let us know where they are or what might have happened to them."

"Okay, here's the next important question. Brigitte, has Will ever taken your blood?"

A slight shake of Brigitte's head answered.

"Does anyone know if Dani has fed on vampire blood?"

"I doubt it. She hasn't really been with anyone since we all got together. I'm sure she hasn't been with a vampire."

"You're probably right. Why don't you all get back in the car and I'll be right there."

Torin watched her as he walked toward the car, well aware of what she was going to do.

Once everyone was clear, she hit another button and waited for an answer, but the call went to voicemail.

"Olivia, I have an urgent question. It involves Will and Dani's safety, so text me the second you get this message."

Staring at the fone after she left her message, she hit one more button. "Call Chione."

Near an abandoned airstrip outside of Brazil

Will woke first, aided, he thought, by his earth magics. Hands tied together with brixstix, releasable only with a coded wand, he assessed the dimly lit room where whoever had taken them kept them secured.

Dani lay beside him, breathing normally, her face pressed into a concrete floor. Sitting upright, he moved his banded hands to gently roll her face away from the rough surface. The movement roused her, and seconds later, she groaned and opened her eyes.

"Will? Where the fuck are we? Why?"

"I just woke up, so I have no idea. Jealous boyfriend?"

"Hardly. You're talking to a girl who had sex so long ago, I'm probably a virgin again."

"Didn't know that could happen. And TMI, darlin'. All right, first, you're okay, nothing seems hurt? Broken?"

Supporting each other, they scooted up against a wall behind them, concrete too, but covered with dirt and organic growth of some kind. It was none too clean, but neither of them were stable enough to sit upright very long without something to lean against.

"Ummm....I don't think so. You?"

"I'm okay. After that healing pool, my body seems to go into hyperdrive to repair itself."

"Handy, especially since we've apparently been abducted."

Will slid his hand down to his pants pocket and grimaced. "Dani, do you have your fone?"

"No. I usually keep it in my side pocket and it's empty."

"Fuck. Next question. Have you fed from any of the vampires?"

"No, never."

"All right, then, they can't find us. No problem, we'll just do this ourselves."

"Break free? Well, let's see, we're locked in what looks like a concrete room and tied up with unbreakable bonds. If you're expecting me to use my sex appeal to convince someone to let us go, you might want to know I suck at flirting."

"Never gonna believe that, but not necessary. No, Dani, I think…"

He stopped when raised voices outside the room were followed with the scrape of stone as a heavy door pushed open. Three large men entered, two holding laser pistols, and one carrying a great big smile.

Artificially tanned skin set off the smiling man's perfect white teeth as he moved close and bumped Will's foot.

"Hello there. How are we feeling tonight? Anyone have a headache? Hungry? You will be happy to know that we all want to get along. If you'd like something to eat or drink, or need to shit, you need to let me know. Our plane arrives in half an hour."

Calmly, Will caught the man's attention.

"Plane? You can't put me on a plane."

"Big motherfucker like you afraid of flying? Wouldn't have guessed it. Of course, you have exactly no choice in the matter. Suck it up, buddy. Now, who's hungry? How about you, beautiful?"

Dani shook her head, although it struck her that since she was going to die soon, she might as well have a last meal.

"Sir, you need to listen to Will. You can't take him off the ground. If you do…"

"Yeah, yeah. Sorry, babe, you two got someplace you need to be by tonight. Boss has sent one of his fastest jets. That thing'll have us in Las Vegas in four hours."

"Listen to me, we'll crash if you put me on any plane, especially one with fast take-offs like those hyperjets. I'm bonded to the earth…"

"Save your breath. You are going into that plane if I have to cut you into pieces to do it. So, no requests? Suit yourselves, we'll be back to get you in thirty minutes or less."

"Stop! Listen to me, asshole! I'm not fucking with you, we'll hit the ground in a big fireball!"

White Teeth shook his head, laughing, as he motioned for the gun-toting sentries to follow him.

The door closed behind them again, neither Dani or Will spoke at first. Both knew how serious this situation was and if they couldn't get their kidnappers to understand it, they were all dead.

Hyperjets took off so fast, they would be high in the sky when Will's earth bond pulled them back, and when it did, with that kind of speed and elevation, no one would survive the yank back to the ground.

His eyes on the nasty room at first, finally Will turned to Dani. He wouldn't be the cause of the death of another woman he cared about. She had a long, beautiful life ahead of her and this, a tragic death at her young age, was *not* going to fucking happen.

"Whoa, this just went sideways fast." Dani's voice defied the nerves that had to be frayed by the situation.

"I won't let them put us on that plane."

"Okay. Well, good. Because death by fire or drowning have always been off my list. Now, smothering in whipped cream, maybe."

"Dani, it's okay."

"No, Will, it's not okay. And it's also not your fault, so don't you fucking dare think it is. If this is our last hour alive, I want you to listen to me. This past year has been electric. I wouldn't give up a moment. And you, you hot, sexy, broody guy, are one of the best things in it. I think you're the first close friend I've had other than my brother, and I won't have you going to your eternal rest thinking that you caused my death."

"I will, if they do this. I'll cause several. Although they might deserve it, you don't."

Dani scooted closer to Will and leaned against him, stretching up to kiss him on the lips. As she dropped back down, her eyes tear-filled, he felt her fingers lace into his.

"It's really okay, Will. It really is. I'll meet you over the rainbow. We both know that this isn't the end."

Tears sliding onto his cheeks, Will couldn't stop shaking his head. *No, no, no...*

"I've lived a lot, Dani, and while I have some major regrets about dying now, I'm okay, I've made peace with mistakes I've made and who I am. But, *you*, sweet girl, I won't let them put you on that plane with me."

"Hum, well, I don't think you have a choice. And if this is our destiny, I'm okay with it too. But Will, if they don't separate us, will you hold onto me? If you can?"

"I'll hold on for all I've got. If this happens, I've got you, but now, this destiny thing, I've yet to embrace as immutable."

Holding her to his chest, Will decided at that moment that there was no fucking way in this world that he would let Dani die tonight.

At Serenity Tower in Las Vegas

All three drunk, Olivia led Corri and Rochelle into her apartment. Rochelle, still dancing, arms swinging, belted out a loud and out-of-tune rendition of an old dance song called *Disco Inferno* from over a century ago.

"Sh-h-h-h." Olivia put a finger to her lips, giggling. "You'll wake the baby."

Corri popped her in the shoulder. "Baby what? Hey, you don't even have a dog. Why don't we have a dog?"

Baby? Olivia wondered why she'd said something so ludicrous. "Let's get some dogs! I'll call the desk clerk."

"Yay!" Corri yelled and started to move along with Rochelle.

"Yup, I'll just call...hey, where's my fone?"

"It was on the table at the club. You didn't grab it?"

"Nope. I'll send one of Sam's guys to get it. Hey, we should get Ro to bed."

Rochelle had just dropped onto the sofa, her head lagging to the side.

"Uh, huh. I'll do it, and then I'm going to sneak out. I'm kinda feelin' like some Vaz tonight."

"Lucky, lucky girl. When am I gonna get *my* Vaz?"

Corri watched Olivia sigh, moving toward the balcony, and followed, slipping off her high-heeled shoes.

"Oh, honey, your Will will..."

"Nope. Don't. No cheering me up tonight. I'm drunk and horny, and I think I want to wallow. Wallowing can be cathartic."

"Yeah, I guess. Honey, we'll talk all this out when we wake. You okay?"

At the railing, overlooking her favorite view in the world, Olivia nodded. "I'm always okay."

"I don't know about that. You know I love you, don't you?"

Her gaze softened, Olivia turned to face her closest friend. "I do. Right back to you, my dear Corri. Get that girl into bed and get out of here. You've got a man waiting for you."

Fifteen minutes later, she heard the door swoosh closed and turned to face her living space. For some odd reason, her stomach was upset tonight, an ailment usually unknown to vampires.

"Stress. Worry. Loneliness. You pitiful fourth-generation first blood vampire. He'll come."

Wandering to her bedroom suite, she instructed the apartment's AI to close the lights to dim, lock the apartment down, and slide all the UV security panels into place.

Rest would help. When the sun dropped, things would be normal again and she'd get back to her life.

After sliding out of her dress, she dropped her black spike heels on the floor and slid between satin sheets that caressed overly sensitive skin. Olivia hadn't been kidding when she admitted she was horny, but the idea of sending for one of her sexy blood-bonds didn't appeal. The idea of anyone else inside her, for the first time in her life, felt wrong and alien.

Sleep finally took her from consciousness, but her unconscious mind wasn't through with her. Much of the night, she saw Will standing distant, a bright sun above his head, and knew, no matter how badly she wanted him, there was no way she could possibly reach him.

Suddenly awakened somewhere mid-day, a sense of panic struck her and she couldn't breathe. Pushing off the bed, she paced, a hand on her chest, confused, because she had no idea why she felt like this, she needed to get out of the apartment and onto the balcony. Daylight locked her into the room more than the three inch thick titanium panels that circled the apartment. A full glass of water later, and a shot of whisky helped to calm her down, and she fell onto her bed, uncovered, her eyes moist, she didn't know why, and finally fell into restless sleep.

At Ife's Compound

"Chione, is there any way to find them?"

"Yes. I need to pull together at least four of the earth warriors and we can reach across the air to discover where they are. You are all so spread out now, it will take a few hours."

"Please hurry. I have no idea who's taken them, but I sense something bad may happen."

"I'll call as soon as I know their whereabouts."

"Thank you."

Ife turned to her waiting friends. Torin sat on the top of one of her best sofas, his feet in the cushions, Scottie still stood at attention waiting for Chione's answer and Brigitte sat rigidly in a chair.

"She may be able to trace them, but she needs physical connection to four of us warriors, and has to put them together. I'm sorry, but that isn't quite good enough. Scottie, call Zia and Caed and get them back here. They only have about an hour to make it before daybreak."

"You're going to try to do a trace with us."

"Yes. There are five warriors right here and we're searching for two more who should still be within this continent. What do you think?"

"It's worth a try. I'm on it."

Crezia and Caedmon had hiked into the interior of one of the jungles to gather samples of both animal and plant life in preparation for an upcoming project. Scottie knew the general vicinity, and it wasn't beyond the timeframe to get back before the sun trapped them.

At an airstrip outside of Brazil

Dani rested against Will's chest. He could feel her heartbeat under his fingers. Her eyes closed, she wasn't sleeping, but it gave him the moment he needed to think about what he could do. Powerful magic rode inside him and now, at this desperate moment, he asked the universe to give him reign over them.

Silently praying to the living planet, he reached for his magics, drawing them from the earth as he had so many times, bidden and unbidden. As expected, they moved into him, waiting for release, stronger than before. Could he do what he hoped?

Dani opened her eyes and slid back. "I feel it, the power moving around us. What are you doing?"

"What I was made to do. Move away from me, Dani."

Without delay, she pushed onto her feet as Will did the same.

Standing now, anchored to the ground, he squatted and placed both hands on the concrete surface. Dani watched, fascinated, as he pressed his fingers into the slab and they began to shake. Seconds later, the unbreakable was broken.

Will's hands were free. He looked at her and smiled.

"There's a bit of magic for you."

His eyes on hers, he walked to her and wrapped his hands around *her* cuffs. Pressure built, the magic swirling around her, almost tangible, and silently, with no warning, the band around her own wrists split and fell to the floor.

Rubbing sore wrists, she nodded. "My hero."

"All in a day's work. Now we have to escape our cinderblock."

"Can you get the door open?"

The look Will shot her made her laugh. "What was I thinking?"

"The question is, what happens when we open it?"

"We have no weapons, no vehicle, and they are probably outside the door. The guy said we would board the plane shortly, so I doubt they're far."

Will's mind working overtime, he knew they couldn't plan without knowing what was out there. He had a thought, and no idea if it would work.

"Dani, pick up the cuff, slide it back around your hands, the opening to the back. When they come to lead us to the plane, I'm going to try to freeze them. If I can do it, we can get to the car and get the hell out of here."

"You really think you can do it?"

"I think I have to try. Dani, we don't know how they're going to react to my attempt. Stay behind me. Promise me."

"Will..."

"Promise me. I can't concentrate if I'm worried about you."

"All right, I promise."

"Okay then, we have a plan. Get your cuff and I'll get mine."

No sooner had they slipped the cuffs back around their wrists, the door opened and the same three men entered. The one who had barked out the orders before motioned to Will. "Come on. You don't have any choice, so no thrilling heroics. Follow Duke, the guy with the awful Mohawk and the biggest gun."

Duke waited at the entrance, and when Dani and Will stepped through, he pushed in front of them. Will immediately began to assess the scene. It was daylight, but he'd already assumed it was. These guys would be stupid to try anything when the vampires could come for them.

Stepping toward a small jet waiting on a paved runway surrounded by nothing but grass, Duke kept a slight distance and the gun on Will. His eyes moving swiftly over the landscape, it was apparent that this was an isolated airstrip for illegal business. No help here.

Dani stayed close as requested. Behind her, the second armed man kept some distance too, the man giving orders taking up the rear, as they proceeded to the open hatch of the high-speed jet.

Careful with his hand motions, Will saw only one other vehicle; a lift-car parked about thirty feet from the jet. The ground vehicle that must have been used to transport them here was nowhere in sight.

That, then, was the only option. He couldn't escape in the lift-car, *but Dani could.*

Time to try out his other new skill. Focusing, he sent his thoughts to Dani, praying that he got it right. First, he spoke her name.

Dani.

Her head shot up and her eyes went to his. Success.

Hi, I wasn't sure this would work. Telepathy is so weird. I am going to try to freeze these guys. If I succeed, you need to run to the lift-car and get out of here. Hopefully, one of these assholes left the keyfob in the ignition.

He could already see the immediate rejection of the idea.

Dani, this is our only chance. I can't go with you, you know that, but if you get out of here, you can bring help. I can see in your eyes that you don't want to leave me behind but I'll be okay. I think I can use my magics to disable the plane. Nod, Dani, to let me know you understand and will go.

Her eyes were wide, but he watched her tamp down her panic, and she nodded.

Good. Just, when I tell you, go and don't stop. Trust me.

She didn't have to speak, he knew what she was thinking. He'd have felt the same about leaving a friend behind, but this was the only way he could be sure she was clear and safe.

Twenty feet from the hatch of the jet, Will stopped suddenly, forcing Duke to turn on him.

"Get movin'! You got a sweet ride to Vegas waiting."

Will did the opposite, dug his center of gravity into the earth and lifted his hands to the sky to reach for earth and universal elements, for power to do what only first blood vampires could do. Air began to whip around them as Will pushed for enough power to do what he needed to.

"Locktite, what the fuck is he doing?" Duke barked, looking to the leader behind them.

"I don't fucking know. They're human, I know that, so they can't do anything dangerous."

The second gunman had noticed the change in the air and felt the unnatural pressure. "I think you guys might be wrong about that."

As suddenly as the moment began when Will stopped to reach for the magics, he lowered his hands and looked at the men. Pushing his need, he waited, breath held, as he watched Duke, the man with the biggest gun.

Duke didn't move.

Will moved his eyes to the second gunman, and the last man. Neither moved, and when he turned back to Duke, touched his cheek and saw shock in his eyes, Will turned to Dani. "Go."

"Will, come with me, I'll fly low."

"No, I don't know what height is dangerous. Get out of here. Dani, go get Torin and a security team."

He just wanted her safe and away from however things happened here. "You promised. I don't know how long I can keep them like this."

Decision made, she turned and ran full out, climbed into the lift-car, and he heard the engine start, saw her lean out, and then head straight up.

"Thank the gods," he whispered. "You guys need to trust me that I cannot go up into a plane without bringing it right back down. I'm going to try to disable it."

Still unmoving, the three who'd abducted them left behind on the grass, Will started toward the plane.

He heard the report of the bullet only a split second before it slammed into him and he went down.

Instantly, able to move again, Locktite twisted his head back and forth, lifted his fingers and wiggled them as he raised a leg and lowered it. *Motherfuck!*

He watched Duke and Sid start to move again as well. Eyes moving to Will's still body lying in the grass several feet from Duke, he sighed.

"What the hell *are* you?" he snapped. Surging forward, he kicked Will in the side using all his strength.

Shit! Villioth wanted him unhurt or at least functional.

A few moments later, staring down at his target, bleeding from the side because his pilot had shot him, and because he'd kicked the fuck out of him, he kicked him again, and then waved to Duke.

"Get him in the plane and see what you can do about his wounds. Tie him up again, and this time, cover his eyes, and tranquilize him heavily. Haven't ever had complications like this one."

Duke hoisted Will's body up, but needed help from Sid to get him into the plane.

"Get us up," Locktite barked and dropped into a wide seat with a glass of Villioth's expensive wine. He admitted that he didn't really get the difference between a 30 dollar bottle of wine and a 300 dollar bottle, but if someone gave him the 300 dollar bottle of wine, yeah, he'd fuckin' kill it.

Sighing with relief that they were finally on their way, he wondered how bad it was gonna be when he showed up in Vegas with just one human who might be able to tell him about his strange vampire?

Ready for go, the pilot, aware that the runway was short, calculated that this hyperjet would have no trouble with the minimal distance, headed down the cracked pavement, gathering speed. When it hit the airspeed required for takeoff, he enjoyed the gorgeous roar of the jet engine as it brought this beautiful bird into the sky and started a fast, steep climb. Banking to the right, he keyed into the flight system all the particulars of the flight, destination, cruising altitude, and turned it over to the highly efficient AI. Sitting back, he scanned the horizon as the plane rose, higher, higher, into the blue.

Some distance away, Dani, in the stolen lift-car, sick to her stomach, ran the car full-out to get back to Ife's and bring help before Will was hurt or worse. The car was stripped down and didn't have a proper GPS or coms system.

"Probably stolen, the assholes," she mumbled as she watched the landscape to make sure she didn't lose direction. Scanning below, Dani assessed the location of Dez's compound to be closer than Ife's and that was the wiser choice. Searching for landmarks, she jumped when a sudden fireball erupted to her left, lighting up the sky, the percussion reaching her even from this distance.

Seconds passed as the implication hit, and even then, somewhere in the back of her mind, she refused to believe it.

No, no, no, no, no…

Heat and moisture filled in behind her eyes as she faced what she knew must be the truth…they'd overtaken Will somehow and put him on that plane. What she'd witnessed just now was the horrific collision of the jet with the hard earth as it stretched its arms to pull its chosen son back to its bosom. If the crash was as bad as it looked, no one aboard would have survived.

Their attempt to rescue themselves had failed, and Will was wrong.

"You were wrong, you were wrong, you were wrong…"

She couldn't stop whispering it to herself as she tried to remember where she was going.

You were wrong, Will. You're not okay.

Eight

Corri opened the door to Olivia's bedroom suite, sliding up the lights just enough to create a pale rose hue over everything. It was meant to be soothing and pleasant to her as she woke to begin her night.

Olivia liked things nice.

Swiping moisture from her eyes, she sat on the side of Olivia's bed and reached across the wide expanse to shake her gently.

"Liv? Liv, you have to wake up." A few seconds later, a heartier shake, and a louder voice. "Olivia."

"Ummm...."

Olivia rolled over, cracked her eyelids, glanced to her side to see Corri, and smiled. "Hey, friendly face. Damn, how much did we drink last night? You're getting really good at designing alcohol that's effective for vampires. I think I have a hangover."

"Olivia, you need to sit up."

Crawling upright, Olivia pushed two of her fat pillows up behind her and leaned into them. "So stern. What's the deal? Oh, by the way, are you going to hold me to that promise to get dogs?"

"I need to tell you something, and this isn't easy."

Somber now, Olivia felt her skin cool. "What is it?"

"Something happened in Brazil today. Liv, there's no easy way to tell you this, but..."

Corri drew a deep breath. "Will was killed today."

Olivia just stared at Corri, unsure of what to say. She couldn't have heard what she thought she heard; it wasn't possible.

Trying to process the words didn't seem to help either. *Will was killed today.*

Finally she was able to respond. "No, he wasn't. Will and I have such a close connection, if something had happened to him, I would have known. Even in my sleep, his spirit would have come to me."

A sudden memory returned, a dream, in her sleep, lying with Will in a sun-filled meadow. But that was just a lovely dream, that's all.

Corri took Olivia's hand and intertwined their fingers.

"It's true, Liv, I'm sorry. They found him. He died in a plane crash."

Olivia shot up, balancing on the soft mattress, laughing, her hair flying around her head. "See, that proves it. Will would *never* get into a plane. *Never!* It's some kind of bizarre mistake."

"Brigitte is on her way here to see you. She's hurting, and she knows you'll be too. Livie, why don't you come out into the galley and I'll make you a hot tea?"

A black cloud descended over Olivia's spirit as suddenly she realized, had to admit, had to understand, to accept, that Corri would never say something so horrible to her if it wasn't true. If she didn't *know* it was true. *And Brigitte?* She wouldn't come here if something hadn't happened to *make* her come.

Collapsing on the bed, her legs out to her side, her hands in her lap, her heart breaking, Olivia lifted wet eyes to Corri. "Tell me."

Forty minutes later, Corri finally convinced Olivia to come from her bedroom into the living space. She set a hot tea filled with honey and whisky in front of Olivia, who sat stone-still on the sofa and looked at the mug in front of her. They waited for Brigitte to arrive, but Olivia had already told Corri to prepare her jet and put her pilot on standby.

"I have to see him."

"It isn't…"

"It doesn't matter. You don't know this yet, Corri, you haven't been alive long enough, but when you've been around for centuries, when awful things happen to rip you apart, the only way to make peace with it, to try somehow to go on, is to face whatever it is and find a way to accept that nothing you say, nothing you do, no prayers, no deals, no begging, is going to change the truth. I have to see him to accept that he's gone."

Hands shaking, Olivia lifted the mug and tried unsuccessfully to take a sip. She held it in her hands for a while until she could hold it steadily. "I have to say goodbye."

"Oh, Liv, my darling, I understand. Can I go with you?"

The mug began to tremble again, and Corri lifted it to place it back on the table.

"I wish you would," Olivia finally was able to answer.

"Do you want to lie back down until Brigitte gets here?"

"I want to go out onto the balcony."

"That's a good idea. It's a lovely warm night and the breeze is perfect."

"It'll never be a warm night again."

"Oh, sweetheart…"

Corri wrapped her arms around Olivia and they stood there in the center of the room, weeping into each other, Olivia crying for Will, Corri crying for both of them.

She'd heard Vaz's pain after losing the first love of his life, and now, to watch her dearest friend facing an even more tragic loss, because they hadn't even had a chance to really find each other in all this mess of a life.

When the door chimed, she spoke softly to accept the visitor, and looked up to see a stunning woman approach, tears welling up immediately when she saw Olivia, and knew it had to be Brigitte.

"Hi," the woman said and turned to Olivia.

"He's gone," she whispered, and the two women dropped to the floor, embracing, weeping openly, as Corri stepped back and wondered how anyone ever survived something like this.

At Ife's compound the following night

Olivia sat expressionless as the discussion continued. Brigitte hadn't moved far from her side since they had lost it in Olivia's apartment, and flown back to confront one of the worst moments of their lives...putting Will's body to rest for the final time. She'd been sitting here in Ife's lounge for less than an hour and she couldn't take another minute.

When they told her how he'd come to be in the plane, that someone had tried to abduct him and Dani, she'd walked out of the building and dropped against the earth to ask how the planet could let him die over some piece of shit that was stalking her. She knew it had to be the person or persons who sought information about her, and now, no matter how long it took, no matter what the sacrifice, she would find the ones responsible, and they would die.

This moment, though, all that remained, all she could do for him, was to give him a proper burial.

Brigitte would accompany her shortly to the little spirit room at the back of the building to see him.

She'd been warned. He had been burned over thirty percent of his body, but otherwise, he barely looked injured by the impact and fire. Brigitte had said it was the magics and Olivia knew it was so.

Still, the moment was near when she would hold him one last time.

"We could bury him in the new flower fields," Ife suggested.

"No."

Everyone looked up at Olivia. "In the cave. We have to lay him to rest in the cave. There's nowhere else Will should be than at the heart of his spirit, where his magics were born. We have to give him back to the earth."

"She's right," Brigitte agreed. "We have to take him to the new cave and let him return to the Mother Earth."

"You're right, of course. Olivia, once you say goodbye, we'll do a procession and take Will home."

Olivia couldn't have spoken for anything at that moment. She just nodded and stood when Brigitte motioned for her to do so.

"Come, let's go see him."

As they passed Dani, Olivia saw her drop her head and look away.

Stopping, she lifted Dani's head and looked into her eyes. Olivia kissed her cheeks, one, then the other, her lips, her nose, and each eyelid. "Will saved you, don't throw away his gift. He's a beautiful man, we'll remember him with joy and love. Dani, don't grieve too long and don't carry the burden of blame. There is none for you."

"But..."

"Will adored you, I know that. Adore him back by embracing the life he protected for you."

Dani held onto Olivia's hand until she continued behind Brigitte down a long hallway, past the dining room and a gaming room, through a music room, and finally into a room separated by a white iron door. Intricate lacework detail covered the door in pale blues, reminiscent of clouds moving through a blue sky.

Brigitte paused with her hand on the old-fashioned door handle. "Are you ready?"

Again, no words would come, so Olivia nodded and followed her into a candlelight-filled room. Near the back of the room, on a satin covered bench, lay a dark form. Olivia stopped. It couldn't be Will, it just couldn't. She shook her head.

"I'm not sure I can."

"You can. I'm going to leave now and let you do this in your own time, in your own way. Olivia, he'll wait until you're ready."

The door closed behind Brigitte, leaving Olivia standing where she'd stopped, unable to go forward or back. Fluttering in her belly overwhelmed her suddenly, and she put her hands to it, amazed that calmness replaced the pain and she stepped forward.

Closer, closer, until she stood in front of Will, and yes, it was him, and *yes*, he was gone.

He looked like he was sleeping, at peace, like he could open his eyes and smile at her. The face that she'd never forgotten after that first night, that she never would, looked untouched, and for him to go through what he had, it was a miracle. Someone had dressed him in a long white robe, which seemed right, aware that it probably hid the damage from the fire.

She slid down to lean against the bench and touched his cool lips with a fingertip.

"Will, what am I going to do with you? I leave and look what happens." It amazed her that she could smile, but seeing him, knowing it would be the last moment with him, was all that she would ever get again. "I'll miss you forever, my beautiful man. My mate. You are my first and only love. I had such plans for us, but..."

Her voice cracked and faded, but she couldn't take her eyes off him. How was she going to face the rest of her life without this man who she was convinced had been her destiny?

When she could speak again, her volume was low but she knew he could hear her. "I waited for you for centuries, Biker. How dare you leave so soon? You're Shoazan, you're supposed to be invincible. I guess that's only if you're pregnant. You aren't, *are* you?"

He didn't answer her pained smile. "Seriously, what am I going to do without you?" she repeated.

Olivia stayed with him for a long time until the door opened and Brigitte spoke.

"Liv, stay as long as you need, but when you're ready, we're going to take him to the cave and have a small service there."

Waiting for a few seconds for a response, Brigitte realized that Olivia couldn't answer, and quietly closed the door.

Her hand on her belly again, as it pitched and rolled, as movement inside felt odd and yet comforting at the same time, Olivia stayed another period of time, how much she did not know, then finally stood. Kissing his lips, her fingers scored Will's face, along the cheekline, the strong chin, across closed eyes, she kissed a trail and ended once more on his lips for a final kiss.

"Until we meet again beyond the veil, past all these earthly concerns, I hope you find joy in the spirit world. Never forget that I wait to join you. I love you, Biker."

Sorrow broke her as she walked from the little room out into the brighter light of the corridor, where, thankfully, she was alone and dropped down against the wall to weep uncontrollably, both hands now on her belly again. Why did that give her such comfort? How could *anything*?

When it felt like there were no other tears left, she pushed up shakily, and, one last glance toward the door, she walked back to the lounge, nodded to Ife and Brigitte, who waited, and continued to the room they'd assigned to her so that she could splash cold water on her face before they left to take Will to his grave.

"Liv."

Olivia whirled and hurried into Dez's arms, grateful to collapse against her, more grateful yet when Zach's arms went around both of them. They stood together, wrapped in warmth and family until Brigitte's voice interrupted.

"We've taken him to the cart. Whenever you guys are ready."

Twenty minutes later, a group of Will's closet friends followed a cart carrying Will's body covered with local flowers, only his face exposed, as the small procession made its way to the cavern of crystals. Lowering him down on a rope pulley designed by Torin, Will was going home forever.

Stepping back into the hole in the earth where she and Will had made love for the first and last time, Olivia nearly lost it again until, from the pit of her spirit, memories invaded; warmth and joy infused her mind and heart. This was not a place for sorrow. Reaching for Brigitte, the two led the group toward a deep hole dug into the corner of the space beneath a wall densely packed with diamond-like crystals. *His grave.*

"This is the right place. Will would like this," Brigitte mused.

"No, he wouldn't." Olivia closed her eyes as Torin and Scottie lowered Will's body into the grave with only the white robe and a shroud of the same material wrapped around his face, so that the dirt wouldn't intrude on those features they loved.

Tears slipped without notice down cheeks, voices cracked, stories told, and it was time.

Torin looked up into Olivia's eyes, his nearly as wet.

"I know you were in love with him. It's okay."

None of that mattered to her anymore, the messed up sexual alliances that were never going to last, the memories sweet, but only that, sweet moments to fade away with the setting sun. What she had with Will had been solid, perfect, and would have spanned millennia.

Brigitte touched her hand and she nodded. None of this was Torin's fault. He just got caught up in her wake.

Reaching for him, she slid a hand into his to let him know that he was right, everything was okay.

Words were spoken, goodbyes said, final kisses bestowed, and as easily as that, or as hard as that, Will was placed in the ground, covered, a sprinkle of the crystals scattered over the spot from each who attended, and it was done.

Will had lived his life, and left it, leaving those who loved him behind to go about their days and wish he could be with them still.

Vampires accepted these truths, these losses, or they could never survive the pain of such long lives. Having been fortunate, Olivia had never lost anyone who meant so much to her, and although she was a pragmatic woman, she already knew that this one would take a very long time to move past.

Dez took her hand. "Let's go home, my child."

"Okay, but Dez, I'm going home to Vegas. I can't be here."

"You'll stay the day at least?"

"No, Dez, my jet is UV protected so I can fly safely and I really don't want to be here. Not now. Please understand."

Dez folded her granddaughter into her arms and held her. They both knew that this kind of hurt stayed and buried itself in the living spirit. She knew that Olivia would be okay, but that would be sometime in the future, not today, and not tomorrow.

"We'll take you to it, then."

Zach reached for Brigitte, a hand on her forearm.

"Do you need a lift?"

"No. My sister is coming to be with me here. Right now, I agree with Liv. Go away, lick the wounds, and live to love another day." Her eyes landed on Dani, in the corner of the cave, a hand in the little pond. "I'm going to see how Dani is doing."

She turned to Corri, who waited nearby. "Take care of her." Corri nodded.

Brigitte turned to Olivia and captured her face in her hands. "Liv." She paused, her smile sweet. "I know he loved you. He was going to tell me that night when I woke, I know he was. I'm sorry you didn't get a chance to find each other and be together. I'll miss him, every day, so if you need to talk with someone who understands, let me know and I'll come to you."

The two women hugged so long, it appeared they didn't want to let go, and for those moments, Olivia didn't. When they finally stepped away from each other, she watched Brigitte disappear beyond the light before she took Dez and Corri's hands.

"I'm through here too. Take me out."

And like that, climbing from the dark hole in the earth, she left behind her future.

Walking away, she stopped and grabbed Dez's arm.

"Does anyone have any photos of Will? Anything to remember his face when time and distance make him fade away?"

Zach slid a hand along the top of her head. "I do. We've taken a lot of candid shots of him along with everyone else who comes to the club. Don't worry, Liv, you'll get them."

"Thank you. You always think everything is going to be all right, that you'll have a chance to fix things, and it just isn't true. No, I have to go home and figure out how to live without him. Right now, the future looks bleak."

In Las Vegas

Frederick Villioth picked up a leaded vase and hurled it across the room, enraged.

"What the fuck did you say?"

"Um, sir, the plane carrying your hostages and the team that captured them, it, uh, went down. No survivors."

Shocked, pissed, he gathered his thoughts, calmed down, and turned to his blood-bond.

"Can you give me any more details? Why did the plane crash? Who discovered it? Where are my men? What the fuck happened?"

"I have very little knowledge. We're, uh, in fact-finding now, but I knew you were waiting for them to arrive, and I thought it prudent to let you know that, uh, they weren't going to."

"Wise thinking. Never keep me out of the loop. So tell me what you *do* know."

"We monitor the news feeds in any country where we have a presence, but this afternoon, we heard a broadcast announce that a hyperjet went down in the old-growth part of the Amazon. Five bodies were recovered."

"Five? *Five?* Your math doesn't add up. There should have been my extraction team, that's three, the pilot, that's four, plus two hostages, a man and a woman. You've confirmed it's mine?"

"Yes, sir. The authorities haven't been able to identify its origins, and any other, they would, so it's gotta be yours."

"Handle it. Make sure nothing can be traced back to me. I imagine Olivia's vampire community will be investigating the incident if the two on board were as close as I believe they were to them. I sure the fuck don't want them on my doorstep."

"I have two vampires on it, sir."

"Good. It seems you have everything in hand. Fuck! When you find out why the plane went down, I want to know."

"At once. I'll go see how things are going."

The bearer of bad news gone now, Frederick punched a heavily tufted pillow. What could have caused that new plane to crash? The hostages fought back? Maybe, but if that were the case, then he'd hired incompetents to secure them, and Locktite was no incompetent.

"Once again, nothing feels right here."

Entering the room, Thalasia, dressed in a short white top, shorter pants, and knee high white boots, had been listening to the conversation.

"You have had a lot of trouble trying to get that vampire's shit. Maybe it's best to let it go. Some things aren't meant to be."

"When I want your opinion, sex doll, I'll let you know. For now, go see if you can find out anything at Olivia's new club. Someone on her staff might know what's going on, and you, my dear gal, blend in well amongst the human trash."

"Whoa. Trash? What the hell?" Thalasia walked toward the door. "You're a pig, Frederick Villioth."

"As long as I get what I want, and, oh, yes, your opinion doesn't matter at all. Find out what you can and come right back to me. Don't linger."

Posed, her nearly exposed ass pointing at Frederick Villioth, Thalasia watched him. He'd used compulsion to make her do what he asked, so, against her will, she sauntered out the door, heading to Serenity Tower to betray people who were a whole hell of a lot better than she was, than the piece of shit she fucked and worked for. It was time to get away from him, but that wasn't likely to happen. He'd kill her long before he'd let her go, and she had no illusions that he wouldn't also kill her long before he made her vampire.

Half an hour later, Thalasia was seated in Serenity's newest club, cozied up, half-drunk, with one of the bouncers, trying to convince him to let her give him a blowjob. Nothing made a man happier to tell everything he knew than when he was under the spell of a good blow.

"So I love your boss. She's just such a classy lady. She here tonight?"

"No. Had an emergency and took off for South America. Second trip there in the past few weeks."

"Wow. Somethin' wrong?"

"I don't know about that. Corri, she's the one who's hands-on here, is really worried about her. She's really sad right now, and that isn't typical for her."

"Aw. Well, hope it isn't anything too tragic."

"Me too. Did you want a refill on that?"

Thalasia handed him her glass. "Yeah, I do. Say, Joey, would you like me to, uh, show you how athletic my tongue is?" *That would loosen him up.*

"I can't fraternize that closely with the guests, sorry. It's a nice offer, but if you'd like to visit our guest services in the back of the club, you'll find everything you need there to leave with great memories."

Fuck! "Nah, I just like you and thought I could give you a good time. I'm very, very skilled."

"I'm sure you are, but, I like this job and can't partake of your kind offer."

"Kind? You think all *this* is *kind*?" Moving her hands up and down her body, Thalasia was ashamed of herself. Joey was a good, hardworking, honest man and here she was trying to force him to risk his job.

Compulsion sucked, but luckily, since he refused her, she couldn't do anything else to convince him, so she left unsatisfied in her mission, but personally pleased to have failed.

After she returned to the vast warehouse building that Villioth had purchased two years ago, Thalasia entered his private rooms, well aware he would want an update.

"Well?" he barked as soon as she arrived.

"Sorry, but he wasn't interested. His job would have been on the line and he has scruples and a strong sense of self-preservation."

"Or you're losing your appeal."

Pissed, sick of her life, Thalasia dropped her clothing on the floor, presenting a body she knew was excellent, and walked up to Frederick Villioth, grabbed his cock, which was hardening under her fingers, then moved away from him. "Not."

"Did you discover anything about Olivia?"

"She's gone. Personal tragedy. I guess we know what. It appears that you've lost your leverage. I'm exhausted, I'm going to bed."

Gone quickly, Thalasia closed the door behind her, leaving Frederick pissed off, but distracted.

For a moment, he considered Thalasia's suggestion to forget about this desire to understand the mystery of what these vampires were, but seconds later, he recommitted.

"You are something special, and I *will* know what it is."

In Serenity Tower

"You're sure you don't want me to stay? I could crawl into bed beside you and we could talk all night."

"Corri, you're wonderful, thank you, but I just need to sleep. Daylight is a few hours yet, but I'm drained."

Corri pushed Olivia's hair back and held her face.

"If you need me, no matter when, call me. You *do* look tired, but after what you've been through, I'd be surprised if you didn't. You're *sure* you're okay?"

"I will be. I'm going to have some bad times, but I have you to help me get through it. Getting back to work will help, but I think I need a few more days to get my head on straight."

Olivia paused, her eyes closed. "I already miss him so much, when I think about him, I can't breathe."

"Oh, honey." Corri held her friend for long moments before Olivia gently pushed her back.

"Go see your mate. I'm going to swallow a gallon of whisky and fall into my bed. Don't let anyone disturb me until I let you know. Honestly, I just want to be alone for a while."

"I understand. Just, please, let me know if you need me *anytime*, okay? Promise."

"I promise. Now, scoot, go see Vaz."

Corri hesitated a moment longer, and when she finally left, Olivia turned to her AI.

"No messages, no visitors, no interruptions until I let you know."

Affirmative, the AI said in the soft feminine voice Olivia preferred.

Her stomach rolled again, and she placed her hands over the offensive area for the twentieth time in the past few days. What the hell was wrong with her? This wasn't typical. It must be the stress and loss tearing her apart, physically as well as emotionally.

Almost by muscle memory, she moved into the galley and stopped in front of the FP.

"Chamomile tea, fifty percent whisky."

Twenty seconds later, the big mug in her hands, Olivia headed into her bedroom.

"Close up for sleep."

The AI activated the UV shields, lowered the lights for rest, and secured the doors.

Crawling into her bed, Olivia set the mug on the nightstand, and looked around the room. Her life was so much more beautiful than it had been before she met her true family a century ago. This tower she'd named Serenity, because it was that to her, held friends and family, a business of clubs and restaurants that she loved, and this home, this entire floor of the tower, always peaceful, always safe, always home.

She would never get to share it with Will, and that made it hurt for now. Closing her eyes, she imagined him in her bed, laughing at some silliness, naked, hovering over her, his hair hanging loose, the beautiful body coming down on top of her; his eyes, serious, in love, as he entered her, pushed deep, where he belonged, filled her in every way. When he moved, she lifted up to force him deeper…

The vision was vivid, seemed so real, that lying alone now, she lifted her body up to him, lifted her core to receive him…except…

He was not there, he would never be there.

Hands on her belly again, she traced circles around it, and cried. Sleep wrapped around her, consciousness sliding away, as Olivia entered the world of dreams.

Would he be here, she wondered, as she walked along a beach lit by early morning sun. No, she didn't see him, and more than that, she didn't *sense* him.

Pushing her toes into the wet sand, Olivia turned to watch the sun move up the bright blue sky pushing away the rose and orange-tones, breathtaking, the lost pleasure of a sunrise. The spirit world gave truth and hope, often needed by first bloods, and *she* did, but Will wasn't here, so why was she?

A voice interrupted her thoughts.

Because you need to know about me.

Not words, but she understood the meaning.

Olivia lifted her dream-self up from the beach and turned in place, searching around her. "Who are you?"

I will call you mother.

Olivia couldn't move at first as the words that were not spoken and yet heard, the *meaning* of the words, came to her. I will call you mother.

Mother.

Warmth like a hot light filled her belly as her hands curved over the place where she hoped, prayed, that what she thought was true. A child in her…*Will's* child in her.

True, *yes*, she could feel it now, the baby; present, new, reaching for the mother it would know someday soon. A fatherless child who would be cherished beyond measure by a grateful and loving mother.

Of course! It had to be; that first time she'd walked into the spirit world to see if Will was who she sought, she'd known that he was Shoazan, capable of bringing life. The idea had spooked her, not ready at that moment to even consider a lifelong mate, let alone a child.

"Oh, precious, precious baby," Olivia whispered, and understood now why she'd had that odd predilection for the past few days to keep her hands on her belly. Will's baby had been there since that night in the cave, and now, even though he was gone, she carried part of him with her.

"Will, look what we've done."

It would be okay because she had a child to raise, to introduce to this world she loved so much, to teach to love it as well.

"Yes, little one, I needed to know about you. Thank you."

Her world would change once again, only this time, a life would come to make hers complete.

"The open window…"

Olivia felt the spirit world fade and finally succumbed to grateful sleep.

Nine

One month later

"Get him!"

"Are you kidding? That puppy moves faster than a vampire, for heaven's sake! Just let him go, Cor, he'll be back. Where's he gonna go anyway?"

"I just don't want him loose on this floor. You know, just in case."

"You worry too much."

"Says the pregnant woman who changed every element of what we eat and drink, even though vampires don't have any problem with the junk food group."

"I've just been reading a lot of books."

"Aarrgh! *Human* books! Liv, take it from one with a medical degree, or nearly, what we are, nothing you do will harm him."

"I know. For some reason, it feels like something that I have control over. Maybe I've gone overboard."

"Then we can have the ice cream back?"

Olivia grinned. "Of course you can. I was actually kidding about that. I just wanted to see how long it would take before one of you broke, and I kind of like seeing how clever Vaz is at sneaking things in. I know about your morning sugar orgies."

"Oh, we do *creative* things with that sugar."

"Oh, can I watch? I get so bored with vids."

"And, *no*. I'm just going to check on Geraldo."

"If you must. And while you're at it, rename him."

"I can't. Vaz really likes that old man in the park. He thinks he's brilliant."

"He's a vagrant. By choice. He's been out there since I opened the tower."

"Vaz invited him to dinner. He wants him to meet his namesake."

"Well, enjoy. I've plans for tonight."

Corri moved close and laid a hand on Olivia's rounding belly. "He's getting so big so soon."

"First bloods come in six months, remember?"

"Yeah."

Corri stared at Olivia's belly, her hand gently moving over the small mound. "I envy you. I would love to have Vaz's child."

"I can't describe what it feels like to have part of Will growing inside me. Especially since he's gone, it's the greatest gift in the universe. Like nothing could ever possibly be this good again. Meeting this little boy will be the one moment in my life that makes everything worth it. Even losing Will, that this boy will be here, will make it worth the pain. I still dream of that man, I don't think that will ever change, but when I wake, and this child is here waiting for me, how could I ever feel sorrow. You would have made an incredible mum. Which, by the way, you kind of will be anyway. Who do you think is going to be nanny?"

"As if you could keep me away." Corri glanced down the corridor. "He's gone. I guess I'd better try to find Geraldo before he finds the elevator."

"I'll see you on the fifth."

"Good. We've finished the remodel, I just want you to approve the final details."

"I'll be there."

Once Corri was gone, Olivia headed into the galley.

Looking at the FP unit, she wanted to order an organic green tea with honey, but instead, placing a forgiving hand over her belly, she spoke. "Chocolate milkshake, thick, with five inches of whipped cream."

Corri was right. Vampires didn't have to worry about healthy food choices, and right now, even the baby seemed to approve.

He was growing quickly, her connection to him stronger each day. Cherise had offered to come from Iceland to help establish the connection but it hadn't been necessary.

"Ah," she'd commented, her French accent still intact even after all these years. "You are fourth generation and this child is fifth. The power curve remains stronger in each generation, and you no longer need a conduit to touch each other through spirit. I cannot wait to meet this boy."

"I want you here, all of you, when he's born. He needs to know the incredible family and community he is born into."

"Of this, he will have no doubt. I will see you soon, chérie."

Her fone beeped and she glanced at a message from Dez. While her grandmother checked on her too often over the past month, Olivia knew it was out of love. This time, though, she asked if Olivia could check in with her restaurant, *Flights*, where she was having some managerial issues that needed a vampire's touch. She texted back a message that she would take care of it with a double heart emoticon, and sent a second to Corri.

Corri, Dez wants me to check on her club before I go to rest tonight. Have kitchen send up last meal in about an hour. Invite Gio and Rochelle. See you soon.

Riding down on her private elevator, Olivia went over a mental list of what she needed when she and Corri started baby shopping next week. Dez had already sent quite a few items to her, but she was surprised at how much it required to set up a nursery the first time.

The evening air was warm tonight with a pleasant moderate breeze that felt nice on her exposed skin as she hurried toward the sporty ground car she used in the city. A sudden shadow to her right startled her and she whirled on a tall man who had come up beside her too fast; handsome, smiling, vampire.

It was obvious he intended to intercept her.

"Yes?" Voice inquiring, expectant, with little warmth. His appearance was at least unwelcome, and at most, suspect.

"Ms. Olivia, my name is Cal Worthington."

Watching her from a distance, Frederick decided to follow through on his plan to befriend Olivia. He didn't know why he hadn't thought of it before. It made sense; he was attractive, charming, vampire, and *she* was unattached. Over time, he imagined they would become close, lovers in fact, and at some point it would be natural for her to reveal her secret to him. The plan was ridiculous in its simplicity; he just had to steer clear of Vaz and Corri. Once he cleaned up his accent, adopting a general American accent, he chose a common local name, donned casual attire, and here he was.

Before he approached her, Frederick handed his fone to a blood-bond he'd held for thirteen years. "You know what to do."

"Mr. Worthington, what do you need?"

"I just wanted to introduce myself. I've been coming into your club, *Serendipity*, for my meals since I came to Vegas a few months ago, and I felt as if I should let you know how much I enjoy the ambience, the service, and the marvelous food."

"Thank you, sir. The goal there is to make everyone feel like an honored guest. It seems we've achieved it."

"You have. I find that I can't make myself visit any other restaurant for first meal, I would miss your fare too much."

"That's wonderful. Well, thank you for letting me know. Have a nice evening."

Pulling forward, Olivia was surprised to feel his hand on her arm. Turning, the suspicion part of her expectation going up, she stared him down.

"I have somewhere I need to be, Mr. Worthington."

"Yes, I'm sure you do, but, if you could indulge me for a moment. Look, I'm quite new to town, haven't made a lot of friends yet, and you intrigue me. May I take you to dinner some night soon?"

A dinner invitation. A date. This was unexpected. Men were often attracted to her, but they rarely made the first move. Olivia admitted she could be intimidating, and she rarely stopped moving long enough for someone to ask.

He seemed nice. Attractive, vampire, so of course his body was excellent, beautiful pale hair much like Vaz's, tipped in purple, which appealed to her. But now was not the time to consider a new relationship. She used trusted blood-bonds for meals, and had no need of sex right now.

"What a lovely invitation, but I am otherwise engaged at this time and it may be a long time before I'm free again. Still, it's nice to be invited, so thank you. Now if you'll excuse me..."

Frederick moved closer, the hand clamping down too tight on her wrist. "Letting you go out of my life seems like a bad idea. You intrigue me, lovely vampire."

Boldness was appreciated, but right now, Olivia had somewhere to be, and he was obstructing her. She pushed his hand off of her. "Again, I am flattered, but no, dinner is not possible. I must go."

There was something about his response, frustration, fury perhaps, that disturbed her. Olivia turned to leave the man when his hand landed on her once more.

"Look into my eyes," she barked, and when he did, she began a quick order, compulsion from vampire to vampire, and told him to forget he'd met her tonight and to go on with his life. Olivia left him in her dust as she rocketed away from him and headed straight to her car.

Left behind, confused, Frederick watched the traffic on the street for several moments as he collected his thoughts. Why was he here? What had happened? Nothing quite looked familiar and he felt a little fuzzy.

Oh, hell, had he been compelled again?

He swept the area for his car, but didn't see it. Thankfully, he finally saw Ravi coming from behind a row of vehicles along the street.

"What do you have?"

"What you wanted. Look at the video, sir."

Pressing the button, Frederick watched the entire brief interchange, especially the part where the female vampire had done it to him again, she'd compelled him to forget he knew her.

Fuck! It had happened again.

Later, at Serenity Tower

Vaz smiled, but Corri laughed.

"You shot him down? Poor man."

"I have no interest in a relationship right now. Can you imagine the conversation when my child grows more obvious? And sex? Not now, or for…"

Olivia almost said forever, but she knew that someday, she would be ready to move forward, and yes, that would include sex with another man. The idea tore her apart right now, so she smiled sweetly, and asked if anyone wanted the last Chinese dumpling.

Two hours afterward, lying in bed, naked, her fingers caressing where her son lay, she thought about the man on the street. Could she imagine someone else inside her? It would be a long time. Will was still in her mind, in her heart, and if she closed her eyes and reached for the memory, she could still *feel* him. She couldn't let anyone else wipe him away.

"Daddy's still with us," she whispered as she fell asleep.

Ten

He felt cradled, loved, held...*whole*.
Not knowing where he was or how he got where he was, he felt cocooned within the Mother's bosom. Sparks of electricity, here and there, fingers, gut, ears, toes, eyes, heart; not pain, just tingles of sensations, pleasant, energizing. He wanted to open his eyes to see where he was, but he couldn't. Somehow, he realized that they had to remain closed.
The sparks of energy increased, and focused, began at his head, heat infusion in his brain growing so exponentially, he wondered if it would explode. Down into his face, eyes twitching now, nose, mouth, ears, tried to do what they were meant to do, but couldn't.
He needed to breathe, didn't he? Drawing breath was where life began, and yet strangely, he knew he didn't and yet didn't need to. Not now. *When had he stopped?*
You are within me, child. I carry you now. All you must do is accept the magics that make you well again. Take what I give you, mind, body, spirit...rebirth.
Where am I? What happened to me?
Child of mine, you rest within me for a little while. Your journey was interrupted, but it is not over. You will go from here soon and not return for several cycles of the moon. Once healed, once remade, you will be unique to the world you come back to.
How did I get here? I can't move my arms or legs. I don't think I'm breathing.

Your mortal ties were cut, which gave you back to me so that I may prepare you for your destined life.

So it was true that I had a destiny all along?

It was always true. Rest now, my son. You are not yet well enough to proceed on your journey. Sleep again, and when you wake, I will show you the world through new eyes.

Will trusted the voice implicitly, but as he fell back into the sleep to wait for his promised future, he wondered if Olivia was okay and if she knew where he was.

Mid-afternoon, outside of Boston

Mies woke abruptly, breathing hard, and pushed from his bed, his eyes on Sarah, who slept peacefully. He rushed into the outer room of their suite, but didn't turn on the lights.

A message...from the spirit world? He hadn't been contacted, hadn't been bothered, for a century. To his knowledge, although he'd been brought forward from his resting place a millennia ago, he'd figured he was like any normal first blood now, his life his own to live as any vampire would.

It appeared he was wrong.

What was that? A mission? For the living planet?

What the hell? Lying back on a cushy recliner, he closed his eyes and, for the first time in over a hundred years, let himself journey back into the spirit world to the strange place he'd first discovered that he would be granted life again.

The disembodied voice that spoke in feelings and not words, began to reveal its goal.

Someone needed his guidance, someone who had passed beyond the mortal veil to heal and live again.

This man was not vampire.

"Humans are not immortal," he reminded the voice. "How does he live again?"

Mies laughed, the answer should not have been unexpected. This time, the words from the spirit world were clear.

The way that you do, vampire. You lost your immortal life forever, and yet here you live. This man lost his *mortal* life, and lives again. You know that rules don't always apply.

"It gets confusing though. All right, tell me what I need to do."

Two weeks later, high in the Himalayan Mountains

Small steps, small steps, small steps...

Will had been here for only eight hours, in yet another cave, and while this one wasn't buried deep under the ground, in some ways, it was, because even though he'd entered through a slit in the rock with the vampire he knew of as Mies, it was carved into the mountainside thousands of feet below the summit of the highest mountain on earth.

It was where much of the earth's magics lay. It was where he knew he had been brought to complete healing.

After helping Will settle into a corner of the cave, Mies proceeded to set up camp. Fire now blazing, he'd placed a pot over it to heat water for coffee, and pulled out two heavy sleeping bags to spread over the dry ground near the fire.

"Do you want to try to eat again?"

Will didn't know what he wanted. His first meal in...he didn't know how long it had been...which Mies had given him several hours earlier, had come back up. Was he hungry? Was that need still there? The answer blasted back to him. *Yes!*

"I would, but do you have something simple? Like crackers?"

"Yes, I do. I remember how difficult it was to begin to eat when I was brought back. Of course, in my case it had been considerably longer, but I think you're experiencing the same thing. Here, try these."

Mies handed him a small pack of thin wafers, and, carefully, Will bit the tip off of one. It had an enticing flavor and proved that he was indeed hungry, so he slowly began nibbling on each until the pack of 4 was gone.

"Things staying down?"

"So far. Thank you. For everything." Will took a moment to scan the huge vampire who had apparently gotten the detail to help Will get to this remote cave in Asia. The man seemed to perform every task with supreme control, calm, measured, assured. He'd commented about being *brought back* too.

"You were dead, like I was?"

"For thousands of years. I was gone forever, until I wasn't. Suffice it to say, nothing is ever lost in the universe, and when you realize that everyone ends up in the spiritual plane somewhere, you understand that, technically, people aren't really gone so much as moved on to the next level of existence. It is rare, though, for ones such as you and I to return. My life was ended much shorter than it should have been, so it's been a gift to be allowed to have the chance. It is true for you too."

Mies lifted the heated pot. "How are you feeling?"

"The food seems to be staying down now."

"Good. Let's add some weak tea with a combination of energy supplements. Then I think you need to rest. This is your first time up since, uh, dying, right?"

"Right. It's been several weeks, I'm not sure how many. Mies, do you know if the people in Brazil know that I'm alive?"

"No. I mean, no, I don't know, but it's doubtful. You are here for a reason, and if the people you cared about knew, they would be here instead of me, yeah? Look, I'm the one put here to help you because I've lived this resurrection thing too. What I can tell you is, take your time, let your mind, body, and soul reconnect and heal as one. In death, they are separated. We'll do this slowly, integrate your magics, which are powerful indeed, and I'll guide you to the best of my ability into adapting to whatever you are now. Will, you are not just a human man anymore, you get that?"

"I'm muddled, but I know that I've changed. I had changed before the death, but now, I don't feel quite the same. Except for..."

"I bet I can guess the except for part. Someone special who is even now grieving for you."

"I think so. It isn't fair to her."

"It never is. Hasn't anyone told you? Fair has nothing to do with life. We struggle because we're made to do so, and somehow, hope we come out stronger and okay on the other side. Let's get you well, trained, and back to your life, deal?"

"Huh. Yeah, deal."

"Now try this tea."

In Las Vegas

"No. No, don't make me do it."

"You will. I tried to charm the bitch, but she's uncharmable. She's a whore, is what she is. My plan was perfect. So now, we're going to try the same thing with you and that weird vampire from Corsica she took in recently. Obviously, he knows what's going on. Give me your best work, Thalasia, and I'll convert you, I promise. Otherwise, I'm so pissed, I'm likely to kill a lot of people just to feel better. Do you want that?"

"No, Frederick, I don't. Fine, you don't even have to use control, I'll do it."

"You bet you will. One thing I know, you cunts have strong survival instincts. You don't have the luxury of failing this assignment, so get your hottest fuck-me dress and heels and get to it. For your sake, I hope he likes women and not men."

Sick to her stomach, but relieved that he actually hadn't used compulsion, Thalasia went to her room and leaned against the wall to calm her shaking nerves. She fully believed he would kill her. He would kill anyone he just felt the itch to kill. It was past time to change her alliances.

So, when she went to Gio, one of Olivia's newest vampire contacts, she would do her best to seduce him, as ordered. In the end, her intention *was* to protect herself, *fuck yeah*, just like Frederick said she would, but by asking to see Olivia and telling her everything. It was time to do the right thing, and finish Frederick Villioth's dangerous obsession.

Across the city, Olivia prepared to go to bed after a ceaselessly busy day. Corri had already gone in even though daylight was two hours away. Both were exhausted.

The nursery was finished, a corner of her suite now repurposed with cute animated animals and pale blues mixed with yellow. And too many ribbons, but she loved the effect. Her baby boy would be here in less than four months. Gods, she couldn't wait!

Her flat belly noticeably rounded, Olivia chose her clothes carefully to hide the shape. Vampires who worked for her, other than the few who knew about first bloods, would eventually be told that she'd adopted a human child. Since the baby would essentially *be* human until he changed one day, it wasn't an unrealistic stretch; he would read entirely human to them.

It would ensure the time-honored tradition of keeping first bloods existence unknown, even from the general vampire community. Most felt it would always be the only way to stay safe.

To protect the coming child, security in the apartment and on the entire floor had been re-assessed by the best in the world. Bas's IT guy, Tim, who had been with him over a hundred and thirty years, had always stayed current with any technology. It would be nearly impossible for anyone, including first bloods, to get into Olivia's apartments now without authorization, a 6-pronged system of redundancies.

The recent threat that had taken Will's life still existed. The bodies of four men found in the wreckage with him had remained unidentified; the plane untraced to an owner or rental agency.

Now, daylight on its way, Olivia wandered through her apartment, smiling to herself. Happy and satisfied with her life like she'd never been before, she'd gone through so much pain and soul searching to arrive here, beyond grateful for this unexpected part of her journey.

Wandering to the rearmost bedroom suite, she opened the door that she usually kept closed. Smiling wider, she entered, a hand out to slide along smooth polished chrome, then along well-tended black leather.

"This was your father's prized possession, my son. It will be yours someday, but not until you're vampire and I know that you will be safe riding it. How he would have loved to have taught you."

With a final loving gaze at Will's vintage Harley-Davidson motorcycle, Olivia closed the door behind her as she walked back through the apartment, ordered a big chocolate milkshake, which had become a nightly habit, and returned to her room.

When she visited the motorcycle, she felt closer to the man she'd loved, and to the child they'd made.

"Less than four months, Biker, and your son will be here." Olivia whispered to Will's memory, and hoped that maybe somewhere in the cosmos, he might hear her. Her belly wiggled, excited. Her son had.

Late that following night

Gio wandered through the club, watching the partiers, some extreme, as they ate, drank, danced, and nearly fucked in the main entertainment room. He'd been working security for *Persistence*, the new club, since Corri assigned it to him, grateful for the opportunity to feel like a functioning member of the world again. She'd set him up with a nice vampire-protected apartment three stories below her own, right next to Rochelle, and given him a community of friends again.

Smiling, he watched an underdressed young woman trying out one of the erotic moves on the visitor's pole as she laughed hysterically when she slid right back down to crash into the platform. He liked the harmless play here in what he had nicknamed, "Sexworld," because it gave people a clean, safe place to live out sexual fantasies. The club strived to make sure that no one felt judged or shamed for their appearance or needs, and as long as no one got hurt or abused, physically or emotionally, it would be business as usual.

While most of the clients were human, a small clientele of vampires visited late at night for consensual paid sex or blood meals.

Olivia had filled a need and the people had embraced the club. Gio was proud to be in charge of protecting what she had built. He'd known from the first moment he met Corri that somehow, she would change his life. Those awful psychotic days with Rocky were long over, and even if he thought of those times now, it was easy to make the memories fade away and remember where he was now.

Near the back of the club, a gorgeous human woman had been ordering drinks and a few appetizer trays all evening, but she'd yet to interact with any of the entertainment or other guests. Once in a while, he saw her lift her eyes and search the room.

As he moved through his rounds, he noticed her watching him, but when their eyes met the first time, she looked away. After that, she kept her gaze locked on his.

Beautiful woman, intriguing, but he used the services of the paid professionals here. It wasn't wise to get involved with the patrons and at this point in his new life, he wasn't looking for a relationship.

He gave her a friendly professional smile and went on with his job.

"Gio."

He turned to Rochelle, who managed the *Pleasure Center*.

"Yes, Roach?"

"Pig."

They still played with some of the ridiculous nicknames from their time with Rocky's cadre. The insults had become endearments.

"Gio, there's a guy in 8 that has me concerned. I don't usually like to access the feeds, but in *his* case, I think we need to. I think he's abusive, but Marli won't admit it."

"You think she's scared of him?"

"I do."

"I'll take care of it."

Each service room, elegantly decorated for a pleasant experience, also had security feeds; never used unless there was a safety issue. Gio trusted Rochelle's instincts without question.

Signing in with his biocode, he watched for only a few moments when he saw the man place his thumbs on Marli's throat and press down using all his weight. Marli couldn't even release a sound of distress, but the panic in her body and eyes was clear. The man was choking her to death.

Inside the room before the client could blink, Gio had him pinned to the wall. The punishment for this type of behavior was banishment and instant behavioral modification. The man stared defiantly at him, struggling against vampire strength he couldn't break.

"Stop. You will never come here to this building again. Before you leave, you will give this woman a thousand dollar tip, and from now forward, sex will be of no interest to you at all. You will *never* harm another living thing. The thought of it will make you violently ill. Now get out of here."

Gio turned to Marli, naked on the bed, terrified. "No, Gio. He told me last time he was here that if I let you know how he hurt me, he'd kill me and my daughter. Gio…"

"Look at me, Marli. You are fine, you feel great, that man never hurt you and he'll never be back. You do not fear him. Go get dressed and report to Rochelle."

Marli's tears stopped at once, she reached for a satin robe, smiled to Gio, and rose. "Gio, what are you doing in here? Did you want serviced? I am always happy to take care of you."

"Not right now, Marli. Go talk to Rochelle."

"Okay, but, just remember me when you're ready. You are my favorite client."

Gone soon after, Gio left the room, walked into the entertainment lounge, saw the woman who'd caught his eye all night, and went out the front doors for some fresh night air. Leaning against the alley, his eyes closed to the traffic and people, he let his mind clear. These brief moments of meditation always helped him to relax.

"Hi."

A throaty, sexy voice interrupted and his eyes popped open to the face of the woman he'd walked away from in the lounge.

"Hi. Uh, weren't you enjoying the lounge?"

"I was. You might have noticed I'm alone at my table, but I like to take it easy and watch everyone else have a good time. I'm, um, kind of shy that way."

"I wouldn't have taken you for shy."

"You caught my eye. I must say, I couldn't stop watching you. Is there any chance I could buy you a drink? Somewhere else, some*time* else, of course."

"That's a nice invitation, but we don't date our guests."

"Oh, good. I wasn't planning to come back. That solves the conflict. Are you involved with someone, or don't I appeal to you?"

His eyes moving over her, from the smooth dark skin to huge expressive eyes, a mouth made for kisses, to a heavenly feminine body wrapped in a tight dress pushing against a firm curvy shape topped with full, and what appeared to be natural, breasts, down to long legs that ended in sexy feet seated in high-heeled slides. Never mind that her smile had grabbed his attention from the first moment.

"You appeal," he said, self-conscious, and aware he'd given her an opening.

"Good. My name is Thalasia. Meet me here, Friday night, at midnight. Please. I'll wait for you for twenty minutes, but not a minute more."

A white card with the name of a streetside café, *Tosh*, slipped into his hand and she was gone.

Shit. Was he going to do it?

Yeah, he was.

Around the corner from Serenity Tower, Thalasia leaned against a wall just as she'd found Gio doing moments earlier. He was so sweet, so handsome, *so* perfect…how could she betray him like Villioth wanted her to? The answer was clear. She couldn't. How to deal with it was up to her.

In the Himalayan Mountains

"I miss you, Sarah. Soon, though, I think I'll be able to come home to you. Sleep well. Kisses and hugs from the other side of the world."

Mies rung off his call and glanced at his companion of two months. Will had filled out and strengthened. Mies, as the oldest living vampire, his body huge, magnificent, felt like he was looking into a mirror. Yes, he and Will had grown close over the months together, but it was more than that. The shared history, the support of being chosen by the universe for a special mission, and given a second chance after the finality of death; Mies had been convinced that no one else in existence had experienced what he had, and while Will's story differed quite a lot, the similarities remained that created a brotherhood between them.

"Your mate doing okay?"

"She's fine. We miss each other, but I think you can relate. We're nearly finished here. Look at you, you're as big as *me*. And the shit you can do, I can't even touch your magics."

"It's daunting. I know I'm not what I was, but I don't have any idea what I *am*. I'm not vampire, I don't read as supernatural, do I?"

Mies shook his head. "No, you don't."

Will shook his head. "And yet I'm not fully human."

"You'll understand why this has happened, I guarantee it. The universe reveals its secrets slowly, but eventually, it does reveal them. My journey was difficult, Will, but worth every second of pain and heartache. For Sarah, for Crezia, I crossed time, came back to life to fall in love and then die again to lose it all. Yet here I humbly stand and thank the powers that rule the universe for giving me the chance to love and find a home. Everything worthwhile has a price, Will."

Will's arms folded now over muscles he was finally getting used to. "But I don't think Olivia is in this deal. I haven't been able to touch her."

"You're shielded, I think. Wait until you're free and see where the next part of your journey sends you."

"I can't go back to them, can I? The people I loved have buried me, have grieved for me, and moved on. How can I put Olivia through this again if I'm not meant to stay? I truly have no idea why I've been brought back and transformed into this strange hybrid supernatural thing."

Placing a heavy hand on Will's shoulder, Mies moved close. "Trust, my friend, the universe has a plan. It's protecting life, and in this case, this world. You are here for a reason, and when you know what it is, you'll be grateful that you are. Don't count out life with the woman you love. I did, thinking that I'd done the noble thing and sacrificed, yet here I am, a century of love with the one woman I know was meant to be with me. Now, let's finish off that honeyed bacon that the Sherpas brought to us."

"I'll start the fire."

"You bet you will."

Grinning, because he always started the fire now, Will turned to the firewood neatly stacked in their makeshift firering, and lifted a hand to draw the fire from the air. Swirls of yellow, then orange, twisted above the firewood and dropped lower to ignite the wood.

"Done," Will announced.

"You *are* a handy man to have around." Mies brought a pack of meat forward and placed a few dozen pieces on a rack. It took a lot to feed them, Mies as first blood vampire, and recently, with his size and metabolic changes, Will ate just as much.

Seated in front of the fire, Mies kept his eyes on Will.

"You know we are nearly done."

"The magics are complete, and I'm changed. You've guided me on the history of magics from those days so long ago. Yes, I think we'll be going back down the mountain tomorrow."

"Whoa, that soon? You already have a timeframe?"

"Not mine. The magics have made it clear. What the fuck I will be doing, I still don't know."

"Will, would you like to come back to Boston with me? Sarah would be thrilled to meet you."

"I really don't have a direction yet. Maybe. Thank you for the invitation. I would love to meet her someday."

Later, ready to rest on his cot, Will admitted...he did have a direction, and it was back to Vegas. He was certain Mies knew it too.

Serenity Tower

"Brigitte, you brought too much!"

Olivia looked over the huge selection of baby gifts Brigitte had brought with her from Zambia.

"Not possible. Listen, this boy is going to be a big strong macho man like his father someday, so I brought him everything he needs to achieve that. Like, in *this* box, I have spirit masks. African totems, symbols of masculinity. This one is the king of beasts. Lions are said to be able to call down thunder and lightning with a roar."

She held up the mentioned items with a grin. "Then there's the *freaking* cute baby clothes and toys. Who knew there were so many adorable things for babies?"

Olivia hadn't, not before, and she was sure that the world of baby stuff was just as alien to Brigitte. "Thank you, but he's first blood, so becoming a huge uber-macho male is a given."

"Ah, true. I just kind of wanted to leave something of me with him. I included rattles carved from natural materials that our blood-bonds make for local children."

When Olivia had first revealed that she was going to have Will's child, a stab of pain had shot through Brigitte.

Will and Olivia had been together…and while she assumed that they had, the pregnancy seemed like a cruel reminder. It wasn't long before she accepted that this boy was an extraordinary gift, part of Will they could keep in their lives.

Laying the rattle down, Olivia took Brigitte's hands in hers. "Bridge, everything is fabulous, but you don't have to bring gifts to be a part of him. You *are* a part of Jasper's life."

"Jasper? You chose his name."

"Last night, after first meal, I just knew who he was. Will's name was Willoughby Jasper, and it fit that his son should carry part of it into the future. When I decided on Jasper," Olivia touched her belly, "He approved."

"It's perfect." Brigitte dropped onto her knees and put her lips to the growing baby mound. "Hi, Jasper, it's your aunt Brigitte."

Suddenly silent, Brigitte closed her eyes and laid her head against Olivia. When she looked up several moments later, tears glistened in her dark eyes.

"I feel him. He let me know that he's going to come soon and wants me to hold him. Olivia…"

"Fifth generation first blood, my dear. The boy already blows me away. Come, let's share a ridiculous dessert, and then go through these gifts."

Eleven

TWO NIGHTS LATER

At the bottom of Serenity Tower

As the sun climbed the morning sky, Will lurked across the street from Serenity Tower. High, so high he couldn't feel her from down here, was the woman he wanted so badly, he almost said "Fuck it!" and went to her. The only thing that stopped him was the fact that it wasn't fair to her.

He knew the pain of loss, and he wouldn't put her through it a second time. If, someday, he had assurances that he could be here for her, he could share a life with her, nothing in the universe would stop him.

For now, it had to be enough to know that she was up there. She would be sleeping, hopefully peacefully, maybe dreaming of him? Or was it cruel to hope she was?

He glanced at the spectacular glass and fabform building that he knew she had designed, a ready smile. He was lucky to have had the chance to be inside her at least that one night before his life went to shit and he died.

Now, though, he had one mission; to find who killed him. Whoever it was, they were a threat to the vampires and earth warriors. After that, he knew instinctively that he would be traveling to the bottom of the world. It would include two of the other earth warriors, so he had carefully chosen those best suited to help him. With one last glance upward, he moved down the street, still quiet in the golden light of the new sun.

At the top of Serenity Tower

She had been sleeping well...as well as possible with a wiggling child inside her. Jasper moved so much, he woke Olivia.

"Buddy, what is it?"

Smoothing her fingers over the stretched skin, she suddenly felt something odd. She sat up, her eyes moving through the darkened room.

A presence? Someone who couldn't be there, someone *gone*, yet the feeling persisted and spawned an intense need, a longing to see him, to hold him.

"Will?" she questioned into the empty room.

It had to be the child's connection to the spirit world, reaching for the father he would never know.

But the presence had felt so real!

"Oh, Jas, I would give anything to have your father back, even for one night, to tell him what he means to us, so he would know how much we need him and miss him. To thank him for the gift of you, my beautiful baby."

Sorrow mixed with joy, even to imagine Will's spirit there with them. Olivia lay back on the soft sheets, fingers spread over their son, Will's face etched in her mind.

That night after the sun dropped

Will lifted his fone.

He remembered that the kidnappers were planning to take them to Vegas, so the person who sought Olivia or her race had to be here in this city. The leader of the group had been referred to as Locktite, a nickname, obviously, for his criminal career. None of the men he'd met had been vampire, so that helped. He was searching for an accomplished mercenary with the moniker of Locktite. That shouldn't be hard to track down.

Since Will had been killed in the plane crash, and he was extremely durable, the others likely perished too. The reputation of a deceased bad guy should offer no resistance as he searched. It was the only lead he had.

Will dialed Mies.

"Hey, there, I need some help. Would you happen to know of an IT genius in the Vegas area?"

"Actually, I do. I'll text the info to you. How are you faring, Will? Doing okay?"

"Making my way. There was a threat several months ago against Olivia and I think the same guys who abducted her friend to interrogate her, and tried to kill her, are the ones who abducted me and Dani. I'm on their trail now."

"Need help?"

"Not yet, but can I keep that offer open?"

"Sure thing. Be careful, Will."

"Yeah. I know I'm powerful, but I'm not bulletproof. I guess it's too much to expect that if they kill me again, I'll come back again."

"What are you looking for?"

"The man who led the group that took us had a highly recognizable handle, so I just need to find a link from him to his last employer."

"Damn. It's a long shot."

"Yep, but it's all I got for now. I'm hoping the magics might help."

"Good luck. Call me if you need me, I can be there in three hours, give or take."

"Thanks. Later."

Moments after ringing off, Mies's contact info came up and Will dialed the number immediately.

"Hi, my name is Will. You were recommended by a friend in Boston. Yeah, I need some research done at once. Can you help me?"

Not too far from Will's hotel room, Thalasia sat nursing a chai tea at a sidewalk table at a favored café she'd found right after they arrived in Vegas.

He wasn't going to come, she was sure of it. There was something about Gio that was too perfect, not because he was vampire, but because he was too good for a girl like her. Before Villioth had blood-bonded her, she'd been a failure; what her mother had called a woman of loose morals. Someone as kind, as honorable, as Gio wouldn't have any interest in her type. Well, yeah, to *fuck* of course, but to be really interested in her as a person? Never.

Lifting her cup, she grimaced, laughing out loud to herself. "I'd be lucky if he'd even *fuck* me."

"So would I."

Thalasia couldn't move. He'd actually shown up and heard her self-pitying comment? She was mortified.

Her eyes on her mug, in her peripheral vision, she saw him come around from behind her to take the other seat at her table.

"Hello."

Damn, even his voice got to her!

"Hello," she barked. Might as well address the comment. She lifted big earnest eyes to his.

"So, uh, I really didn't think you'd come, and so, uh, I'm sorry for that crass statement."

"Was it crass? It sounded like a wish."

"Yeah, well, wishes usually don't come true, so it was just stupid."

"I came. I didn't tell you that I wouldn't, and I didn't want to stand you up."

"So you're just being polite." Thalasia drained her teacup. "I *hate* polite."

"Then tell me what you *like*."

God, he was too good for her! Not only was he out of her league, she'd been sent to betray him and his friends.

She pushed her chair back so quickly it tilted over.

"I can't do this."

Gio stood, his brows drawn together. "Can't do what?"

Thalasia moved close. Fuck, he even *smelled* amazing.

"Look. Believe me when I say, you don't want anything to do with me. Walk away, handsome, and, uh, watch your back. And your friend's backs. Something bad is coming for you."

When she turned to leave, Gio grabbed her shoulders. She noticed he didn't hurt her, but she couldn't pull free either.

"Stop."

He was trying to compel her, but with the amount of vampire blood and a compulsion from Villioth to refuse other compulsions, she was able to resist.

"Gio, you're a good man, but you're fighting out of your weight class. I've been forbidden to tell you anything specific, just know that *your* boss is my boss's target."

"Who's your boss? What does he want?"

"I want to tell you, but I can't."

"Come with me. Olivia can…"

"Excuse me."

A rotund man bumped hard into Gio, knocking him against the table. Thalasia, shocked, watched as the man grabbed Gio, now unconscious, and lowered him into his chair, seamlessly resting his head on his arms on the tabletop. Instantly, he grabbed Thalasia's shoulders and pushed her past the café.

"What the fuck!" she yelled.

"Quiet. I'm with Villioth. He had me tail you to keep an eye on the situation."

"I was just doing what he told me to do."

The man's smile crooked, he cackled. "Yeah, sure. Look, it ain't my job to get you killed, lady, so I'm not telling him that you were about to spill to this guy. You're gonna have to cover your own ass. I just had to cover mine."

Was this guy for real? She didn't recognize him, but if he did tell Villioth about her conversation with Gio, it was *goodbye World*.

"I wasn't gonna spill. I can't, I'm compelled."

"I know, but we both know there are ways around a direct order. Anyway, I'm done here. Good luck back at the hub."

After he disappeared into the traffic, she eased closer and peered at Gio from behind another wide man. Someone had noticed he hadn't moved and was poking his shoulder. Shit, she'd better get gone.

Gio would be fine, no matter what the guy had done to him, it couldn't kill a vampire permanently.

Fifteen minutes later above the city

Gio woke in an emergency lift-car, strapped to a trolley.

"Shit," he whispered. Someone had tazed him with enough high voltage to electrocute him. Someone who knew he was vampire. It didn't make any sense that it was his beautiful date, she'd been warning him off something. Either way, he was en route to the hospital on the edge of Vegas, an enormous medical complex vampires avoided.

He looked up at the single attendant, a youthful redheaded girl with pale creamy skin. "Hi."

"Oh, hi, you're awake. Good. We're monitoring your vitals and are currently on our way to Vegas Med. Do you have any idea why you passed out?"

"Yeah. Would you unstrap me?"

The girl looked back at Gio after checking his latest vitals. "It's not wise. So why did you lose consciousness?"

"Look at me please."

"Sir..." Frustrated, she looked directly into his eyes.

"Release me."

Once she had, Gio moved to the front of the car. When the driver saw him, he smiled.

"Feeling better?"

"Yes. Return me to Serenity Tower."

Without delay, the pilot complied.

Feeling for his fone, Gio was grateful to find he still had it and dialed a number.

"Sam," he said, when it picked up. "My fone may have been compromised, but you need to secure Olivia and those close to her. Thanks. I'll explain when I'm back in about twenty minutes."

So the threat was real, and he'd just been a target. There was no reason to trust Thalasia, other than the attempt to *warn* him. He'd just have to wait to see how things turned out to find out if she was bad news or a victim too. It wasn't the first time he'd felt stung by the dangerous nature of compulsion.

Back on the ground, he used the same ability he'd just condemned to send the EMS vehicle back to the hospital. Using the private elevator to the top floor, he was outside Olivia's room in minutes.

Sam chimed him in, his face a study of interest, concern, and impatience. "Fill us in."

Olivia sat on the sofa, her feet up, Corri and Vaz beside her. Brigitte, at the bar pouring drinks, looked up.

"Anybody want anything?"

Rochelle strolled from the galley. "You okay, Gee?"

"I'm okay, but wait until you hear about my adventure tonight."

Fifteen minutes later, Sam bolted up, his fone in his hand. "I want all surveillance feeds on a café on Capital Lane called *Tosh*. I need feeds at approximately midnight, and then entrance and exit feeds for the two hours leading up to that timeframe and leading away. I'll be in the office in half an hour to review them."

He looked at Gio. "You say you met her at *Persistence* the night before? Okay, we have a starting point for her contact."

Sam looked at Olivia and rolled his eyes, a hand smacking his forehead. "I don't suppose it'll make any difference whether I ask you guys to stay clear of the clubs or any common schedules until I check out this threat?"

Her smile guileless, Olivia nodded. "Of course it will, Sam. Whatever you suggest."

"Oh, now you're just playing with me like a cat toy."

Corri laughed. "Sam, go do your job. We'll all stay here. There's plenty we can do from this floor."

"It's just that it's obvious we're dealing with a ruthless asshole and he knows how to take down vampires. A little prudence never hurts."

Olivia, groaning as Brigitte rubbed her ankles, caught his gaze. "I really have nowhere I need to go, so I'll stay here. Go take care of business, but keep me informed."

"You know I will, and thank you for keeping me from worrying about you while I *worry* about you."

"You're a doll, Sam. Go. I think we all will take a nice swim."

Gio followed Sam to the door. "I'm coming with you, in case there's anything I can contribute. I might see something you miss only because I was there."

Sam nodded.

After they left, Corri turned on Olivia. "Good job playing it cool."

"I deserve an award. Listen, Corri, we haven't discussed this, I know you think it'll upset me, but I've been thinking about the people who had you abducted and dumped in the desert. What if they had been watching you afterward, followed you, saw Will rescue you, and then bring you back to Serenity Tower. I know, it's a long shot, but if it happened like that, what if those same people or person who took you, took Will and Dani? For the same goal, to find out what I am. They're human, the kidnapper might have wizened up and decided to try compulsion on humans who know me. They wouldn't have known that compulsion doesn't work on Will or Dani."

"But why take so long to decide to abduct them? Will was down there for over a month."

"Maybe because *I* flew down. Because I became a part of their story. Maybe it was *my* joining them that brought the kidnappers to Will and Dani. Dear gods, it is likely *all* my fault. Will is dead because I decided to follow him."

"Stop that right now. Your choices aren't responsible for this creep's behavior. This is first blood trouble. You told me once that there is a long history of first blood threats, that's why you guys stay hidden. It isn't you."

Pushing from the sofa, Olivia grabbed her drink. "Let's get in the pool. I need to calm down for Jasper's sake, I've upset him. Vaz, could you bring my fone?"

Vaz nodded, but he wasn't paying attention. Corri noticed how distracted he was.

"Liv, we'll join you and Brigitte in a moment. Vaz, what's on your mind?"

"Something that you just said, that there are always threats to the first bloods. There was a vampire, the owner of the *Warehouse Erotica* in Corsica, you remember? He found out that Koen could use compulsion on a vampire. He offered to help search for you, but only if I would reveal how Koen could do that. I knew before we located you that he couldn't be trusted and Koen came back to do a final compulsion to purge his memories. He shouldn't remember the events with Koen. And yet…"

"You think it's possible he's involved?"

"Damn, it *seems* unlikely, but we've seen unlikely things happen too many times to ignore it. Yeah, it's possible. I have no idea what his link to Olivia might be, but I'm going to find out."

"Not alone, you're not."

"Corri…"

"Call Koen, or Tam, or Dez. Or at least take Bas with you."

"You're bossy, you know that."

"If you're right, he's already killed for this secret. You need back up."

"All right. I'll call Bas and see if he will fly over with Koen."

"Okay, then. Let's go help Olivia get rid of the crazy idea that she's responsible for Will's death. And you *like* me bossy."

A small office in the old section of the Vegas strip

"Here's what I found. I tracked covert messages on the Black web."

Will leaned over Michael's shoulder. "*Gotts Wettbewerb*? What's that?"

"It's German. It means *God's Competition*. It's the name of a covercorp, which used to be called shell companies a long time ago. In this case, it doesn't actually exist, but any, uh, unsavory business, your Locktite guy for instance, is processed through the covercorp. They're supposed to be impossible to trace back to the real user."

One word he said got Will's attention. "*Supposed* to?"

"Yup. Unless you're fucking amazing with hackable tech. And it's *all* hackable to me."

"So you have him? The guy who hired Locktite?"

"Take a look."

Michael Conner turned his vidscreen to face Will. He couldn't believe he had his information this quickly. It had only been 24 hours ago that he'd contacted Conner to ask if he could help him.

"Villioth Worldwide Entertainment."

"Yup. And here are his Las Vegas offices. Now, I tell ya, though, you better take a small army. Look at this."

Michael pointed to a line-item list deeper on the page.

"I don't know what the guy does, but he hires a lot of mercenaries. Good folks, folks *not* lookin' to fuck others, they don't usually do that. So, what I mean is, he's real, *real* bad news."

"I can't explain how much this means. You wouldn't let me negotiate your fee last night. What do I owe you?"

"Paid. Mies helped me out two years ago, something I can never repay him for, so he needs me to help a friend, especially something this easy, no charge. I'm happy to do it. Also, it's nice to ruin a bad guy's night."

"Much appreciated, Michael. I'm in your debt, then, so if you need something from me, let me know."

"That I will do. Good luck, Will."

At Serenity Tower

Sam punched the button announcing his arrival at Corri and Vaz's apartment. He'd been summoned there tonight, and with this recent threat he was actively dealing with, he hoped it would be quick.

The door slid back and Sam moved in quickly to see Corri and Vaz waiting just inside. Vaz nodded to him.

"Would you like some Scotch? It's old, horribly expensive, and heady."

"Sure. You guys always have the best booze. Not too much, though."

As Vaz walked to the bar to get the drinks, Sam smiled to Corri, then looked back to Vaz.

"You said you have some news for me?"

"Yes, we do. I think I may know who's behind these abductions and the threat to the first bloods."

"Interesting. We're still tracing back vid-feeds. What do you have?"

"The name and location of the man who may be responsible. You remember the problems we had in Corsica? The owner of the club where Corri disappeared from was a vampire named Frederick Villioth. He accidently recorded Koen using compulsion on him and insisted I tell him how he was able to do it. I didn't, of course, and Koen used compulsion again to purge any memory of him. The man has clubs here in Vegas, and I think, somehow, he knows Olivia is first blood. I believe it may be why Corri was taken and abused, and why Will and Dani were taken in Brazil."

Vaz held up his fone. "I have his address. Bas and Koen are on their way here as we speak. Do you want to come with us?"

"You bet your hairy vampire ass."

"Thought you'd say that." Vaz winced. "Although, not, uh, in exactly those terms."

"Hey, a guy gets excited about getting the villain."

"I hope I'm right, and I hope I'm not. It pisses me off to think that asshole fell through our fingers, and we could have stopped all this, and yet, at least if he is the culprit, we can stop it here and now."

An hour later

"This is it." Koen glanced at Vaz as they pulled up outside the address Vaz had given him.

"It's unassuming. Isn't this an old warehouse? Seems underwhelming from what I remember of him. I would have expected his offices to be in some fancy high rise."

"I would have expected him to be a neutralized asshole, but I was wrong." Koen had been pissed at the idea that he might not have squashed Villioth as a potential threat back in Corsica.

"Enough recriminations. Let's go find him and see if Vaz is right," Olivia barked. "Besides, I have to go to the bathroom."

"You shouldn't have come."

"Koen, I'm indestructible, this man might have killed the father of my child, I'm hot, and I have to pee. Don't *fuck* with me, just someone help me out of this van."

Olivia, feeling the weight of her child, and, not unlike other first blood mothers, found it unacceptable that her vampire nature didn't protect her from the same stupid issues that a human mother had to deal with during pregnancy.

Bas understood completely, having lived through four pregnancies with *his* first blood mate. "Here, Liv, I'll help you."

"There's my gentleman. Thank you, Bas." Olivia took his warm hand as she stepped from the van that carried Koen, Vaz, Sam, Bas, and herself to confront Frederick Villioth.

Koen paused as they headed to the back entrance of the large building. "I know you're nearly invincible, but you're still an expectant mother, and family. Please, Olivia, let me be the big strapping hero and protect you. Would you stay behind me?"

"Yes, Koen, I'll let you be the hero, but if Villioth is responsible for Will's death, I won't keep that promise."

"I get that. Bas, Vaz, take point and take us in."

Easily moving past the locked doors, they found an expansive space stretching in both directions, nearly empty of merchandise, people, or anything else.

"Fuck, you could hear a pin drop." Koen moved to a corridor on his left, carefully peering down it. "Office doors. We'll have to search each, but it means we give up the valuable element of surprise. We have to go door to door."

Breaking her first promise, Olivia stepped around him.

"Then we check each one. There are five of us, of which four can be anywhere in seconds, so if you find him, run into him, call the others at once. We've seen Villioth's profile picture, so we know who we're looking for."

Olivia's pragmatic plan met agreement without anyone responding. In an orderly fashion, they moved down the corridor, opened doors, entered, then proceeded on to the next. At the end of the corridor, the five gathered.

"Well, that's unnerving. Not one person, and little evidence that anyone actually works here."

Sam, showing solidarity with Olivia, nodded and, his handgun near, looked at a wide doorway similar to the type used in airplane hangars. "The building has three stories. Lots to check out, so on to the next."

Two stories above

Villioth grinned at Will, who had surprised him in his massive office that included a dance floor with disco lights and the ubiquitous mirror ball.

Working behind his desk, Villioth had looked up when the big man entered. "Nice place you got here. I'm going to guess your business is doing very well."

"Quite."

Now, five minutes later, Will kept ten feet between them, his eyes moving around the room, then back to land on Villioth. "Do you recognize me?"

Villioth stared, his eyes locked, that smile sly.

"No. Should I?"

"Yes, you should. You do. Or maybe it's the fact that I'm half again larger than I was when you sent your guy to abduct me and finally, kill me."

"I truly have no idea what you refer to since you appear to be quite alive. Apparently, you are a sadly confused man. Perhaps I should call the authorities."

"You wouldn't. You know I'm a risk to you, and you'd kill me first. Except that I still know something that you, apparently, would *kill* to know. So here's what I think. Since I'm here, you're already planning to use compulsion to force me to tell you a secret that, and listen to me carefully…"

Will moved closer, now only three feet from his murderer. "You will *never* know."

That was what it took to force Villioth to reveal himself. First, he laughed, then casually turned to his desk, opened a drawer, and pulled out two whisky glasses.

Drawing a long breath, Villioth glanced toward Will.

"Scotch? You might be wise to take it; it will be the last you'll ever taste."

Villioth was playing with him. Fine.

"Aged? The good shit? Sure."

"Please, have a seat."

As if in a business meeting, the two men sat, Villioth behind his desk, Will in the fine leather seat in front of it, as he reached for the glass. "Very nice. You have good taste."

"Indeed I do. I've had a few centuries to develop one."

After a pause, Villioth continued. "So, that doesn't surprise you, that I'm vampire."

"Not at all. I know you well. I did some research."

"Clever. Of course," Villioth took a large gulp of his drink. "It won't help in the end. As you know, I'm faster than you could ever imagine, you really can't hurt me, and I can force you to do whatever I want you to do."

"Ah."

Throwing down the remaining contents of his glass, Will crashed it onto the desk top. "Does it surprise you that I'm alive?"

"No. I assume you were never really on that plane. It would be of interest to me to find out how you managed to bring it down, but I'll find out in a few moments. And yes, I will know the beautiful Olivia's secret. Amazing how you can socialize with us, but you humans never really get it, do you? We are superior to you in every way. You are a toy to those of us with vampire blood in our veins. Would you like a refill?"

"All right." Will wondered how long they were going to sit here and play nice. "So, *God's Competition*. Really? God complex or jealousy of his status?"

"Neither. Just a healthy admission that, compared with you, with your race, we're like Gods. Your weak, powerless status puts you in the same category as farm animals."

"Wow. Yet you're feeding a farm animal your best Scotch?"

"I'm not cruel, and it seems appropriate to provide you something nice before I, how did you phrase it? Kill you again?"

Setting the glass carefully onto the top of Villioth's desk, Will leaned forward, his hands clasped loosely, his body relaxed, his demeanor easy. "Before you *try*."

Repeating Will's moves, Villioth set his glass down, and smiled. "Before I succeed. It's kind of cute, though, that you think you have any control over what happens now."

"It *is* cute, isn't it? Try to move."

The smile unwavering, Villioth pushed from his seat. *Tried to*. His smile gone, lips tight, he tried again, but couldn't budge. Eyes on Will in a hard stare, he scanned the oversized body that looked vampire, but didn't *read* vampire. "What the fuck is happening here? You aren't capable of this."

Standing now, no hurry, Will nodded. "And yet, here you are, locked in your chair, and yes, I do know what kills a vampire forever. What was that you called me just a few seconds ago...*powerless?* See, I *did* die in that crash, and

I wouldn't give a shit much about that, except that you're still a threat to people I love, and that is the deal-breaker. You won't ever touch one of them again. I am not a killer, but I will do what I have to do to protect those you threaten, so someone *is* going to die today, only it isn't me."

Will moved to the back of the desk where Villioth struggled.

"I can make you wealthy. You can have anything you want."

"I have what I want. Once you're gone, Olivia and Dani and all my friends are safe. Make your peace, Villioth."

Air began to swirl, to whip, in the enclosed space of this office where that couldn't happen. Realization finally struck him that Will was far more than just human, that he held powers such as he had been seeking from Olivia or Koen.

"What are you?"

"I'm the man who is going to remove you from existence. Pure love, *good*, exists, and so does evil. Evil can be as simple as the act of taking a life because it in some way benefits you. Life, living on this world, is a privilege and an honor, and you have betrayed that honor. The result is that you lose the privilege."

Before Will could make another move, he heard voices in the corridor, and the door slammed wide. Reaching for his expansive magics, he lifted his hands and cloaked himself from view. Standing near Villioth, ready to end his life, Will watched a huge vampire enter the room, glance around, and stop on the unmoving Villioth behind his desk. Will suddenly realized it was Koen, the vampire he'd met in Africa. Koen smiled wide, and leaned back out the door.

"I've got the motherfucker!"

Turning back, Koen came deeper into the room. "You should have stayed down. What happens next is your fault. In Corsica, I wiped you, tried to protect you, but you fucked it up. Now it's out of my hands."

Within moments, two other men walked into the room, both vampire, and right behind them, a fourth man, human. Will's eyes teared instantly when he saw that Olivia follow behind him. She stayed behind the human man, her eyes locked on Villioth.

"This is the piece of shit?"

The pain in her eyes was deep and hurt him to the core of his soul. He knew at once she missed him and sought vengeance on the man who had caused his death.

More than anything in his life, he wanted to unveil himself and take her into his arms. The desire, the need, was almost too great when he saw fury surge in her eyes and the human man turn to block her from moving toward Villioth.

"Liv, stop. You don't want this legacy for Jasper. Let us take care of this. For you, for Jasper."

Koen faced her. "Aye. Olivia, Let us do this. We'll take care of him so you stay safe and keep your heart and hands clean."

He moved near her and whispered to her, his lips close to hers, and Will nearly broke cover to beat the vampire senseless.

It had been months, though, since he'd been in her life, and it was obvious she had an incredible support system. This wasn't the time to reveal that the man she had loved was still alive.

Olivia stared into Villioth's eyes. "Make him admit it."

Will wasn't sure she'd go, but she nodded, and left the room with the human man. Whatever Koen had said to her, she'd complied.

Good, he didn't want her to have the blood of this creep on her hands.

The vampire moved back to the frozen Villioth.

"What the fuck is wrong with you asshole?"

"Koen, please, you need to help me. There's a man here, he's done this to me. He has ungodly unnatural talents."

"Really? And where is this superman?"

"When you arrived, he disappeared, but I'm still stuck!"

"Frozen with fear? You should be. First, you need to help me. I already know the answer, but I promised the lady. You are the one responsible for the abductions in Brazil a few months ago. You want to know what we are?"

After a long hesitation, Villioth nodded. "Yes, I am the one. Now can you help me?"

Will knew that Koen was also a first blood like Olivia, but he couldn't recall…was he mated? Perhaps an old lover? Controlling the piercing jealousy, he dropped his head and stepped back.

This was not his life anymore, destiny had made it clear. He knew that he would be in a frozen cave in Antarctica by next week. If this man could console her, protect her, *love* her, Will had to stay away and let it be.

It was the hardest thing he'd ever done in his life.

"Villioth," Koen began, "You've placed your life in our hands now, because you threatened a first blood. I am going to help you. You want to know what we are? We're the first vampires to inhabit this world. We've been here over 6000 years, and we'll be here long after you are gone. We are sentries to this planet; protectors of life, and you've killed. Harsh choices have to be made. I hope you have made peace with who you are and how you've treated people in your life. Believe me, there are punishments and rewards beyond this life. Good luck with that."

Will stayed long enough to ensure the deed had been done. Five minutes later, still frozen, still trading his life for his greed and cruelty, Frederick Villioth left this corporeal form for whatever lay beyond.

Now that the threat had been neutralized, Will remained hidden, torn between leaving or rushing out to take Olivia in his arms, find a private place, and make love to her until he vanquished all her pain.

But then he would have to leave her again, and that kind of pain, he could not be responsible for. His future, the path that he was meant to walk, he had no idea where he would go or how long he would be gone. With the level of magics he'd been granted, it may be the rest of his life. How could that be right for her?

No, for this point in time, he had to follow the designed journey to fulfill the destiny he had apparently been born to. While he'd sought the possibility of that destiny, the reality that he'd actually *had* one, that it fully encompassed the life he was building, had been unsettling. Waiting for the vampire group to go, he stood in Villioth's office and wished that he had been free to live the life he had been building, but he knew that his mission was too important to deny.

"Off to Antarctica," he whispered, waiting still. Olivia and her group lingered, but when they finally disappeared out the door to the warehouse, Will was free to move. It hurt too much to stay and hurt too much to go, so he slammed himself into the rental car he'd signed for and headed back outside the city to a small hotel.

Settled again in his tiny room, he ordered room service, and as he waited for the meal to be delivered, he dialed his fone.

"Eras, this is Will. You may have been informed that I died, and while it was true, things have changed. For now, though, please don't tell Cari or anyone else, it needs to remain secret. Thing is, I need the help of a couple of our warriors. I think that you and Bura would be perfect. I wonder if you two would be able to join me in Antarctica? Let me explain."

Twelve

"Holy shit!"

"You can fucking say that again, Bura."

"Holy shit!"

"Damn, it's really fucking cold. I think we're underdressed. Will, did you know this when you called me? This is really our mission?"

"It really is, Eras. I guess you should have asked more questions before you said yes. Although I admit, I have never been to Antarctica, so I didn't know what to expect. This is obscenely, freaking un-survivably cold. I don't think we're underdressed, I think it isn't possible to be appropriately dressed."

"I'm wearing five layers, I have a thick bear coat, and I'm still freezing my paws off." Bura, the biggest of the three, a totem with a bear *spirit animal*, wasn't kidding when he said he had a bear coat. He spent the first thirty minutes after they left their transport shaking, rubbing his hands up and down his arms to try to create friction, and up and down his cheeks to try to keep them from freezing into chunks and falling off. He didn't feel as if he accomplished any of those things.

"How deep do we go, Will?"

"All I know is that it's deep. I can lower myself down on a column of air, so that will be easy, but I need an assist from you two to pull off the ascent. As far as sealing the fissure, I don't know how much that'll take out of me. I get images, impressions, but not details. Something tells me that the future of this job isn't looking like a picnic."

"Everything we do as earth warriors isn't a picnic. That's why we're here, to fix things that either we've done to the world to fuck it up, or natural occurrences that can destroy it too. Per your permission, last night I told Cari about you, with a gag order. She wants to tell Dani. Dani still feels strong guilt over leaving you."

"God, yes. Let Cari know to do so immediately. None of this was Dani's fault, she should have no guilt at all! I guess I should have called her."

"It's okay, I get why you are keeping your survival mum for now. Eventually, though, everyone will have to know."

"Likely, but until I know what the universe and Mother Earth require of me, I want Brigitte and Olivia to have peace."

"They do. Did you know that Brigitte's been spending a lot of time with Olivia in Vegas?"

Olivia and Brigitte had become close? Ah, had they bonded over his loss? Interesting. He hoped they were supporting each other to make the pain less. Suddenly all he wanted was to go to them and wrap them in his arms.

Screeching winds brought him back to the moment. Bura had pulled a heavy piece of scaffolding away from the entrance to an ice cave. They'd just crossed a storm-driven blizzard to the brutally cold, but wind-sheltered cavern where a huge fissure had opened up, and according to Will, the building earthquake they were there to stop.

"Thanks, Bura. Earpieces in? Testing."

Seconds later, both Eras and Bura nodded.

"Communications up." Eras looked at the long nycor rope that they'd carried. "This won't even come close to reaching, will it?"

Lips pursed, Will looked into the crevice that had opened from the fissure below, shaking his head.

"Not even close. Besides, the heat down there would overwhelm you in minutes, even with your vampire nature."

"You're sure you can survive this? Will, we can call in everybody and give you full earth warrior support."

"It won't help. None of you can survive down there. In addition to the heat, the outgassing, the steam would be fatal. Please understand, even I could still succumb and die. The earth and her magics have prepared me as much as possible, but if the unstable ground gives away, I won't make it out. In that case, you guys get back to the transport and get out of here."

"We can't leave you."

"If I go, if the ground collapses, there won't be anything to leave. I'll just become part of the planet in a very real way. That's why I didn't want to let Olivia know I was still alive. I may not remain that way. This is important. If I don't make it out, don't ever let her know that I came back. She'll feel betrayed by the universe, all the pain coming back. I don't want to be a memory filled with pain and regret."

"We understand, don't we Bura?"

"Yeah," the big Bear said. "But don't die again."

"That's the plan." With another long sigh, Will looked back into the fiery hole. "Okay, my earpiece should survive the conditions, I've wrapped magics around it. I'm going in, and when I've finished, *if* I finish, I'll let you know, and then I need you two to connect with me and help me rise back out."

"You're sure your magic will help us to connect? Neither of us have ever had that skill."

"Eras, that's why I chose you two. Your own connection is strong, and it extends to me. I'll be able to boost the power and between the three of us, you should be able to help me come back. Like I said, best laid plans."

Bura surged forward and wrapped his big mylar-covered hands around Will, gave him a cushioned hug, and stepped back. "Be safe."

Nodding agreement, Eras moved up and smacked Will on the arm. "We'll be waiting."

One last moment of hesitation, eyes on his two companions, Will drew a long breath, and jumped.

He'd already called up the air, and it responded by creating a pillow of support around his body, slowing the descent, controlling the speed so that when Will reached the bottom long minutes later, he landed hard, but with no damage. It took a little work to recover his respiration, but when he had, he stayed down as he scanned the place he'd jumped into based solely on universal guidance.

As expected, the temperature wasn't survivable for a human body unless earth magic protected him, and it seemed to be doing so. Magics didn't stop his body's reaction to the heat, though, as sweat surged and he found himself panting. When they'd fought to contain the power and explosion of the magma at Yellowstone last year, he had journeyed into the magma chamber spiritually, but this, being here physically, was beyond that, past imagining, suffocating. The intensity of heat, the vibrant electric colors of fire breathed from the core of this world, the sounds that split the steam-filled air…he didn't have the words to explain. Now, though, he needed to find a way to convince this fissure to calm down, to seal, and stabilize this land.

An earthquake in this area, along this part of the faultline, would devastate Australia, the United Islands of Indonesia, Malaysia, and the Philippines, the resulting tsunami possibly striking the Asian continent. Millions would die and the irreplaceable food farms supplied by Australia would be wiped away.

It was up to him, a failure in life; a heavy drinking motorcyclist from the desert southwest who's greatest achievement before being drafted with the earth warriors last year was inadvertently killing his fiancée and unborn child.

Who the fuck made *that* decision?

He couldn't let this happen, so he drew from within, pulled from every corner of the world, reached into the sky to new airborne powers he'd never had before, focused deep into the bowels of this world, sucked every molecule of magics that rode through rock and flesh, and balled it all, turned it into a force to seal the rip in the earth that threatened to tear itself apart.

How he'd been chosen didn't matter now, all that did was that he *was* the chosen one to wield magics beyond his understanding to fix this geographic event.

The building magics carried power that he alone could not contain and he realized quickly that while he drew the powers, the magics, together, he was not the conduit that carried them, but the thing that focused the power and guided it to where it was needed, sent it to where it belonged to accomplish this feat of protection.

Will wondered how his body could do what it did as the force of the magics, the heavy air, the fire and brimstone walls of stone around him, drove him to his knees.

Was his head on fire? It felt like it was. At one moment, Will was sure his eyeballs were melting, and then his skin, but he kept pushing the magics, kept feeding them in, kept guiding them. Minutes passed...*no*, hours, trapped against the rock floor, every muscle spasming, his knees ached, and that was the least of it.

A roar had set up above him that rocketed off the walls from each side except below, and at its peak, sent shrieks through his ears, deafness assured, but it never came.

Finally, *when,* he did not know, Will collapsed like an airless balloon onto the jagged stone floor, grateful for lost consciousness. If he was done, he was done, and it would be okay.

Will did not wake.

Anxious, far above, Eras and Bura waited through sounds and heat that shot from the fissure so nasty, so extreme, they'd had to move back and take cover under a heavy rock ledge. Hands over ears, eyes closed, they knew they couldn't even imagine what Will was going through.

Eras believed that what Will was doing couldn't be survivable, and at the same time, remembered the things they'd all accomplished last year in Yellowstone.

It was a new world they inhabited now, with magic beyond anything they'd ever known or ever heard about.

Collapsed against a boulder, cold on the side that faced the opening of the cave, hot on the side that faced the fissure, the two men sat wordlessly waiting for Will's voice in their earpieces. Eras thought that there was no way the earpiece would function, given the conditions in the hole, but he still hoped like hell he was wrong. Bura expected it to work, because he wanted so badly to trust in the process and the magics. Both just prayed that Will would get back out safely, and that what he'd gone down to do, would work.

Every few minutes their eyes drifted back to each other's in solidarity and hope. Finally, after what felt like hours and was probably only one, the desperately hoped-for *bing* announced the earpiece's engagement.

"Gentlemen, help a brother out. World safe again. For now."

Relief and gratitude surged as they pushed off the ground, stiff from sitting so long wrapped in polartex, and carefully made their way to the opening of the fissure.

"I'm going to begin to spin a web of magics from this side. Honestly, guys, I'm so exhausted, I don't even know if I have the strength, but I have to try. I passed out, how long ago I don't know, and that seemed to help. Once you feel the magics rise, all you need to do is tap into them and feed your own magic into the web. If it goes well, I should be pulled through the web and back up the tunnel, defying gravity. Ready?"

"Ready," Eras agreed once Bura nodded that he was, too.

Faces over the edge, scalding heat blowing against them, Eras and Bura maintained their positions, and when, ten or so minutes later, they felt the bizarre movement of magic curling away from the opening, they knew what to do and how to do it. Eyes closed, both reached into the spiritual realm and pulled their own magics forth, tying them in with the framework of earth magic that Will commandeered. At the top of the tunnel, Eras and Bura supported the webbed magics that held and lifted Will up from below. There was relief when Will finally came near the mouth of the tunnel and the two grabbed his hands to pull him from the ladderless chasm dropping into what seemed like a bottomless pit. They all tumbled, crashing hard onto the ground, laughing. Will righted himself first and stared at the two men who'd saved his life by bringing him back from hell.

"Brothers," he whispered, the volume low, the best his scorched throat could produce.

"Brother," Eras and Bura said simultaneously.

Bura clapped his hands together. "Booze, pizza, and endless junk food tonight, right?"

"Anything you want. My treat. Heroes don't buy." Eras stood and held out a hand to Will, who stumbled getting on his feet, but once up, stayed steady.

"I'll take you up on that, guys. I may be a hero of the earth, but no one's said anything about a payday."

"Aw, what you do is its own reward."

"Still gotta eat. Gotta be able to buy gas…"

For the first time, Will wondered what had happened to his Harley.

"I've got your back, Will. We're in this together, and the children of the moon are financially sound, so anything you need for living expenses, just let me know."

"Eras…"

"Whatever you're going to say, bullshit. You've taken the hit for the rest of us, let us take care of you."

Will wasn't accustomed to this kind of family, to being part of a whole, and while the past year had been leading him from his solitary life toward this kind of communion, he still didn't know what to say.

Sliding a hand behind his neck, Eras gave him a little shake. "Just say *thank you*."

The words didn't come easily, but it seemed the right thing to do, so, swallowing, he looked into Eras's eyes.

"Thank you."

"Good. Shit, guys, is it getting hotter in here? I'm suddenly feeling like I'm smoked salmon."

Moving back to the opening, Will glanced down.

"The captured heat is feeding back up into the cave. You're right. Shortly it should feel like summer in Vegas."

"Oh, shit, and me without my shorts and swimmies. Let's take this party back to *Farscape Base* and get hammered. I think we all deserve it."

"That's the first good thing I've heard since you called and said, 'Hey, Bear, wanna go to Antarctica?'"

Thirteen

TWO MONTHS LATER

Covered in mud, Bura struggled, but finally succeeded in pulling the rope free.

"Fuck. Done."

Will and Eras had been lowered beneath a waterfall in Austria to repair damage to a mountain caused by a fallen satellite. The water had been feeding back into a valley and would have destroyed thousands of acres of grasslands where hundreds of species of animals had been re-introduced only twenty years earlier.

All three looked like they were covered in chocolate, tired, hungry, filthy, and hot, they looked at each other, and then, at once, jumped the fifty feet into the water below where the waterfall now flowed again.

Once down in the calmer part of the river, the men peeled their clothing off as they pitched everything up onto a pebbled shore.

Ripped, naked men rinsing off in the water, laughing, shoving each other beneath the surface, drew the attention of a group of four young women on a narrow lane above them. Bura saw them first.

"Oh, look lads, we've got admirers."

"Have at it, Big Bear. I'm taken, of course." Eras watched Will treading water. "Are you ready for some female companionship? You've earned it."

"Naw. I'm good. Bura, we're here to monitor the repair for two days, go ahead."

"Think I will."

Bura waded from the water, the drips cascading off his hairy powerful chest and thighs. Two of the women looked at their companions, and then headed toward him as he reached down for his pants and slowly slid them on to make sure they saw all his charms.

Eras lowered his head back into the water to rinse his hair. "Still pining."

"Always will. Have you heard from your sister recently?"

"Bridge? No. Sadly, we often go up to a year before we check in. Time just flies and we're all so busy now. It just gets away from us. I know she's still in Vegas."

"Huh. It seems that she and Olivia must have gotten along well."

"I think so. She's living in Olivia's building."

"I miss them both, every moment of every day."

"You should go see them."

"Someday, yeah. It's not time yet."

"I guess you'll know. Anyway, let's get cleaned up and get some food. This is hungry work."

In Serenity Tower

Jasper gurgled and made a sound like a laugh.

Brigitte picked him up and looked into his huge blue eyes. "He's laughing at me. He knows I'm a newbie at this baby thing."

Coming into the room, Olivia gently nudged Geraldo aside. The dog was obsessed with her son.

"Then he's laughing at both of us. I know less than you do." She tickled him on the cheek. "Yet I think between us, we're doing an incredible job."

"I agree. Lucky for us, he's first blood and we'd have a tough time breaking him."

"Luckily." She noticed that Brigitte wore a sexy satin dress and high heels. "Are you on your way to see Russell?"

"I think so. He's taking me to dinner, and I kind of miss his goofy smile. Plus, for human, he's not bad in bed."

"Oh, no details."

"I know I promised."

"Have a good night."

"I think I will. I'll be in before daylight."

"Doesn't he have a secure room?"

"Yeah, but I prefer to be at home."

Olivia nodded. Neither commented on the fact that Brigitte considered this home now. It had been odd how they'd bonded over Will's son, and now, Olivia couldn't imagine her life without Brigitte. Between Corri and Brigitte, the boy had the best godmothers in the world.

And while Brigitte had found someone to enjoy, had gotten back to sex, blood, and romance, Olivia hadn't been interested yet.

Following Jasper's birth three weeks ago, she'd thought that might change, but it hadn't. She still missed Will as much as she ever had.

Besides, she'd been extremely tired since the mid-part of the pregnancy, which Park had told her was natural.

"Growing a first blood baby saps your own magical strength and can leave you weak for even a month after delivery. I found that out with baby number two. It will right itself with time. Just enjoy your son."

Now, tonight, she would feed him, use the FP to make a nice dinner, eat in her room and watch a nice sci-fi show, no romance, and fall asleep. Jasper lay in his lace bassinette, already snoozing.

Quiet nights had become a favorite, post-pregnancy, the old partying Olivia happy to just relax and enjoy herself with Jasper or friends. Tonight, since it was Saturday, everyone had plans. So, a solitary dinner and a fun new vid program...perfect.

Set up in her bed an hour later, comfortable, a nice meal relished and gone, the baby gurgling now, Olivia shut off the vidscreen and checked on Jasper.

Diaper clean, recently fed, he was ready for sleep and so was she. A wide yawn later, she kissed her son goodnight, his bassinette within reach of her bed, the U.V. panels drawn so that Brigitte didn't have to think about it when she came in, and Olivia scooted down to sleep.

ON THE OTHER SIDE OF THE WORLD IN AUSTRIA

Filling up the entire floor, his arms outstretched, Bura was dead to the world, having been up most of the night with a very pretty blonde local. Eras had succumbed to the daylight sleep of a vampire.

Will, wide awake, restless, his body buzzed, like tiny pins and needles in his arms and legs. Careful to make sure the room was secured, he left their hotel and headed to the waterfall. This was the final day to check it, and then Eras would go home to Cari, and Bura would check in with his crew in Australia where he managed the continental farms.

Will didn't know where he would go. For the past few months, he'd had assignments every week, but *this* week, after completing the mission, there had been no odd cryptic messages telling him where he needed to be or what he would be needed to do. For the first time since he'd been brought back to life, he didn't know where he would be next week.

It was a good thing for his companions. Eras missed Cari, and Bura was concerned that without his steady influence, problems may arise back on the continental farm that would be difficult to fix. They needed to go home. Will just...

He knew what he needed, he just couldn't have it.

It was warm today, the sky cerulean, the water cascaded over the falls as it was meant to do. Perhaps he would stay here for a while. The disaster diverted, this valley was truly a paradise. Walking along the shoreline, the large pebbles finely polished by the water tickling his feet, he stopped to perch on a boulder to watch some white soaring birds sail over the waterfall.

Suddenly a stone sailed past him, waist high, and flew into the calm water, skipping, one, two, three times before it sunk.

"Cool."

Will turned to see who had thrown the rock. A child? Yes, a little boy with dark hair and pastel blue eyes, maybe five years old, stood just behind him.

"Oh, hey." Will lifted his eyes to scan the trees, but didn't see anyone else. "Who are you with, young man?"

"I am with *you*."

Smiling, Will slid off the rock and dropped to the boy's level. What incredibly expressive, pale blue eyes.

"I see that. But who did you come here with?"

"I came alone to see *you*."

Well, this was strange. "You must have a parent or adult with you. You're too young to be by yourself out here."

"I'm not by myself."

"I guess you're right about that. Let's try this a different way. What is your name?"

"I'm Jasper."

The name jolted Will at the bizarre coincidence.

"That's funny. Jasper is my middle name."

"I know."

"How is that?"

"Mommy told me."

The boy was looking for another rock to throw.

Will stood, an eerie feeling traveling along his spine.

"Jasper, what is your last name?"

"I don't have a last name. What is yours?"

"It's Collins."

The boy's smile widened and he moved around Will to climb up on top of the same boulder Will had just slipped off of.

Spotting the boy to make sure he didn't fall, Will stayed beside him until he reached the top and stood watching the water pass.

"Then that's my last name too." The boy's gaze dropped to Will's. "You have to come to me. I've waited, and you haven't come."

His stomach rolling now, Will lifted the boy from the rock and lowered him back to the ground, kneeling beside him again. "Who is your mother?"

The unexpected giggle echoed off the mountain that fed the waterfall. "You know who she is!"

"Uh, no, I don't." *Did he? What the hell was happening?*

After rolling his eyes, Jasper put one little hand on each of Will's cheeks. "Daddy, you know who my mother is. We're waiting for you to come to us so we can be a family. Mommy is happy, but sometimes, she's sad too."

Will could feel magics pouring around them, around this beautiful child. He stood, lifting Jasper with him, holding the boy close as he wrapped his short arms around Will.

"Your mother. Is her name Olivia?"

"Of course, silly."

"It isn't possible." Whispering, Will looked into the eyes of a boy who *did* remind him of Olivia, the kid *did* have *his* eyes, when it suddenly struck him...*he must be dreaming!*

"I'm asleep, I'm dreaming this."

The child paid no attention to Will's rambling.

"Mommy talks to me all the time and she tells me about you. She says my daddy would be so sorry he couldn't meet me. She says my daddy would be proud of me, so why won't you come home to me?"

Will set the boy down.

"Because you are wishful dreaming. But she's right. If I had a boy like you, I'd never leave you. If you were my little guy, I would kiss you every night just before you go to bed and kiss you awake every morning. Yes, I would be *so* proud of you."

It was remarkable, Will realized, how well he'd envisioned a perfect blend between himself and Olivia. Their son would have been exactly like this imaginary boy.

"Walk with me."

Will kept his steps short so the child could keep up with him. "Jasper. Wow, I'm getting this right. I think Olivia would have chosen that name. Especially with me gone, as a memorial."

"It's my name."

"I know. If I *did* have a son, I would want him to be *just like you*."

The boy stopped. "I *am* your son."

"If you existed, yeah, in about five years."

"Daddy, come home."

"Hey, Will, wait up!"

Will turned to Bura's voice behind him, yelling out, waving. What was Bura doing in his dream?

As he caught up, Bura handed Will a mocha pop.

"I figured you didn't make any coffee this morning, so I brought you one of these. I don't know if you've ever tried them, but they're great."

Bura looked around. "Where'd the kid go?"

"What?" Ah, it was a dream, Bura would have seen him too.

"It's my son. He's disappeared."

"Funny. Sure. Yeah, that would have been cool."

Will still couldn't figure out why Bura was in his dream. The magics swelled again.

It *had* been a dream, right? *Had* to have.

Why did this suddenly feel like it *wasn't* a dream?

"Bura, I'm dreaming right now. This isn't real."

Bura watched Will for a moment, his mocha pop halfway to his lips. "No, Will, this is the real world."

"It can't be. That kid, he doesn't exist."

"I saw the kid. Who was he?"

Silent now, lost in thought, the magics confusing him when they usually made things clearer.

"Bura, you saw the child I was talking to? And you say this is real?"

"Will, this is real life. No dream. I woke up, Eras was sleeping, so I came out to find you, figured you'd be near the waterfall, and saw you talking to a kid, who, yeah, kind of disappeared. I don't know how else to tell you."

If the boy was here, and if the magics were wrapped around him, as they seemed to be...*was it possible?*

Fuck, anything was possible!

"Bura, I need to go right now. I have to be back in Vegas as soon as possible. Thank you for everything you've done for me, with me, for the past two months. We're not finished, I know that, but the magics are telling me something and if it's what I think it is, I'm way overdue to meet someone."

"Sure, Will, sure. Just let us know and we'll be there. It's been rough at times, but in the end, I feel good about what we've accomplished."

"I hoped you would. Tell Eras the same thing I said to you. I consider you brothers."

"We feel the same way, Will. Good luck and I hope what you think is true, really is."

"Thank you, big guy."

Will left, using speed not unlike that of a vampire, and when he entered the hotel room and grabbed the small pack that held everything he owned in the world, he laid a hand on Eras, wished him well, and headed to the airport.

Thank the universe for giving him magic of the air so that he was no longer strictly bound to the earth. The pull was there, but it never overrode him, so, finally, he could safely fly.

Three hours later, Eras woke, groggy, thirsty.

Bura was pressed against his leg, the result of throwing a couple of thick comforters on the floor and just camping out. He looked around, but didn't see Will. No worry, he wasn't bound by night like Eras. Pushing off the sheet, he bumped Bura's foot.

Groaning, Bura shoved against Eras. "We really need more space."

"I agree. Hey, do you know where Will is?"

"In a plane, bound for Vegas."

"Vegas? Why? And why so suddenly?"

"Thinks he has a kid there. A little boy. The crazy part is that I think I actually saw the kid. Fucking magics'll really mess with your head."

Lying still, Eras smiled. "About time."

The next night at the bottom of Serenity Tower

Will had no idea where to start. To begin with, Olivia, Brigitte, *everyone*, thought he was dead. It wouldn't be the kindest thing to just walk right into their apartment and announce, "Guess that death thing didn't stick, eh?"

But he had to see if he was right, and if he was, if Olivia had borne a son with him, there wasn't anything on this earth or above it that would stop him from being with her and the child. Just, how does a man suddenly show up, alive, after a woman has accepted his death and moved on? Fuck, she might even have another man in her life.

Fuck this, he thought. It has to be simple, I'll go to her, she'll be shocked, I'll explain, and it will be all right.

No, it won't.

As he waited, trying to figure out the best way to let Olivia know that her son's father was alive, he watched a small party leaving the building under the huge covered pavilion at the main entrance.

It was Corri, accompanied by the three vampires he'd seen at Villioth's office before he was eliminated. And Olivia, even more exquisite than he remembered. Wearing a dark purple strap dress, skin tight to show off her excellent body, and high heeled pumps, it didn't look like she'd given birth recently. As soon as he thought that, it struck him that a first blood likely wouldn't have any trouble getting those amazing bodies back following the rare pregnancy.

"You'd be perfect either way," he whispered. Then his eyes landed on Koen, at Olivia's side. His blood heated as he watched the giant vampire turn to Olivia with a warm smile and lift his hand to cup her chin.

What the hell did that mean? Was he her lover? Had Olivia taken a lover? She should have, it had been over half a year since he'd *died*.

Will had never been a jealous man, but here he was, rage surging, fighting the desire to race forward and confront the vampire, to shove that offensive hand away from his woman. *To show the asshole what earth magics could do!*

His woman? He hadn't claimed her. He'd let her send him away to make his decision, even though at that point he already knew…*it would always be Olivia.*

All he could do now was shadow this group. Carefully surveil them to see he had been replaced, and if he determined that he had, Will decided he would stay away until he could control himself, could accept that she'd moved past him, and that what they had had died with his first death.

From there, he'd find out if she really had carried his child, and if so, he would have no choice. Whatever her future with another man, Will *would* be father to that boy who'd come to him across the globe to tell him that he needed him. No power would change that.

Sliding into his *city car* rental, the small cars available in any large city to use while within the limits of the city, he kept his distance as he followed the big van.

At *Flights* restaurant

First night out in a long time, and Olivia was nervous. She'd left her son with Brigitte while she went out to celebrate their victory a few months ago over the man who'd threatened the first blood race. Koen had insisted.

"Get on a pretty dress, lass, and let's have a fine dinner. I've heard that Dez's sky-high dining is the best in the city."

"I'm going to have to take a small exception with that. My restaurants are excellent. I will, however, agree, that *Flights* offers an incredible variety of unique food. On a 5 star scale, it's a 6."

"Then get all prettied-up and let's go. I'm starving."

Now, seated at a corner table with a view of the other diners on one side, and a view outside a glass wall of the city 83 stories below them, Olivia had to force herself to stop worrying about Jasper.

"He's fine, Liv." Corri placed a tray of appetizers in front of Olivia. "Dig in. Koen is such a character. I just adore him."

Vaz shot her a look and Corri leaned in to bump his shoulder. "Not as much as you, of course. He's just kind of…bigger than life."

Nodding, Vaz let her off the hook. "He kind of is. I'm not jealous, he really is mythic."

Olivia's eyes went to Koen. Her great-grandmother was very close to him; she had lived with him and his family for over a century now. He was family, there whenever anyone needed him. "Yes, he *is* mythic."

"Let's get this party on. Waiter!"

Koen had never been shy about demanding what he wanted. As soon as the waiter hurried to their table, he ordered a second round of appetizer trays and four bottles of *Flights* finest champagne.

"When ya bring it back, we'll order the entrees, thank ya, lad."

"So, all quiet on the vampire front these days?" Olivia asked.

Koen nodded. "Mostly. Some incidences here in the U.S., but nothing unusual. Vampires do have accidents sometimes. A concern here or there, but we don't manage issues in North America."

"Good. I've been kind of cloistered during the pregnancy."

"I'm glad you came out. You needed this."

"I did, Cor. It's been an odd six months, with Will's loss, carrying his child, and now the joy of holding Jasper in my arms. I am ready to get my life back on track."

"We're all here to help."

"It took Park a while after each child to get back to normal. Enjoy this, Livie. You won't get a chance to feel exactly like this again." Bas lifted a glass. "To family."

"To family," everyone said, and saluted the one stable force in first blood lives, the fact that they were all in this together and that they would always be there for each other. Olivia felt once again the blessing that Zach had found her, and that through him, she'd found her family.

As she sipped, her eyes lifted to Koen across the table, but movement beyond him caught her gaze instead. In the shadows, several rows in from the aisle, a table in the corner held a single diner, a man. She couldn't see him clearly, but there was something about the way he moved that drew her attention. What was it? Try as she would, she couldn't make out his face; the distance and darkened corner obscured him too much.

Shaking her head, Olivia turned her attention back to the remarkable people at her table who had gone the extra mile to protect her, her loved ones, and give her peace at a time when she needed it most. Any threat would have been unacceptable now with her son here.

She raised her glass again. "To the special people around this table, all of you family, and to a happy safe world for all of us. Namasté."

Koen rose and went to Olivia, leaning in to kiss each cheek. "To our new little mother, the first vampire to have a baby in many years. Park tries to keep track and no one has had a first blood child since my great-granddaughter. As close as I am to Tam, I consider young Jasper to be my grandson too. Know that I will always come when you or he calls."

Tears welled up fast, and Olivia moved in close for a tight hug. Her face buried against his warmth, the hard muscles under her fingers, the memory of Will's body very like this after the healing pool, gave her shivers.

"Thank you, Koen. It means the world to me."

"Aye. And the boy is the only fifth-gen I know of. It will be interesting to see how powerful he might be."

"Right now, he's just a little boy."

"Aye. It's a gift that our children get to have a real childhood."

"I agree. Ah, here comes Tito with the appetizer trays. Ohhh, those will take a while to polish off."

"Nay, there are five hungry vampires here. I give it ten minutes."

They did take longer, since they enjoyed the company, lively conversations, and copious amounts of champagne.

Her gaze continued to wander back to the corner, where, oddly, the man still kept his face out of view. Was it on purpose? The way he held his head, the wild dark hair, his demeanor, were all familiar, but that couldn't be unusual since she'd met a lot of people over the many years she'd been in Vegas.

Trying hard to ignore him, Olivia failed. He remained a distraction, and she had to solve the mystery. When he suddenly rose and disappeared through a balcony door, she decided to follow him.

"Please excuse me for a moment."

Across the room, Will curled his fingers around the edge of the table. The huge vampire had his hands on Olivia again, and when she stood to hug him and didn't let him go for long moments, he couldn't take it anymore.

The intention had been to quietly, covertly watch them until he was satisfied either way, and then disappear from the building before she ever saw him. The waiter set a bottle of vodka on the table and Will poured himself a glass of the powerful clear liquid, but he couldn't drink it. He couldn't watch this or he'd explode, the magics surging around him. Afraid of losing control, he grabbed the glass and busted across the floor away from Olivia's table and out onto the glass balcony. Distance and fresh air would help, and at least give him a place to release some of the pent-up magic.

Once he was out there, alone, thank God, he could breathe. Below him, over eighty stories above the city, the lights created an incredible eye-catching landscape. Good, anything to distract him. *Anything…*

"Excuse me, sir."

Her voice…

Olivia? *Behind him?*

Fuck! What foul twist of fate had created this moment? *She couldn't find him like this!* For a second, he thought about jumping over the edge of the balcony, hoping to land on the one below. Not likely. Could he deflect her?

"I hope I'm not disturbing you, but you look familiar, like someone I used to know. Sir, I need to see your face."

No, she didn't.

He didn't have a choice. Olivia was here, close behind, alone on this balcony with him, and all he had to do was turn around and face her. It would shock her to her core.

Careful, he thought. *Protect her however you can.*

"Please don't come any closer."

Will kept his face averted by looking straight over the balcony. After he'd spoken, he didn't hear or see her, but she hadn't moved. When she spoke again, he knew she'd recognized his voice.

"Who are you?" Olivia's voice was hard, suspicious, shocked.

"Just stay where you are and let me tell you. It's going to be a bit jarring."

Instantly, he felt her behind him.

"Turn and face me."

"Olivia…"

Her voice cracked. "Who *are* you?" she insisted.

Just do it.

Slowly, hoping to give her a moment to adjust, Will turned to face Olivia, leaning against the railing for support.

"I need to explain."

Shocked was the right word, she moved back a few steps, her eyes wide, mouth open. "Will?"

Nodding, he lowered his head. "It's me, Olivia. Really."

"What? Um..." Silence, then, "How?"

Her eyes moved over him, devoured him, and as he prepared to answer her, she was in front of him, her hands on his chest, her eyes searching over him. Then she closed hers, drew in his scent, and opened them again, visibly shaken; now quivering.

"It *is*," she whispered. "How?" she repeated, so quietly, it was only her nearness that let him hear her.

"Earth magic. Celestial intervention."

Her hands moved from his chest to his face; her fingers tracing each feature, across his cheeks, along the edge of his nose, and then up to his eyes as her own sought his again.

"I've missed you, more than I can tell you with words."

Still touching him, lingering, she moved in and up to kiss his lips lightly, testing, but that ended fast when Will yanked her against him.

The kiss went beyond passion, beyond desperate, tongues intertwining that never expected to ever do this again.

In his arms, Olivia, finally...

Need was the only word that met the insistence, the need, the depth at which their emotions shot through them as they touched and connected after all connections had been torn away.

Olivia jumped on Will, she couldn't get close enough, buried her face into his neck, hands burrowed into his hair.

He wasn't the same, she could feel it, saw it right away, but *this was Will*, and she was wrapped around him.

A horrible thought suddenly stabbed her in the belly and she looked up. "You can stay? Will, you can stay, can't you?"

"I'm staying. God, Olivia, it hurt not to come to you, to make love to you, to tell you that I choose you, would *always* choose *you*."

He felt her body stiffen, and she slid off him. Pulling the tight dress back into place, she looked up.

"Will, how long have you been back?"

Confusion filled her eyes. Will needed time to help her understand. "Um, can we go somewhere private and talk?"

Olivia's head jerked as she looked around the balcony where only she and Will were present.

"This is private. How *long*, Will?"

"It's complicated."

"Not really. Just give me a number and a unit. Two. Days. Three weeks. Four months. Like that. How *long*?"

"I can't say exactly. I was buried in the healing cave, I'm sure you know that, and I came awake there. I'm not sure how long after I was buried."

Flinching, she moved closer again. "Oh, Will, you came awake beneath the ground?"

"Cradled in the earth. It was okay. I easily dug out, and when I remembered how I got there, I remembered that I had died. That I should still be dead. But the magics inside me, and without, needed me alive. They repaired me, and here I am."

Olivia went into his arms again, holding tight in case this was an illusion and he might dissipate like smoke.

"I'm just...*you're back*." Another whisper as she continued to adjust and accept. In that moment, Will knew that this was all he needed. Olivia. Nothing else in this world beyond her. Unless...

It wasn't time to ask about Jasper yet.

"Would you like to go back to your apartment to talk? Just to talk. I know you need a chance to process this after thinking I was dead for six months."

For moments, she didn't answer, and when she did, her smile softened. "I've only been able to touch you in my dreams, and I have needed you for so long. I haven't been with anyone else since..."

"Not even the big vampire I saw you hug earlier?"

"Koen? I'm like a granddaughter to him. He's family."

"So you haven't...it isn't my business."

"I can't think of anything else now other than that you are here, standing here, alive, warm, and I can touch you. Will, come with me, meet everyone."

"I'm not ready for that yet. Can I come to you tonight?"

"Yes, of course. Will, Brigitte is staying with me."

"It's fine. Eras told me."

"Eras?"

"I'll explain, I promise. This is my number. Call me when it's clear and I'll come to you."

Will lifted her fone from her hand and keyed something in. Afterward, he handed it back to her, kissed her, a far too chaste kiss, and went through the balcony doors.

As soon as he was gone, the moments on the balcony with him felt like a fantasy. Suddenly, without tangible evidence, Will was already a ghost again.

Lifting her fingers to her lips, Olivia tried to remember every second with him just now, every word he spoke.

"Liv? Are you okay? You've been gone awhile, I was worried."

Olivia turned to Corri, trying to decide whether to tell her about the bizarre event. Without a conscious decision to do so, she realized she didn't want to tell anyone about Will yet. If he *was* an illusion, a magical creation in her mind, she wanted to hold on to it a little longer.

"Sorry, just needed some fresh air and ended up ruminating. You know what that's like. Have the entrees been served?"

"And how. Koen really knows how to bring it."

"He always has. Let's go feast."

Outside Serenity Tower, after a wonderful evening of drinks, food, and wickedly funny conversation, Koen and Bas said goodbye to Vaz, Corri, and Olivia under the pavilion cover before they got into their car.

It was always sad saying goodbye to friends and family.

"I'll get back to France soon," Olivia told Koen.

"Tam will be happy to hear that. Even though she was here for the baby's birth, she already says it's been too long."

"I'll text her and tell her to come back and stay a while. I have a newly decorated apartment suite at the end of the hall that will be just right for her and Marc."

"She might come at once. Take care of my little guy and make sure he isn't riding that godawful bike too soon."

"I think we have a little while before we have to worry about that, Koen. À *bientôt*."

"À *bientôt*."

At the top of the tower, grateful to be home, Olivia slipped out of her high heels as Corri followed her into the apartment.

"You're sure you're okay."

"Cor, I'm fine. Bridge and I'll probably have some ice cream, watch an old vid, and close up for daylight."

"I can stay. You seem...troubled."

"My friend, I'm good. I'm going to get into my comfies and hug my son. Go home to your mate."

"Hey guys! Good party?" Brigitte came from Olivia's bedroom wearing a slinky dress and boots.

"Good eats. I brought you three of *Flights* best entrees."

"Yummy. But can you stash them for me until tomorrow? Russell called and I'm heading to his place now that you're home and I'll probably stay the rest of the night and day there. I just feel very horny tonight. Must have been that sexy vid I put on after Jasper fell asleep."

"Thank you for staying with him. It was nice to get out, but it's still tough to leave him."

"He's a darling. Sleeping like a little trooper. Good night, ladies." Brigitte lifted a lightweight overnighter and headed out.

"You too, Corri. Tell Vaz goodnight for me. It's because of his brilliant insight that we finally got to celebrate tonight."

"I'm so glad we did. Get some rest. I'll see you tonight."

After the usual end-of-day hug, Olivia headed to her bedroom to make sure her sleeping baby was still sleeping comfortably.

Curled up, his soft dark hair sticking out in all directions, she gently smoothed it back down, well aware that in no time, it would be all wild again. From birth, he'd had too much hair, and now it had some length, and had already thickened. Long, soft strands so like his father's sifted through her fingers.

Sighing, she looked at her fone. If she searched her contacts, would there be a new listing for Will? Or were those moments with him on the balcony at *Flights* only the fantastic imagination of a lonely mind? Had he really been there? Had he left a number?

Finger hovering over the button, she gave herself one last second to believe, just in case...and then touched the *contacts* button.

There, in black letters on a blue field, the name *Will* and 9 digits beside it. He'd told her to let him know when she wanted him to come.

"He's real," she whispered to her sleeping son.

Moving back to her living space and beyond it to the balcony, she sought the sky and stars, cool air, in her place of peace. *Will was alive!*

No hesitation this time, she pressed the button, and it seemed like it took a million years to connect through, but then...

His voice came through the tiny box, sparking tears.

"Olivia." *Strong, alive, beautiful.* "May I come to you?"

"Right away. Just come through the door, everything is unlocked for you. You know where I am?"

"I know. I'm close and I'll be with you very soon."

"Okay."

After staring at her fone for long seconds, she placed it on a table and wandered back inside.

Nine minutes later, her door slid open and there he was. Will was in her apartment, near her, near their son that he did not know existed. A night of revelation and explanation...love, maybe, *hope*? An interesting night, at least.

Olivia moved toward him. This time she took a moment to search the man who came back from the other side. He was bigger than Will had been before, his hair even longer, even fuller and wilder. He wore a black short-sleeved tee shirt and black denim pants, both too tight, like Will would have before. This newly resurrected man *was* Will, but ramped up, vampire big, muscles harder, more heavily defined, certainly more powerful.

All that mattered to her was that he was back. She went into his arms instantly, he gathered her close, lifting her from the floor, their heads buried into each other. How long they stayed that way, they had no idea, but just that closeness was all they needed.

Finally, Olivia slipped to the floor, took his hand, and led him to a curved seat on the balcony where the only light was what traveled out from the living space.

"Will you tell me what happened, where you've been, what you're doing? Will, I asked this question before, and I realize I sounded hostile, but when it seemed like you've been back some time, I don't understand why you never let me know. Why you didn't come to me? Unless you didn't want to be with me anymore."

"I *always* want to be with you. Forever, make no mistake about that, but there is a very real reason I didn't, *couldn't*, come to you. Okay, here is the tale. Yes, I've been back for a while. Months. Part of the time I stayed in the healing cave, where this transformation happened. Part of the time I was training to become a soldier of the earth. More than what I was with the other warriors. My magics are obscenely powerful now. I've been all around the world with Eras and Bura, protecting the earth, the land, the people, all life endangered by events we stopped."

"But you couldn't let me know?"

"I *wouldn't* let you know. Olivia, you are my heart. When I knew you had been through my death, my funeral, and had gone home, when I knew that you were beginning to heal from my loss, I couldn't come to you because I didn't know if I could stay, or what the universe wanted from me. Olivia, I would come to you through fire if I had to, but not if it hurt you."

"So you've been here almost from the beginning?"

"I think so, yes."

"Okay. Wow."

Shoving off her seat, Olivia moved to the wall to look out over the city. He'd been here so long and she hadn't known. All those months, she'd carried his child and he had been out there, oblivious.

The universe, destiny, the living planet, all played a part in their lives and she *did* understand. "You were trying to protect me."

"You had a life to live, and for all purposes, I didn't know if I could ever be part of it again. Why contact you to say that I could never come to you?"

Turning, Olivia, arms crossed, leaned against the wall.

"So why did you? Why come now?"

"I had a messenger."

"Messenger? Who?"

"That's an even more bizarre tale. I was walking along a river in Austria when a little boy followed me. He was about five, bright, friendly, a beautiful child. He asked me why I hadn't come to him."

Olivia's heart beat faster. What did he mean? A five year old child? A boy?

"He told me his name was Jasper."

The air blew out of her, and she panted. "Jasper?"

Will was beside her, his hands gentle on her upper arms, holding her still. "Do I have a son?"

Tears streaming now, she nodded, over and over, because the words wouldn't come. All she could think of was the bizarre manifestation of Jasper five years older, across the world, asking his father to come home.

Now, both dumbstruck, dealing with what they'd each learned, Will led her back to the lounger and set her on the cushion. He dropped to his knees in front of her.

"It's true, then?" Tears had filled Will's eyes, streaming down his cheeks too. Olivia pushed into his arms.

"He's so perfect, Will. I guess he already knew you were alive."

"How could...could he have done that? I thought I had dreamed him up."

"He's fifth generation first blood, he is capable of that. Projecting his future self to you, the emotional tie so strong, he found you no matter where you were in the world. Will, come with me."

Standing, she took his hand and led him through the big living space, down the brief corridor, and into the biggest bedroom he'd ever seen. Everything was soft colors and light except for a corner of the room, dark now, but he could see bright colors on the walls and a huge fabric bin on the opposite wall filled with stuffed animals and toys.

"He's right here, and yes, his name is Jasper."

Stepping up to a white crib, Will peered over the lowered railing at a tiny baby, asleep, breathing softly, little hands over a head covered with lots of dark hair. Instantly, his hand went to him, his fingers exploring through the thick hair and over the perfect tiny skull.

"Jasper?"

"Yes. A reminder of you. I wouldn't let your memory die."

"Thank you. We made him. You and I."

"He's happy. Healthy, of course. When he wakes, he's going to be overjoyed to find you here. Will, you're going to be an incredible father. If you want to. If you stay."

If he stayed.

Scooping Olivia into his arms, he swung her around.

"If I stay? I'm staying, fuck the universe. My family is my heart, my life, my mate and my son, nothing will take me from you two. I am here and yours until the world ends, Liv. If you want me?"

Olivia's tongue invaded his mouth, her hands tugging hard on his hair, the pain exquisite, as she kissed away any doubts. "If I *want* you?"

Wiggling free, she dropped to the floor and pulled him to her bed. "I want you, this very second, Will, don't even think about refusing me on any technicality. If you say you want to give me time, that you can wait until I'm ready, or any other shit like that, I'll hurt you."

He was underneath her and naked before he could respond to the demand.

His eyes moved to the dark corner where the white color of the crib glowed.

Will shoved Olivia off him and picked her up, carried her to the balcony, and lay her on another lounge out there built for two. "Fuck, no, I won't refuse you, but, that kid is just too self-aware for a baby. Not in your bed, not now."

"Fine."

Pushing him back against the lounge, she slid down to the bottom, his cock in her hand, perched over him. Her tongue dived to run a course around the tip before Olivia lifted her head, her eyes boring into his.

"Humans have weak scents, did you know that? The pheromone levels are low, so that sexual identifier usually doesn't affect a vampire much, but you...*yours*, is intense, and, uh, unique. When you rose from that pool the night we met, your scent struck me almost as much as the erotic image of this body dripping with water."

Olivia nipped up and down the edges of his cock, and it jumped in her hand. She moaned. "I have never purged your scent or image from my mind, it's embedded on my soul. I still smelled your scent even after you were gone."

Will couldn't control the loud groan that tore from him when she pulled him into her mouth, all the way, closing around him, her tongue sliding along the back, teeth nipping as she moved around from tip to base, up and down, down and up, while he fingered her hair and lay back to centuries of skill. Pressure built fast as she drove him to explode, tickling the sensitive skin, the head soaked, until his orgasm hit hard. As she drew away, she nipped him again with sharp teeth, the pleasure/pain striking once again.

"Liv..." he barked out.

Moving up to stretch out alongside Will, Olivia nuzzled beneath his hair and bit his ear too. "I'm overdue for my blood meal. I *need* to taste you."

"I think you just did."

"Ummm, I did, but now..."

"Bite me, Liv. I am yours."

"Oh, you're mine, Biker, that's been settled."

Swinging a leg over Will, bare skin to bare skin, the feel of Olivia's body moving against his, her heat pressed to his spent cock, she lowered to nuzzle beneath his neck. Just as his lips went around a nipple, her fangs sunk into his neck, another pain/pleasure sensation hit him in the groin, his cock filling again. The sound of her pulling his blood into her body, Olivia pressed to his cock, her opening right there, he started to thrust to get inside her, but she resisted, using her superior strength to capture his legs as she finished feeding.

Had he ever been more aroused? The feeding had shot him into overdrive and he could feel her need too, wet and breathing hard, and yet she slipped off the lounger and walked into the apartment.

"Follow me."

Will lay still for a moment, his hand on the now hard organ between his legs, not sure if he could get off the lounger. Desire pushed him, sliding to the edge, lifting on shaking legs to enter the living space where he saw his naked woman disappear down another hallway. She'd said follow and he had no choice. Three doors led off the hallway, all closed except the last one.

As he moved through the hall, he palmed the head of his penis, still in his hand as he came around the doorway and saw the most amazing sight.

Olivia, stretched out on his Harley, her legs open, waiting for him. He'd been wrong when he wondered after the feeding if he'd ever been more aroused...*this*, Olivia, waiting, ready for him to enter her, on his bike, *this was it*.

"Fuck me, Biker."

Moving toward the bike, legs still shaky, harder than he'd ever been, he swung his left leg over the seat of the bike, facing the back, and facing Olivia, her full breasts in his face, his cock perched on the leather just an inch from her.

"I never forgot one detail of you, but, gods, woman, you're even more incredible than I remember."

"That's because nothing beats having someone you can touch and taste. Like this."

At the same second she scooted toward him, Olivia pulled him forward, then Will took over. He scooped her buttocks into his hands and lifted her to meet him as he thrust his cock into her, all the way until he couldn't bury himself any deeper. Her hands on the seat supporting herself, Olivia lifted to him as her head dropped back, lost in the ecstasy, then raised it up to watch the thick wet organ moving in and out of her. She rode him until she was almost there, then stopped, holding him inside as deep as she could.

After feeding from Will and now capturing him inside her, the blood bond, the sexual connection, and his sudden thrust brought her home and she came so hard, she held tight to the side of Will's bike to keep from falling off. Olivia's orgasm brought Will with her and he did the same, struggling to make sure that neither he or she, or the bike, went over onto the floor.

Olivia collapsed back onto the seat, her eyes moving back to Will's face, no more than 12 inches from her, a face that she was sure she'd never see again, which hit her with a force that shook her.

Will saw her emotions crash, tears in her eyes, knew they were joy that he was there, knew that they held fear too.

"Liv, Liv, it's all right. I'm really here and I'm not leaving you or Jasper. We have earned this, the chance to be a family. I love you, Olivia, more than anything I've ever expected in my life, and I already feel the same way about our son. Baby, it's all okay now."

Her arms so tight around him, they hurt, Olivia held on, and even though she believed what Will said, that the universe had kindly given him back to her, the loss still felt too raw. And somewhere in her mind she didn't trust the universe to allow him to stay.

"Will, please don't let them take you back."

"They won't. *I* won't. I'm your mate, Olivia, I plan to be here with you for a great many centuries."

With a nod, she pushed him back, using her hand to wipe her eyes, and punched him in the gut. "See to it that you don't break that promise."

"I'll do that. Liv, you have to be exhausted."

"So do you. Please stay here."

"Wasn't planning to leave."

"Good. Come."

Sliding off the bike, Olivia, resplendent in nothing at all, walked to the doorway and turned back to Will when she saw he lingered. "Coming?"

"That's a leading question and perhaps an invitation? Yeah, I am, but Liv, thank you for saving my bike. It really has been my one companion through nearly my entire life."

"It meant so much to you, Biker, so it became important to me too. I had her cleaned and serviced before I brought her up here. I was going to give her to Jasper someday."

"I couldn't think of a better memorial for my son. So, I'm still following."

Olivia turned again and headed down the hall, this time, Will right behind her. As they entered the living area, she stopped to look back.

"Can you live here? This high above the earth?"

"I think I can. I'll have to return to the ground, and sometimes to the caves, but I'll always come home to you."

"Nothing you could say right now would make me happier."

Following Olivia into her bedroom suite once again, Will crawled into the biggest bed he'd ever seen on the softest sheets he'd ever felt, and pulled his woman up next to him. Before he dropped off to sleep, he lay there, perched up on his arms, and watched as she slept, grateful that finally, after all the troubles, they were together. His eyes wandered to the baby sleeping peacefully in his crib. Tonight, he would hold his son for the first time.

Just before dawn

"Liv?"

Brigitte whispered, praying she didn't wake the baby.

"Liv?" Easing herself into Olivia's darkened room, she leaned close to her ear to quietly let her know that she was home.

She couldn't believe what she saw. Olivia was in bed with a man. Moving around to the other side, too curious not to, stunned when she realized who it was. Shock struck her and reality twisted. "Will?"

He woke and saw her, distressed. When their eyes met, she bolted from the room.

Out in the living space, her shoes still clutched tight in her hands, Brigitte stood, statue still, and watched a man who looked like Will walk from Olivia's room wearing jeans zipped, but not snapped.

"Will?" she repeated, barely breathing.

"Bridge, don't freak out, I'm really here. Earth magics brought me back. I've been with your brother for six months working for the living planet. It's okay. Breathe."

Slowly, she moved closer, and planted a hand gingerly on his chest, then pushed, then plunged at him to feel him against her.

"Holy shit," she whispered. After a long hug, she pushed back, swiping at her eyes. "Um, obviously Liv knows."

"Just tonight. She's just as shocked. Brigitte, before I, um, died, you knew I was falling in love with Olivia, didn't you?"

She nodded. "Yeah, we've reconciled, and yeah, I knew it. I'm okay with you two, really. Of course, I didn't expect there to be any, you know, conflict. You being dead and all." Staring, she looked at this ghost from her past, *alive*, breathing, warm, in front of her after accepting his loss.

"I can't believe it. Gods. You're really here. I'm *so* happy to see you. I kind of still love you, ya dope."

"I kind of still love you too."

"Aw, look at us. A threesome. I'm kidding! Although…"

"If I ever would, it would be with you."

"Yeah, you're not the type. You are an old-fashioned one-woman man. It's one of the things I loved about you. So, welcome back, handsome. Where have you been all this time?"

"I know it's your bedtime, why don't we talk tonight? If you're really curious, call Eras."

"That bully. Yeah, I might."

One last hug, Will kissed her lightly on the cheek, then walked back into Olivia's room where he wandered over to the crib.

Jasper, awake, stared up at his father, and smiled.

Will slid a fingertip over his cheek and felt overwhelming love. Yes, this was the boy he met in Austria. "Hey, Jasper. I did what you asked, I came home to you. Thank you for letting me know you were waiting. Daddy's home, and he loves you beyond the sun and moon and stars."

The sheet still turned down, as if it, too, had been waiting, Will crawled back into the bed and rolled in next to his mate. His last thought before he fell into a deep sleep was that he'd finally found his destiny.

The End

The following night on Sunset Strip

Gio finished his task, and headed to his car. Where the hell had he put that keyfob? So forgetful lately; too much on his mind, too many strange things happening.

Finally, in the back pocket of his pants, there it was, the elusive keyfob.

"Thank God." Groaning in relief, he was grateful he didn't have to look for a station to give him remote electronic access to the car.

Loading his package in the trunk, he turned to get in to head back to Serenity Tower when a woman passed by on the sidewalk. He did a double take. Was that...? Sliding back out of the car, he hurried onto the pavement sparkling with embedded glass.

Squinting, he wondered...*could it be*?

"Thalasia?"

The woman didn't stop, but, fuck, it looked like her. Gio followed her and when he finally got a look at her face, he moved to intercept her and gently took her by the shoulders. "Thalasia, it's me, Gio."

She looked at him with blank eyes. "Gio?"

"Yeah, you know me. I mean, not well, but I've been looking for you. I wondered if you were okay."

She wasn't. He could tell, she looked at him as if he was a complete stranger. Oh, fucking shit...*had that bastard*...?

He caught her eye, and used compulsion to cut through any crap.

"Do you know your name?"

She didn't respond at first, but the look of confusion increased. Her eyes moved back and forth like she was searching for the answer. "No."

The simple answer told him all he needed to know.

"Motherfucking asshole," Gio hissed.

Thalasia winced.

"No, not you, honey. Look, I'm going to help you. Come with me. Please, I won't hurt you."

He pushed that last command with compulsion so she would come with him without question or panic.

"Get in this car." Gio gently sat her in his car and got in the driver's side.

He'd looked for her after they'd gotten her boss, but he couldn't find her. It seemed logical that she'd just taken off before she was somehow implicated in his crimes. She'd known he was vampire, was likely Villioth's blood-bond and sex slave.

Too bad for her that she hadn't just gone. What he'd done to her was so much worse.

Villioth had purged her. He'd removed any memory she had of her life, and while she was still technically functional, she had no idea who she was, how she'd lived, where she was, or anyone or anything that had defined her life. She was an empty slate, a lost soul. It was one of the cruelest things a vampire could do to someone.

Catching her eyes again, Gio promised. "I'm going to take care of you, Thalasia. That's your name, Thalasia. Is that familiar at all?"

Shaking her head, she dropped her gaze. "All I know is that I'm nobody. That keeps repeating in my mind."

Fuck that fucker! He'd seen cruel before, but this one was one of the worst.

"Look at me again. You are not nobody, you're a beautiful, vibrant, smart woman, and your name is Thalasia. We have some work to do, but you are going to be perfectly fine. Believe me."

"Perfectly fine. Okay."

Gio smiled when something struck him. "I've become the champion of vampire-damaged women. I wonder what my superhero name would be."

Serenity Tower was ahead on the right.

"We're almost home."

Thalasia watched his face for the rest of the ride, a spark of interest in her eyes.

Two weeks later on the coast of Oregon

Ife watched the sea, each wave as mesmerizing as the first time she'd seen it in France, but this time she was alone. This time there was no one at her side and nothing to influence this moment. It was terrifying...*and freeing.* A high moon cast silvered light on the pale sand where she sat, the air warm, sparkling water at her feet.

Her dress felt oppressive and unwelcome, so she lifted it over her head and dropped it to her side. Naked now, she burrowed deeper into the sand that still held the heat of the sun.

After a rough year, she needed to escape for a while, and she was here for one thing, and one thing only...to do nothing. Nothing for her to fix, no one to take care of, no one needing her. All she had to do was take care of herself and enjoy the nights. So many times, people forgot to stop, appreciate, and just...*be.*

For the next two months, Ife's only job was to enjoy every moment, trouble free. Vampires didn't do it often, but today she began a much-desired vacation.

She fell back into the sand, and drew in a deep cleansing breath.

"Heaven," she sighed.

Up on a hill, near a lookout designed to stop and enjoy the scenery, Jack Remington had pulled over to watch a bright full moon set over the sea and grab a sandwich. How long had it been since he ate? Shit, there were a lot of times he didn't *remember* to eat.

Lifting the paper, he looked at what Stacey had packed for him. Ham and Swiss on wheat with mayonnaise. That would do nicely.

Leaning against the concrete railing, he sighed. Not enough of these quiet, trouble-free moments. He took a bite of the sandwich, and moaned. Oh, that was good. He'd have to thank Stacey for thinking about it. She might be the best assistant he'd ever had. If she kept this kind of shit up, he'd give her a trophy saying so.

"What I wouldn't do for a few months off," he told the surf.

When was the last time? Oh, yeah, six years ago, for a few weeks, he'd spent some time with a cute little hottie in Oklahoma. Grinning, he took another bite of the sandwich. His father had busted his ass for that, but it had fucking been worth it.

Nope, not too many company sanctioned days off in his business. His family had been in it for centuries, from his great-great grandfather right up to his father, himself and his younger brother.

An insistent *chinging* interrupted his peaceful moment. Dad. He'd ignored the last two calls, hoping to avoid his father.

Jack lingered before he pulled his fone out. "Yeah?"

"Where the fuck *are* you?"

"Took a moment to take a breath. Why?"

"Ben needs you."

"Didn't he have the night off?"

"Got in trouble, so answer your fucking fone and go help him."

"Yeah, yeah, I'll call him."

Ringing off, Jack let his finger rest above the return call button while he watched the rolling sea and silvery sparkles dancing on the waves from the low moon.

Something bright white on the sand below caught his eye. What was that? It fluttered like a huge white bird and fell to the sand. Laying his fone on the wall, he reached inside his car for binoculars and focused them in on the white shape.

It continued to flutter from where it lay on the sand, but it wasn't a bird. A piece of fabric maybe? Moving the binoculars to the left, he saw another shape, and used the electronic zoom to move in closer.

Whoa. A woman lay on the sand, naked, full breasts lifting to the sky, a hand lazily drawing circles in the sand. He zoomed closer on the breasts, well aware it was an invasion, but he was an overworked horny guy and what guy wouldn't look at such a spectacular body? Those were seriously lickable nipples. Moving lower, to the pale hair between her legs, he lingered on a place he liked to call *heaven*.

Moving back up, the binoculars showed her face, in repose. Hair as pale as the moon blew around her as she tried to capture and contain it. Suddenly she sat up and turned to face the hill where he stood.

Now he got a good look at what he thought might be the most beautiful face he'd ever seen. The light from the moon and the effective optics of the binoculars revealed pale eyes, probably blue, that he thought might actually be able to see him watching her. It was impossible, of course, without ancillary optics. Still, he lowered the device and watched her form as she stood and kept staring up at the hillside.

Fuck, he enjoyed watching her standing, that body displayed for his eyes only. *Bad boy*, he chided with a grin.

Anyway, he fucking had to go and see what his little brother needed. Reluctantly, he lowered the binoculars, and as he walked back to his car, he redialed the missed call.

"Yeah?"

Ben's voice was calm. "Hey, I need you. I found the group that was on Barkley's radar."

"Aw, shit. I was heading home to crash."

"It's night. No sleep for vampire hunters, J. I sent the coordinates. See you soon."

Shaking his head, Jack slipped behind the controls of the car and snapped his tazer back on his belt. Time to go to work again.

We're on our way to Oregon next to frolic in the sea with Ife, except that her peaceful vacation will be quite a lot less peaceful than expected.

Thanks for staying with my unique vampire world.

Keep an eye on all new releases and any news on my Facebook page C.L.Quinn Writer. Take a moment to check out my new series set in central New York, a lovely series set in a different world than the Firsts…*this* one.

Namasté, Charlie.

Readers, don't forget to try the book that created the idea for this series…

Last Best Hope, *by T.C.Butts is the tale of an ordinary woman faced with extraordinary circumstances when fireballs destroy the world one night. She'd been living a happy life in the Colorado Rocky Mountains, writing highly successful vampire romance novels for living. Sound familiar? Try Charlie Quinn's story on Amazon.com.*

All of the books up through Book 12 are available on audio if you would like to hear the stories come to life.

Thank you so much!

Made in the USA
Monee, IL
29 August 2024

64814575R00134